She would say *her life depended on it.*

Which it might.

Fear of failure sent her pulse thundering in her ears as his face lowered to hers.

Her throat felt bone-dry, unused. "I still love you, Mac." She repeated the line he had fed her. A lie spun to tell her his name, and imply it was a lot longer than five minutes since they first met.

"That's better," he murmured.

The touch of his mouth was cool, dry and almost impersonal, yet, *too* much. And they were being watched.

Her hand clutched a fistful of supple leather jacket to make it look real. Feeling herself lifted as if she were no bigger than a doll, she clung as she'd never clung to a man before, praying this man named Mac wouldn't continue the wild scary ride that had begun with her staring down the muzzle of a gun.

Dear Reader,

November is full of excitement—vengeance, murder, international espionage and exploding yachts. Not in real life, of course, but in those stories you love to read from Silhouette Intimate Moments. This month's romantic selections will be the perfect break from those unexpected snowstorms or, if you're like me, overeating at Thanksgiving (my mother challenges me to eat at least half my body weight). Oh, and what better way to forget about how many shopping days are left until the holidays?

Popular author Marilyn Pappano returns to the line with *The Bluest Eyes in Texas* (#1391), in which an embittered hero wants revenge against his parents' murder and only a beautiful private investigator can help him. *In Third Sight* (#1392), the second story in Suzanne McMinn's PAX miniseries, a D.C. cop with a special gift must save an anthropologist from danger and the world from a deadly threat.

You'll love Frances Housden's *Honeymoon with a Stranger* (#1393), the next book in her INTERNATIONAL AFFAIRS miniseries. Here, a design apprentice mistakenly walks into a biological-weapons deal, and as a result, she and a secret agent must pose as a couple. Can they contain their real-life passion as they stop a global menace? Brenda Harlen will excite readers with *Dangerous Passions* (#1394), in which a woman falls in love with her private investigator guardian. When an impostor posing as her protector is sent to kidnap her, she has to trust that her true love will keep her safe.

Have a joyous November and be sure to return next month to Silhouette Intimate Moments, where your thirst for suspense and romance is sure to be satisfied. Happy reading!

Sincerely,

Patience Smith
Associate Senior Editor

Please address questions and book requests to:
Silhouette Reader Service
U.S.: 3010 Walden Ave., P.O. Box 1325, Buffalo, NY 14269
Canadian: P.O. Box 609, Fort Erie, Ont. L2A 5X3

HONEYMOON
WITH A
STRANGER

FRANCES
HOUSDEN

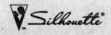

INTIMATE MOMENTS™

Published by Silhouette Books

America's Publisher of Contemporary Romance

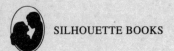 SILHOUETTE BOOKS

ISBN 0-373-27463-7

HONEYMOON WITH A STRANGER

Copyright © 2005 by Frances Housden

All rights reserved. Except for use in any review, the reproduction
or utilization of this work in whole or in part in any form by any
electronic, mechanical or other means, now known or hereafter
invented, including xerography, photocopying and recording, or in
any information storage or retrieval system, is forbidden without
the written permission of the editorial office, Silhouette Books,
233 Broadway, New York, NY 10279 U.S.A.

All characters in this book have no existence outside the imagination of
the author and have no relation whatsoever to anyone bearing the same
name or names. They are not even distantly inspired by any individual
known or unknown to the author, and all incidents are pure invention.

This edition published by arrangement with Harlequin Books S.A.

® and TM are trademarks of Harlequin Books S.A., used under license.
Trademarks indicated with ® are registered in the United States Patent
and Trademark Office, the Canadian Trade Marks Office and in other
countries.

Visit Silhouette Books at www.eHarlequin.com

Printed in U.S.A.

Books by Frances Housden

Silhouette Intimate Moments

The Man for Maggie #1056
Love under Fire #1168
Heartbreak Hero #1241
Shadows of the Past #1289
Stranded with a Stranger #1354
Honeymoon with a Stranger #1393

FRANCES HOUSDEN

has always been a voracious reader, but she never thought of being a writer until a teacher gave her the encouragement she needed to put pen to paper. As a result, Frances was a finalist in the 1998 Clendon Award and won the award in 1999, which led to the sale of her first book for Silhouette, *The Man for Maggie.*

Frances's marriage to a navy man took her from her birthplace in Scotland all the way to the ends of the earth in New Zealand. Now that he's a landlubber, they try to do most of their traveling together. They live on a ten-acre bush block in the heart of Auckland's Wine District. She has two large sons, two small grandsons and a tiny granddaughter who can twist her around her finger, as well as a wheaten terrier who thinks she's boss. Thanks to one teacher's dedication, Frances now gets to write about the kind of heroes a woman would travel to the ends of the earth for. Frances loves to hear from readers. Get in touch with Frances through her Web site at www.franceshousden.com.

I want to dedicate this book to my editor, Julie Barrett, a lady of infinite patience. Thank you, Julie.

Chapter 1

It was November in Paris, a bleak, damp month when the City of Lights turned petulant, more given to dampen a lover's shoulder with tears than blow a warm kiss, the way the capital would come spring.

The long nights and foggy weather suited Mac McBride's calling just fine, but then, Mac wasn't your typical American in Paris. As an agent for IBIS, the Intelligence Bureau for International Security on call 24/7, his days weren't anyone's idea of routine.

A snub-nosed pistol sat comfortably inside his left boot, and a 9 mm Glock, his favorite piece, was tucked neatly under the waistband in the back of his black jeans. Mac felt ready for anything.

His fingertips tingled with edgy anticipation as he fitted the PM53 Makarov pistol into his shoulder holster, knowing all his hard work was about to pay off.

The only important decision now was whether or not he

should keep on the gray tie with the black shirt? Did his outward appearance say Jeirgif Makjzajev, Chechen rebel, or did the slick oily sheen of the stuff he'd put on his hair yell Mafia lieutenant instead?

Mulling over the appointment ahead of him, he ditched the tie, then scraped his fingernails through this rough face stubble.

He drew his thick brown eyebrows into a frown that quickly disappeared once he was satisfied his reflection fitted the hard-ass look he'd intended.

The small break that took his nose off the straight and narrow became an asset on gigs like these. Though, he had to admit, he hadn't thought that at the time when he was training at Annapolis, but then life had been all about girls—women—and what attracted them. Now it was about terrorists.

His face hadn't seen a razor in more than six days, and the stubble looked darker where a dimple made a hollow in his chin.

Six days of dragging his heels on top of the month he'd already spent inveigling his way into the confidence of the slightly down-at-heel Algerian arms dealer he was setting up.

Meanwhile, his firm had made short work of any competitors without arousing suspicion.

He'd laughed when they told him he'd got this gig because of his razor-sharp cheekbones. Laughed to realize they thought he could pass for Chechen, and him with his true-blue American bloodline and a family history spanning 250-odd years since the first McBride set foot in America.

What the hell, he was more than willing to be involved in one of the craziest operations he'd yet encountered. And it helped that he spoke fluent Russian.

Though the Algerian didn't, so the odd curse word was enough to fool him.

Luckily, Mac's ability to finesse a deal speaking French was every bit as effortless as working in English, Russian or any of the other languages he'd picked up while his father's career took the McBrides to U.S. embassies around the world.

Mac was shrugging his broad shoulders into the soft well-worn creases and shoulder-hugging cut of his black leather bomber jacket, almost ready to leave, when the phone rang.

Without looking, he shot out an arm, snagging the receiver, thankful it no longer took a guessing game to locate things he needed in the Le Sentier apartment. Reciting his number, he heard, "Zukah is on his way up to the apartment."

The voice was Thierry's, one of the other IBIS agents—French—working with Mac. "Damn, how far away?"

The importance IBIS placed on this case showed in the amount of money they were willing to commit. Thierry's assignment was to tail the Algerian and his men; he and three others covered that end, but only Thierry was a master at disguise.

"They entered the building as I punched in your number, three of them. Want me to follow them up?" he asked.

"No, wait. Pick up their trail again when they leave. Zukah probably thinks there's safety in numbers, but three shouldn't be a problem now I've been warned."

Mac only stated the facts as he knew them. The word *arrogance* didn't raise a ripple on his conscience.

After focusing most of his adult life training to be the best, able to kill with his bare hands if need be, he now took those abilities for granted.

Roxanne Kincaid looked back over her shoulder, wondering if it was the last time she would see the little Renault.

She hadn't worried about the car when she'd stolen a heart-racing gap in the traffic from under the wheels of the one alongside her, or while she swerved into the corner to cross the Seine at the Pont Neuf, but parking in Le Sentier?

This dark, dank *quartier* of Paris was the contrast that proved the rule when they spoke of the City of Lights. It would be just her luck to find the wheels missing when she returned.

She looked along the sidewalk, saw three men walking ahead of her and slowed her pace.

Earlier that evening the couturier Charles Fortier had caught her eye as he spun his bright glance round the avenue Montaigne workroom, and before he could say *"Bon soir, Roxie,"* she'd known he had a special job for her.

One she couldn't refuse.

And now here she was, outside a six-story apartment building that hadn't been on her agenda for this evening's entertainment.

Gathering the upstanding collar of her charcoal-colored coat closer to her ears, she cast a baleful frown up at the persistent drizzle, sniffing air that had long since lost the dusty scent of autumn.

Everyone said winter had come early this year, but what it meant to Roxie was that all the straightening lotion in Paris wasn't going stop her hair curling.

Standing under the dismal street lamp, she checked the washed-out number painted on pitted plaster as she swayed against a gust of wind that funneled through the narrow streets. This *quartier* really hadn't changed much over the years.

She found it hard to imagine her grandmother growing up not a two-minute walk from this very doorway. Grandmère's neat Dorset cottage, where Roxie grew up, had been a far cry from the dark, sightless windows crowding the narrow cobbled streets.

Though, if Grandmère were alive to see her now, she wouldn't be delighted to see Roxie visiting her old haunts.

No, Anastasia Perdieu Kincaid hadn't been the type of woman who minced words or called a spade a shovel.

A quick twist of the wrist and Mac checked the time on the flashy gold watch—Russian—and checked it against the plain clock, the only piece of decor on his apartment walls. The transient feeling of the place was exactly what he'd had in mind.

The Algerian was thirty minutes early, but if he'd thought to surprise Mac…?

As far as he'd discovered, Ahmed Zukah had only lately begun playing out of his league. Until now the worst crimes listed on the Algerian's rap sheet were shady arms deals.

But this one was bigger, much bigger, a deal deadly enough to be brought to the attention of the IBIS.

Though Zukah acted as front man and had two Frenchmen working for him, none of them had the cojones to put this together, but the IBIS had still to discover who was running the Algerian.

Mac wondered if tonight would bring him any closer to the man he really wanted to lay hands on, the fourth man. These others were small potatoes compared to the brain behind the scheme.

Right on time, a fist hammered on the door of the third-floor apartment. Mac sniffed; they could wait.

The wooden door received three more poundings while he finished pulling his shirt collar over the neck of his jacket.

His dark gold eyes narrowed, fierce lights burning in them, sparked from his resentment of the impatient demand on his door.

It was a look those who knew him had come to dread, but then, the bad guys outside the door didn't know that.

Yet.

Roxie's foot hit the first step of the two leading to the dark aperture of the six-story building. Stairs led to the floors above, but she ignored them.

At the end of the hallway she heard the courtyard gate clang shut and decided it would be wisest to let the men she'd seen get well in front of her.

She'd just mimicked Grandmère, saying, "Better safe than sorry," when her eyes caught a movement in the darkness ahead that was hardly more than a shift in the dank air.

An uncanny flicker crept up the nape of her neck, and she dragged in a deep calming breath as her pulse fluttered.

The lighting was so poor, the electric globe sticking out from the wall sconce had to be as low wattage as they could buy and still have it give off light.

"So it's dark, get over it," she muttered. "It's not that bad." She'd heard some Parisians broke their necks trying to find an apartment round here so close to the heart of French culture that the Louvre was a mere ten-minute walk away.

With a couple of twists of the leather strap of her purse, she pulled its weight securely against her knuckles in case she needed a weapon.

She laughed unapologetically under her breath, fanciful maybe, but her instincts never let her down. Setting a brisk pace, she directed her toes toward the silhouette of an iron gate breaking up the gray light pooling in the courtyard.

Clamping her lips shut so the stale smell wouldn't taint her mouth, Roxie took the last few steps at a run before her lungs exploded.

Almost there, she desperately gulped down air only to be swamped by a miasma of cheap wine and garlic fumes.

With the courtyard less than a yard away, a figure lurched out of the shadows under the stairs. Roxie's heart leapt up to her throat, reducing her scream of fear to a squeal.

Unfortunately, the sound wasn't loud enough to drown out the man's slurred words, or the suggestions she read in them.

He wanted to intimidate her, but he didn't succeed.

Wine sloshed wildly as she dodged the bottle waved in her face. She batted it out of her way with a forehand swipe of her purse before swooping low to avoid retaliation.

"Missed me," she taunted under her breath, more for her than for him, and dove into the courtyard like a runner crossing the winning line.

With any luck the drunk would have gone by the time she'd completed her task, and if not, she'd be ready for him.

Without due haste, Mac flicked his black shirt collar up 'til it brushed the curled ends of his longer-than-usual hair, framing the planes and angles of his hawkish features.

Just as casually, he removed the Makarov from its snug place under his arm, then strode across the sparsely furnished living space of the apartment.

Even in boots his footsteps were soft, silent, those of a hunter. And, as if someone stage left called out, "Lights, cameras, action," his expression took on the appearance of fierce determination before he wrenched open the door to an enemy who hadn't heard him coming.

Butt of his pistol held high to knock, Zukah took a couple of involuntary backward steps, landing up against the men with him.

With his forearm resting on top of the door frame, McBride let his broad shoulders fill the doorway. He kept the hand gripping the Makarov hidden alongside his thigh, then slipped it behind a door that wasn't built to stop a bullet.

Mac eyed the pistol in the Algerian's red-knuckled fist with a lift of an unimpressed eyebrow, before his gaze dropped to Zukah.

A slovenly dresser, the man always looked as if he'd just stepped off the boat at Marseille, but Mac's eyes saw beyond the front Zukah put on public view. Zukah was a hell of a lot shrewder than he wanted generally known.

Almost as quickly as he dropped his hand, a peevish frown drew the Algerian's bushy eyebrows into a saturnine line. Looking foolish obviously wasn't part of the act he cultivated.

That performance seemed confined to his beige crumpled suit straining over a creased shirt and protruding gut.

Sticking with French so there could be no misunderstanding, Mac said, "I see you brought your calling card, Monsieur Zukah, and some *compagnie*. There was no need for such diligent precautions. I'm quite aware who I'm dealing with."

Zukah's tar-colored mustache quivered above a smirk. "As I do, Makj…pah, your name is unpronounceable."

"Stick with Mac, everyone does. And forgive me if I'm wrong, hadn't we arranged to meet at La Grappe d'Orgueil?"

Mac's eyelids narrowed as he spoke, and his smile when it arrived, though lethal, was a mere feral-baring of white teeth.

Only he knew that the smile was because his cover had withstood the test that he'd assumed the Algerian would put it through.

IBIS was nothing if not thorough when it came to cover stories. If only they'd been as successful at discovering how the Algerian had gotten his hands on a biotech weapon called Green Shield that the French military had supposedly destroyed.

Ahmed's dark irises disappeared behind a mass of wrinkles as he grunted. No way could the sound erupting be taken for a laugh. "Precisely, *mon ami*. I decided meeting you here might save time."

Mac couldn't summon up any humor.

Though the bureau knew who had designed the weapon Zukah had on offer, no one had discovered how it had come into his hands.

Green Shield—named after a sap-sucking beetle—was a designation that gave no hint of the true nature of the beast.

Even the slick gel in Mac's hair wasn't enough to prevent it from lifting at the back of his neck, as he pondered the kind of sick mind it had taken to devise such a weapon.

"A pity you didn't think to call first," he said. "I'm particular about whom I invite into my place."

Mac perused the Algerian's self-loading pistol, a small Mauser, old, well-cared-for but no longer seen on the streets for sale. "For you, I'll make an exception," he said, stepping back, allowing Zukah a view of the Makarov he'd had pointing through the door at an extremely vulnerable target.

He'd never entertained the notion that the two men covering Ahmed's back wouldn't be armed. Though they'd hardly make a move with the Algerian's bulk blocking the line of fire.

That Zukah was aware of the danger in his position showed in a sideways movement of his eyes that revealed their whites.

In or out, there was no way to dodge a bullet.

Mac generously decided to let him off the hook.

It was too late to back off now. The damn biotech weapon was reputed to be of awesome consequence. And no matter what, Mac's mission was to obtain it at all cost.

He didn't need telling his life was on the line.

What was one man's life when millions might face a slow, lingering death from starvation? With that in mind, he said, "Since you and your friends don't appear overly dangerous, come on in and let's deal."

To put a spin of honesty on his announcement, Mac turned his back on the Algerian filling his doorway to return to the living room, wondering, where was a Kevlar vest when you needed one?

Roxie paused, at the other side of the courtyard, winded by her frantic pace. Her boots were made for walking, not the hundred-yard dash.

Besides, she'd heard nothing to suggest the man had followed her, no shambling footsteps that signaled his approach.

The open square she'd crossed appeared dependent on the windows facing down into it for light. Luckily, the bleak weather had kept people at home and the lights showed her the way as she ran.

By now, she'd come to the sensible conclusion that the man was *un clochard,* one of the homeless, who'd been sheltering in the entrance to escape the worst of the weather.

Still breathing hard, she stood at the foot of the stairs and heard a door close, and wondered which floor the men ahead of her in the gloom had been going to.

As the apartment door closed, Mac decided that for the moment, he had nothing to fear from these wiseguys.

The dealer running Zukah and Co. was asking an arm and two legs for the weapon, and only the wealthiest terrorist groups could afford that kind of lump sum.

Al Qaeda hadn't come sniffing around as far as IBIS knew, but then they preferred their weapons to go off with a bang, not the whimper of dying vegetation.

That was one of the few facts on Mac's side.

The Palestinians couldn't afford it, and since most of North Africa was pretty barren, anyway, the Israelis weren't interested.

No, this weapon was designed to turn lush green countries, thanking God for their daily bread, into yellow deserts.

From what he'd been told, one miniscule drop could do more damage than a planeload of Agent Orange had done in Vietnam.

Perching on the arm of the only easy chair, Mac nonchalantly waved Zukah toward the sofa. *"Asseyez-vous."*

"I prefer to stand."

Stubborn, Mac concluded as the Algerian held his ground, the two men with him ranging themselves on either side like a pair of fierce black cats guarding a king's ransom.

The closemouthed Frenchmen weren't strangers to Mac. He'd seen them at previous meetings, always dressed like twins in dark suits and ties.

Mac stood, saying, "Your choice. Have you brought the goods?"

Zukah sniffed derisively, and had Mac still been seated he would have looked at him down the length of his nose.

"You think I would carry it around in my pocket? I am not foolish. It would be far too dangerous. I enjoy living in *la belle*

France. If I had a passion for desert sands I could have stayed in Algeria."

Mac caught a hint of something in Ahmed's explanation that tightened the skin at the back of his neck.

Damn, the weapon sounded worse than he'd heard. "It's really that potent?" he probed. "I was led to believe its specifics named grain crops, wheat, corn…?"

The Algerian shrugged. "Believe what you like. I refuse to take chances…and, anyway, I haven't decided who gets it yet."

Mac whirled toward the door. "Then don't waste my time!" he snarled, privately wondering if another buyer had come on the scene to make his life more complicated than it already was.

Roxie took the stairs on the other side of the courtyard entrance and began to climb. A mumble of French drifted down from an upper landing, then cut off abruptly.

Though it was dark enough to make her want to hurry, she took her time, just in case the men she'd seen thought they were being followed. At this time of night most deals being done in Le Sentier would be dirty.

At the top of the first flight, the sign on the door facing read Claudette's Lingerie. Not as startling as it might sound since Le Sentier was the garment district of Paris.

Halfway up a third flight, she heard raised voices and, nearing the top, was relieved to see light leaking under a door.

Her pace quickened with revived confidence,

Charles had trusted her to do this for him.

She hurried the last few stairs, the four-inch heels of her boots sounding an uneven tattoo on the wooden treads.

The Algerian soon made it known he hadn't done with Mac. "I want to know what makes this your fight? You tell me you want to bring the Russian bear to its knees, yet you were born in America."

Zukah spoke urgently, the soft sibilant accent of his homeland making it hard to follow. "The Cold War is over and those two old enemies are already swapping pillow talk. I would be a fool to take you at face value."

Mac's tempered flared; though he kept his voice low, it sounded harsh, in keeping with the role he'd taken on. "When you were selling guns, did you always ask who your customer was going to shoot with them?"

Mac had learned to be particular about his cover story, to fit into the skin of the character. Lip curling, he asked, "In your small conflicted world, did you ever hear of Grozny?"

Zukah gave him a blank stare, but Mac noticed one of his men nod as if remembering the siege.

Mac's nose flared as he looked down on the Algerian. Zukah had a lot of native cunning but obviously wasn't interested in events that didn't affect him personally.

"Not that it's any of your damn business, but my mother's family were there. Not one of them survived the siege." A single step brought Mac chest-to-chest with Zukah. "So, you might say I have a large stake in acquiring that weapon."

It was a one-sided pissing match with only Mac speaking, but he continued, "And before you sell to someone else, it would be in your best interest to discover the punishments we mete out to those who cross us Chechens."

The uncomprehending expression reminded Mac that a threat was redundant if the one being menaced lived in blissful ignorance, but the same guy shifted his feet as if in discomfort.

Mac reckoned it would pay to remember which one could be more easily unsettled, anything that gave him an edge.

Not to be outdone, the Algerian blustered, "And we have to be sure of your—" All at once Zukah broke off and as one their heads turned in the direction of the swift footsteps outside.

Mac spat out a curse and cast a murderous glance toward the door, wondering what else could go wrong. "If this is another trick, Zukah, it doesn't sit at all well with me, so be warned."

* * *

It was silent as Roxie crossed the landing, as if someone had turned the sound down on a TV. Roxie put her ear close to the door and heard nothing. Not a sound.

It could be the wrong apartment.

She knocked lightly. Nothing. .

About to reach for the handle, she hesitated, thinking it could be very awkward if she was wrong. Then told herself, don't be a coward. All you have to say is you're looking for Madame Billaud, the seamstress who's doing some specialized work for Charles Fortier, the couturier.

Everyone had heard of Charles.

Yes, if she made a mistake, she would simply ask them to redirect her. She tried the handle.

The door to the apartment opened easily. She took a deep breath and called loudly, *"Bon soir. C'est Roxie...."*

The rest of her announcement stuttered to a halt in the face of a deadly looking gun. She blinked in the bright lights for a few seconds, and still none of the men facing her spoke a word.

It was she who broke the ominous silence by blurting out, "Bloody hell!" in English, the second of the languages she'd grown up speaking.

The gun never wavered an inch.

Not even when the thin, hollow-cheeked man grabbed the shoulder she was desperately trying to ease back through the open door. He pulled her into the room.

Her eyes winced at the sudden transition from dark to light. But all the same, it looked as if she'd stumbled into the middle of a home invasion.

Four strange men and one solitary woman. Latent instincts stirred in her brain, telling her that the danger she felt could come from more than just a gun.

Chapter 2

At first, Roxie's shocked eyes merely grazed the others in the room. Now her gaze lit on the largest man, who held it with the fierce, glittering-gold intensity of his own.

She drew a shuddering breath to still the mind-numbing fear crawling under her skin.

The Kincaid family never showed weakness, and Grand-mère had bred strong women. Yet she doubted if they'd ever met anyone like the huge, broad-shouldered man dominating the others.

Not with physical force, but by the leashed power of his expression and the glittering light in his eyes.

Consumed by a frantic need for survival, she latched onto the notion that this was the man to deal with. The one who could mend the faux pas she'd made by barging in without permission.

Might this be the time to mention her muddle with the directions?

As though in a dream, she watched the big man's lips purse,

a wry expression softening the sharp angles of ruggedly blocked features. *Handsome* features.

She felt hypnotized, compelled to react, though her intense response to the fiery shimmer in his eyes lost its impact when she felt the thin guy holding the gun tighten his grip on her.

It was as if she was caught in limbo, between sheer unadulterated terror and bewilderment. Pick one.

Her intuition told her it was entirely reasonable to expect the big guy to take her fear in the palm of one large hand and crush it into extinction.

But what did he want, *expect,* from her in return?

Yet, he was the antithesis of everything she'd built her career around. Miles away from the tailoring that made her designs work and had caught Charles's eye at her grandmother's funeral.

Madame Fortier accompanied Charles to Père-Lachaise, the old Paris cemetery where Grandmère had been buried. It was then Roxie discovered that Grandmère and Charles's mother went way back, even before they fought together in the French Resistance.

That meeting had changed Roxie's life.

And though she had left the London School of Design for Charles's workroom to a chorus of it's-not-what-you-know-it's-who, Grandmère had brought her up to be practical, not stupid.

A survival trait she'd always managed to adhere to until now. She stared at the guy with slicked-back hair, designer stubble and a black leather jacket that shouted "Biker!"

She must be mad. Her normal reaction would be to run a mile, not beg for this huge stranger's help.

"Roxie." When he spoke, none of the softness she had noticed before lingered in the rasp of his voice, but he knew her name!

It took a second to remember he'd heard her call out.

"Didn't I tell you I would be out tonight and not to bother me?" Once he'd spoken her name, each dry consonant that followed cut her hopes into rags with the sharpness of a knife.

Through the mists of apprehension clouding her mind, she perceived he expected something in return for the verbal lifeline he had thrown her…but what?

She metaphorically reached out with trembling hands, certain beyond all reason that her future depended on her response. "I saw the light from the courtyard…and, I thought…that, well I would surprise you."

He strode lazily toward her, as she desperately tried not to cower while watching him pocket a gun that hadn't registered with her before.

And though her every instinct screamed it was a bad move, her hand flew to her lips as her stomach somersaulted nearer to her mouth.

Behind him, the narrowest hand on the utilitarian clock counted out what might be the last seconds of her life.

His long legs covered the distance in half the steps it would have taken her. But she wasn't fooled by the perception of indolence; this big man was more dangerous than the razor-jawed creature holding her shoulder.

"So, *chérie*," he drawled as he halted in front of her, "I guess I surprised you instead?"

His fingers prized her hand away from her mouth as she nodded, unable to deny the obvious. Then her head whirled as the man she hoped was her savior grabbed the wrist of the one holding her.

Without effort he sent both clinging hand and its owner spinning back a few feet. "Your kind of help we can do without."

Such blatant force was alien to Roxie. In fact, she'd never encountered even a suggestion of the energized enmity circling, gathering, waiting to ambush them all without provocation.

Her hopes took a dive as the shortest man of the group barked out, "Who is this woman? Why is she here?"

She hoped the big guy had a good explanation up his sleeve, for she was too frightened to see past her blunder, or to worry how annoyed her boss was going to be with her when she reported back, if ever.

With his leather-covered arm casually circling her shoulders, Roxie's heart raced out of control.

Her designated protector gave the appearance of nonchalance, yet she wasn't too dumbstruck to notice the hand closest to his gun was kept free, as she stared at the broad-palmed hand cupping her shoulder.

Dark gold hairs softened the wide sinewy shape. His fingers were long, blunt-tipped, more like a carpenter's than a gunman's.

As she glanced across at the other armed men, she wondered if his hand was large enough to hold his life as well as her own.

"This is *ma petite amie.*" *Girlfriend.* He directed the conversation to the fat man. "If you'd waited where we originally arranged, her being here wouldn't be a problem. But if it bothers you, Zukah, speak up."

Roxie was scared out of her wits, yet as she was pressed close to his side as he uttered his unequivocal statement, and though the situation more closely resembled a funeral than a wedding, she wanted to say, "Or forever hold your peace."

Though trembling inside, she felt grateful this man had ranged his overwhelming presence on her side.

By the tension in the air, she could tell the game they'd been playing when she arrived hadn't been going too well.

She mentally crossed her fingers.

Dear God, please let her be on the side of the angels.

The Algerian made a grudging concession. "As long as she doesn't interfere in matters that aren't her concern, she'd better stay."

Angels, she decided were in a minority of one.

She looked up, hoping for reassurance as the big guy's fingers squeezed her arm to attract her attention.

"You've always known what I was, *chérie,*" he said, "Though you tried to ignore it. Now the blinkers are off, tell me once more."

Utter confusion made her stammer, "T-tell you what?"

"Say, I still love you, Mac." Wow, she knew his name.

Her heart climbed back to her throat, fluttering in panic.

Uh-uh, this wasn't the time to be chickenhearted. She would say the words as if her life depended on it.

Which it just might?

Fear of failure sent her pulse thundering in her ears as his face lowered to hers. Massive shoulders loomed, shaded her.

Unpredictably, his open jacket seemed like a place she could hide. Her throat felt bone-dry, unused. "I still love you, Mac."

"That's better," he murmured.

The touch of his mouth was cool, dry and almost impersonal. Yet too much to ask of synapses scattered by feeling herself being lifted as if she were no bigger than a doll.

Her hand clutched a fistful of supple leather to make it look real as well as for support. They were being watched.

She clung as she'd never clung to a man before, praying her association with this man named Mac wouldn't make her continue the wild, scary ride that had begun with staring down the muzzle of a gun.

Mac was fit to be tied.

It wasn't often he allowed himself be cornered, and until now he had never been locked into an impossible situation with a woman hardly big enough to be an armful.

He'd brought it all on with his insistence he meet with Zukah's boss. His mistake was evident the moment the Algerian agreed, saying, "You will of course consider yourselves our guests."

Right about then, Mac felt the trap close.

Hell, he personally didn't give a damn. He wanted to meet the fourth man, but he'd lumbered himself with an unknown quantity, albeit a frightened one who trembled like a mouse facing a cat.

All he knew about her was her big gray eyes had made his heart constrict and take pity on her. Bizarre reactions from a guy who hadn't known he could feel that stupid kind of emotion.

To cap it off, Zukah had failed to mention they would be unarmed guests, though if his head had been on straight he would have realized.

The Algerian waved his pistol around laconically as if directing his foot soldiers was an effort. "Jean-Luc, collect his weapons and, Yves, you can search the woman."

Comprehension that they were about to be taken hostage had come slowly to Roxie. He caught the first flash of new panic lightening her eyes to silver as she turned, hand tightening on his sleeve while the Algerian concluded his gruff orders to his men with, *"Vite, vite."*

If she could read his mind she'd have even more reason to be apprehensive. No way could he allow her to act on the impulse he sensed racing through her.

A moment's madness on her part could send a month's work crashing down on him.

This was his game and they'd play it by his rules.

He didn't have time for niceties, or considering her sensibilities as if she were indeed simply someone who had blundered into a fraught situation, which he didn't believe for a moment.

He pulled her closer, whispering words as harsh and hard as their meaning in her ear. "Don't you dare try to escape. They'll shoot you like a dog and I'll let them because today's horoscope said nothing about taking a bullet for a beautiful bimbo."

So? He wasn't actually sure about the *beautiful*, and most likely the *bimbo* was out of line, but his words had the desired affect.

Her face darkened as he let her go, and now it was a question of which one of them she was more annoyed with, him or Zukah.

Relieved, Mac watched her shoulders straighten as she pulled herself together, instead of hiding her face inside her high-collared coat.

Bottom lip pouting, she lifted her chin. Mac sighed. Looked like he might have whispered the magic words to put some much-needed fire in her belly. Anger suited her better than panic.

About time, too. Mac had never been a great believer in co-incidences. Roxie's arrival at his door couldn't have been acci-dental. No woman in her right mind wandered around the back streets of Le Sentier in the dark without a special reason.

But, from the way events were shaping up, it was going to take him a little while longer to discover who she was, and ex-actly which organization she worked for.

Hell, in Paris there were almost too many to choose from. Though her French was great, when she'd blurted out "Bloody hell!" in that English accent, MI6 had reached top of his list.

No one could call him a two-time loser—he'd been suckered by a woman before—but for the life of him he hadn't been able to throw this gray-eyed mouse to Zukah's sleek black cats.

One of whom in particular, Roxie was glaring at now.

Zukah's years in France were signaled by his typically Parisian shrug. "Don't look at it as being taken hostage, *petite.* Think of it as a trial honeymoon."

Mac muttered a mental "oops." Zukah might think he was being helpful, but he wasn't doing *him* any favors.

The Algerian's humor didn't sit well with Roxie. But, for what must be the first time in her life, she kept quiet.

Not because she'd been struck speechless, because she hadn't a clue what was happening. Playing dumb meant she couldn't say the wrong thing or have Mac's lukewarm rescue blow up in their faces.

If she gave in to the urge to run zinging through her, it might be the last impulse she ever acted upon. Though, the differences between being shot or facing a so-called honeymoon with a stranger didn't seem particularly large.

Neither of them was on her top-ten list of things to do next.

The one called Yves approached her, once more sparking the fight-or-flight factor through her synapses.

Tensions coiled in the muscles hidden by her long coat.

Yves was the man who'd grabbed her as she entered the apartment and he looked like a man who enjoyed his work *far too much.* She held her breath as he began patting her down.

Never had she felt so alone, not even when Grandmère died. All she'd felt then was numb, until the Fortier family took her under their wing, distracting her with work she loved.

It took every inch of her control to ignore Yves. Ignore his enjoyment as his hands slid over her. She turned away and watched the other Frenchman relieve Mac of his guns.

When they totaled three her initial panic segued to deep-seated dread, and its by-product, shudders, ran through her.

It was impossible to keep fear at bay.

Her breath hitched as Yves's fingers circled her ankle and began inching upward.

Gasping, she took a step back, her gaze flying to Mac for help. But all she saw in response was the glittering warning he'd already verbalized. Blast!

What had she landed into?

How had she gotten surrounded by strangers, all of whom looked as if they'd been ripped from the underbelly of Paris?

Bottom line, it had been her own stupidity, and the urge to impress her bosses.

God help her, when she didn't dare trust the best of them. Mac. And he, as the finest of a bad bunch, wasn't saying much.

Darn it, the man had had the cheek to call her a bimbo.

There and then she decided if it were the last thing she did, she'd pay him back. Her spurt of righteous anger replaced fear.

Only once had a man made her feel like a victim. He'd

showed his love with one hand and stolen her designs with the other.

It wasn't a sensation she was comfortable with, or intended becoming used to.

Being a hostage hadn't exactly been part of Mac's plans, but crap happened when you least expected. And if Roxie was looking for a hero, she'd picked the wrong *quartier* of Paris to shop in.

Out on the landing Zukah lined them both up at the top of the stairs and began issuing orders, sending the Frenchman who'd pawed Roxie off to bring the car round.

"*Enfin,* we can go." Zukah poked Mac in the back with his Mauser. "Remember, I'm right behind you."

Beside him, Roxie practically jumped out of her knee-high boots as Zukah barked. Until now, Mac had never come in contact with a female agent whose footwear were impossible to run in, but there was a first time for everything.

He was curious to know what kind of cover story demanded heels higher than the Eiffel Tower. A couple of inches off them might have given her more of a chance.

Though it sounded clichéd, in Mac's line of work he knew to expect the unexpected. That's why he was prepared to tie a knot in his original plans and turn any new contingency into a plus. He hoped the same could be said for his new lady friend.

The woman posed a huge problem. Hell, she had more unknown quantity in her little finger than the other three put together.

Sure, she was putting on a good show of being scared. And she'd done right to keep up the act. The hot, resentful sparks she'd shot at Zukah had been her only sign of emotion in a while.

Talk about sex rearing its ugly head.

Yves *had* enjoyed running his hands over her a little too much.

Carrying out the role he'd assigned himself to the full meant he should have protested. Should have—would have—if her pleading glance hadn't reminded him of Lucia approximately five minutes before she stuck a six-inch blade in his back.

That said, he wouldn't be turning his back on Roxie anytime soon, not until he was certain she wasn't carrying a knife.

His trust was on the meager side when it came to beautiful female agents.

Mac had felt disappointment coming off Roxie in waves, but there was no point in giving too much away to look better in her eyes.

He'd been there, done that, and learned one helluva huge lesson. One he wouldn't forget in a hurry. Being a woman didn't make her any less lethal to his health.

Happiness came in all guises, and this opportunity to go with Zukah suited him just fine. Damn fine.

Mac heard the car draw up outside as they splashed across the cold rain-soaked courtyard to the exit.

Juggling bodies, they ended up dancing the do-si-do, squeezing through the half-open double doors leading to the sidewalk.

In the watery glow from the street lamp, Mac caught her glance while their bodies brushed close, as if her puzzled eyes wondered what made him tick. Her conclusions would be wrong.

Hell, tonight he'd done something so off the wall it could take *him* years to figure it out.

He was an undercover agent, not anyone's idea of a knight in shining armor, certainly not Jason Hart's. When all this was over Mac would have to do some explaining to the chief of IBIS.

Maybe by then he'd have come up with an answer.

A blue minivan—the type with three rows of seats that soccer moms used—sat waiting at the edge of the sidewalk.

It didn't take a huge leap of imagination to know who'd be

sitting in the middle row. "Get in," Zukah growled, playing the big man, nudging them toward the vehicle with the dangerous end of his pistol.

The guy was dumber than Mac had given him credit for. A wise man would be wondering if his plans had gone a little *too* well.

They'd hardly gone more than a couple of feet when someone staggered out of the shadows and grabbed Zukah's gun arm.

Roxie squawked as the gun swung her way, while Zukah cursed roundly through the cloud of cheap-wine fumes as pandemonium ruled.

In the poor light the drunk could easily be taken for one of the many homeless found sleeping in doorways around Le Sentier and Les Halles.

But Mac wasn't deceived.

He pushed Roxie behind him while the drunk grappled with the Algerian. Zukah rained blows down on the guy's head and they were all treated to a stream of slurred French invectives.

Seeking to escape, the guy ducked under Zukah's arm to clutch the front of Mac's jacket as if begging for help.

But that close the drunk couldn't hide the bright intelligence in his eyes, or the question in them he directed at Mac.

The smell of garlic breath was a good touch. Trust Thierry to think of it. Mac narrowed his gaze in warning at his fellow agent and slightly shook his head.

Message received.

"Get off him!" shouted the Algerian, but before Jean-Luc could pull Thierry away, Mac felt something slide into his pocket.

Seconds later, Thierry staggered away into the night, leaving Mac curious as to which of their many gadgets his second in command had slipped him.

Curiosity that would have to remain unsatisfied until they reached their destination.

"You first." Zukah gave him a push in the back.

Mac looked at the smaller seat opposite the door. He couldn't trust Roxie not to try escaping. "No," he said, "she can sit by the window. I need more room for my legs."

No one argued with him.

It was Yves who pulled Roxie out of her cat's-got-her-tongue mode once again. *"Cochon!"* she yelled, slapping the Frenchman. "Keep your hands off me. I can manage."

As the car pulled into the road Mac decided there was going to be a reckoning between those two. He just hoped Roxie held off long enough for him to accomplish his mission.

"Lean your head on my shoulder," he said companionably as the minivan squeezed through the crush in rue Montorgueil. "You might as well try to sleep. God knows how far we're going."

Through the golden haze of a better-lit street it was impossible to miss that her long-suffering look was essentially female. It shouted "I wouldn't be caught dead."

Damn, he thought as he gave a rueful shake of his head. Didn't the woman realize that if it hadn't been for him tonight, "dead" had definitely been her short-term destiny?

Chapter 3

Roxie woke with a start, her head clunking back against Mac's shoulder. The car had stopped, but the only illumination came from the headlights. "Where are we?"

"No idea, but it looks like more than a comfort stop. I'd say we've arrived." Mac sounded more alert than she felt.

She pushed away from him, annoyed that in sleep she'd taken advantage of the shoulder she'd refused earlier.

Keeping her voice level to a murmur, she spoke English, hoping Jean-Luc sitting behind wouldn't understand as she touched the warm spot where her cheek had rested. "That wasn't intentional, so don't get the wrong idea."

Turning away, she combed her fingers through her hair to fluff it out. But before she could snag another breath his big hand curved round the back of her neck, pulling her close.

Face-to-face.

Her heart pounded, thundering in her temple as his lips pressed against her ear. She needn't have worried.

Sweet nothings weren't in Mac's repertoire. "You mean like Yves? I think the guy has a case for you. Better look out."

As he followed her example by using English, his hand forked through her curls, holding her head in an apparently passionate embrace that meant she couldn't move.

"Don't worry, *chérie,* you're safe from me. Just take a little time to remember who walked into whose territory."

The hand on her neck stroked, a subtle caress that drew a reluctant shudder from her. "Time to compromise, *chérie,* you help me out and I'll look after you. Just keep in mind that this is my show, not yours, and everything will turn out fine and dandy."

It seemed she had no choice but to follow his lead.

Earlier, before she'd fallen asleep, she'd stared out into the wine-dark countryside and railed against the impulse that had brought her to this place in time.

Annoying though it felt, Mac was her lifeline.

He was big and tough, and at least she was aware that she couldn't trust him as far as she could throw him.

While it suited her, she would go along with his suggestions.

Mac at least acted as if he knew what he was doing.

Fully awake now, she observed Yves and Zukah exit the front of the minivan, then latched onto a new subject. "How long would you say we'd been on the road?"

"Without being able to read my watch I'd say around four hours, probably more. It took almost an hour to get out of Paris. But judging by lack of lights and noise, this is pretty rural."

Did Mac have to be right all the time?

The small château they were ushered into didn't look *grand* but it was more than a farmhouse deep in the heart of the French countryside. Not a lit window for miles.

Roxie blinked, blinded as she stepped onto a floor laid in ancient gray flagstones. Compared to outside, this was obviously where the owner had spent his money.

The rug covering them, although old, glowed like a ruby.

Half a dozen large sconces lit gold-paneled walls, explaining the glare that had dazzled her as she entered.

Mac had no such problem, asking, "What, no welcome party?"

Zukah fussed, as if out of his comfort zone surrounded by impressive antiques. In his crumpled suit, he looked more like a hostage than they did. *"Le patron* hopes to be here tomorrow."

Did that mean she might be back in Paris by tomorrow evening? It felt childish, but she couldn't help crossing her fingers.

All she wanted was to get back to her own world.

She would put up with bitchy models and the complaints of the patternmakers without a murmur if they could leave this place as soon as possible.

She desperately needed to talk to her boss—to Charles—but Yves had destroyed any hope of that by wrecking the cell phone he'd found in her purse when he searched her.

Mac's reaction to the news was "Might as well go to our room, then, since there's nothing to be gained here. No point in talking to the dummy when the man you need is the ventriloquist."

To herself, Roxie admitted she was in awe of Mac. All that air of control should have been on the other side.

They were armed, he wasn't.

She wished she could take a leaf from his rule book and act as if she were a VIP instead of a hostage.

"Everything is ready for you, though we weren't expecting your *petite amie.* The bed will be a squeeze, but I don't suppose you'll mind."

The bed, as in one bed?

She was caught up in her own nervous interpretation of what that meant, when she realized Mac wasn't overjoyed with the arrangement, either.

A soft growl issued from his throat that throttled back into a curse. "You're a twisted bastard, Zukah. If you wanted me here,

I only needed an invitation, not this French farce. When word gets out, no one will want to deal with you. And it'll get out."

Mac left the words, "And I'll see about it," unsaid.

"Calm yourself. I'm only granting your wish to meet the head of our organization." Zukah's smile didn't reach his eyes. "Of course, word will only get out if you leave the château."

She would never understand why Mac had trusted this guy in the first place. One look convinced her Zukah was the kind of guy she would rather cross the street than pass on the sidewalk.

She watched Mac's whole demeanor poker-up as he noted the threat. His big body loomed over Zukah, and Roxie's stomach sank level with the tops of her knee-high boots.

She would never understand men, and *men* like Mac had never come within whistling distance of her before tonight.

Which meant she had no idea how to handle him.

No idea how to handle sharing a room with a virtual stranger. A man who might be no better than the thugs he was dealing with. A man looking as if he was about to create mayhem.

"When you threaten someone, Zukah, you have to be prepared to back it up. You can thank Roxie for the fact you're still breathing. I don't like to see her upset."

She knew his words comprised an explicit warning, though his tone and expression scared her most.

Maybe she should have ignored Mac's advice and taken a chance on being shot. Something told her it might have been wiser than taking a chance on Mac.

They'd located them in the attic, which Mac found promising. It showed him that even unarmed Zukah considered him dangerous.

The window was barred and behind it lay a sheer drop, at least forty feet straight down. The only way out was through the door that Yves and Jean-Luc would more than likely lock as they left.

As he looked around, the Frenchmen remained standing immediately inside the threshold, Yves armed with Mac's own Glock.

Narrowing his gaze to laser intensity, Mac dismissed Jean-Luc's status and took a dig at Yves's manhood. He glanced down at Roxie to emphasize her lack of inches. "Well, I'll be…don't tell me you're in awe of an unarmed man and woman?"

Yves's glance slanted in Jean-Luc's direction. "We will leave you in peace. What can you do? There is no way to escape. We will quell any attempt you make. So save your energy."

"Never entered my mind," Mac lied. "I'm willing to stay here as Zukah's guest until the boss man arrives to negotiate the deal. Just remind him that, though my resources are almost limitless, my patience has a use-by date."

He let the indictment hang in the air for a moment then turned the tables on them. "We'll expect breakfast around seven-thirty, eight o'clock at the latest. Lock the door on the way out, we'd like a little privacy."

Before they could leave, Roxie asked, "Hey, this place is like an icebox. What do we do for heat?"

Yves smiled, the first one to cross his face since he'd followed the Algerian into Mac's apartment. "You have each other," he mocked, earning a ferocious look for his trouble.

Walking desultorily, Roxie left Mac's side and sat down on one of the small blue-painted wooden chairs on either side of a table that had been placed in front of the uncurtained window.

Though his back was to the door, he heard it close, listening with interest to the tumblers clicking in the old-fashioned lock.

So, two covert agents alone at last.

He wondered which one of them would break their cover first?

Mac shrugged off the notion it would be him, but he hoped Roxie knew better than to reveal the nature of her mission while every little thing they said was most likely being recorded.

"Are you always so confrontational when a guy's holding a gun on you?" she asked as she unbuttoned the top button of her coat.

Mac raised his eyebrows in mock surprise. Maybe she wasn't as green as he'd thought. "Talk about me? I saw you cut those guys off at the knees with a glance."

Her small heart-shaped face scrunched into a grimace. "It's a French thing," she said reverting to English. "Those guys should be used to it. I learned that look at my grandmother's knee."

"Did she teach you to cook as well?"

"As a matter of fact, she did."

"Now, that's what I call an asset."

She pouted, leaning one elbow on the table, as if the sleep she'd had as they traveled hadn't done much good. "I should have known you were one of those guys who believe in keeping their wives barefoot, pregnant and chained to the kitchen...and talking about plumbing, did anyone mention a bathroom?"

"No one did, but since there is only one possibility, I'd try that door in the corner next to the armoire."

No sooner said than she was off. "Hey," she called out, her voice echoing. "There must be a tower on the corner, this room curves on three sides." Then the door clicked shut behind her.

And then there was one, he thought, remembering an old black-and-white movie set in a remote house.

Mac shivered. Roxie was right about it feeling colder up here, colder still now Roxie had left the room. Her personality could almost be termed sunny when she wasn't pretending to be scared out of her wits.

He gave the low-ceilinged room the once-over, not that he expected Zukah to be that obvious in his placement of listening devices.

The furniture was about what one would expect in an attic,

remnants no longer wanted downstairs. The brass bed was set against a backdrop of faded yellow wallpaper.

Its size hardly made a dent in the open floor space.

Mac sat on the edge of the bed to test the mattress and it complained. Quilts had been piled on top to disguise a thin mattress on an even thinner wire-sprung base. But it was chilly enough to make the down-filled covers necessary.

He huffed out a breath that hung in the air like mist.

It wouldn't surprise him if they were near a river, the Loire maybe, for he hadn't noticed the loaded minivan being tested by many hills.

The bed creaked as his weight came off it.

What were the odds of Roxie allowing him to share? That way he wouldn't be forced to sleep on the lumpy easy chair Zukah had provided, or, God forbid, lie on the floor?

What would it take to convince her that just because she was female and breathing, he had no intention of hitting on her?

When her eyes lit up, she seemed pretty enough. That's when she wasn't hiding behind her coat collar.

In fact, once he'd gotten over the annoyance of her arrival, and hauled her out of her jam, he'd wondered if MI6 were so short of volunteers, they'd begun giving their secretaries assignments.

He laughed to himself, imagining her toffee-nosed SAC saying, "Take a note, Roxie. Collect a semiautomatic on your way out, you have a mission in France."

Yeah, and that was likely. As far as he could see, she hadn't been armed with anything larger than her cell phone. And for the first time he paused to wonder, why not?

Roxie sat on the commode with the lid down. All she'd wanted was a little privacy to have a nervous breakdown. And now thank heaven, she was over it.

Charles would be having fits tomorrow when she didn't call in.

She stood up, swiped at her cheeks with the backs of her knuckles, hoping her outburst hadn't left streaks of mascara.

The mirror was old, freckled with green-mottled patches where dampness had invaded the backing, but it was clear enough to show the giveaway red blotches under her eyes.

Compared to some French bathrooms she'd visited, this one was large, but somewhat utilitarian. It had been a surprise to twist the faucet and feel the water run hot.

The metal bath was so ancient its claw-foot style had been in vogue and out again at least twice since the original was cast.

However, she was pleased to note some thoughtful person had jerry-rigged a shower over the bath, as well as a circular rod and curtain. That was as far as privacy went.

The first thing she'd discovered on entering the bathroom was it had no lock on the door.

Soap and clean towels were piled on the counter by the basin, so she hung her coat on a hook on the back of the door until she tidied up.

Just as she'd thought, her shoulder-length brown hair was curling at the ends. She tucked the long, loose waves that fell over one eye behind her ear as she washed her face, washing off the results of her disastrous evening while listening to Mac moving around in the next room.

Sucking in a deep breath, she held it till she had no choice but to let go or explode. She'd taken so long that any moment now he would come looking for her.

And she wasn't certain how to handle that, handle him.

Sure, he'd been kind in a rough sort of way, but there was just no getting away from the fact that his career designation came under the heading Criminal or, even worse, Terrorist.

The knock at the bathroom door came before she'd made up her mind about her companion and now it was too late.

"Hey, Roxie. Are you decent? Can I come in?"

She flashed a glance in the mirror. It was okay, not a trace of red to give her away. Her hands worked at the towel, folding and tucking it over the rail as she called, "It's not locked."

The bathroom had seemed fairly large until Mac entered and it shrunk to half its original size.

Feeling small was something she'd grown used to, but his presence was intimidating, a combination of height and breadth, plus she was uncertain about his part in this evening's events.

Without saying another word, he tilted the mirror to one side to look behind it.

Before she could ask what he was searching for, he put a finger to his lips, then turned on the faucet, letting the water run. That done, he checked out the other fixtures, crouching low to squint behind the pipes.

He was acting more like a plumber than the guy who'd rescued her life like a regulation white knight. Though she knew for sure now that his armor was tarnished.

And knowing that, why did she feel a sudden buzz in her nerve endings as she looked at him?

Sure, he was handsome when you got past the greasy hair and what passed for designer stubble but looked like laziness....

The mental criticism of him ground to a halt as he drawled, "So, what happened to the mouse?"

She spun around, searching the floor. "What mouse, where?"

"You, in that damn coat. The way your nose peeked out the collar. Suddenly you've turned into a kingfisher all yellow, black and blue-green."

A glance in the mirror reassured her there was nothing unusual in her image. This morning, because it had turned cold, she'd worn layers, a short turquoise cardigan sweater she'd buttoned across her breasts, over a yellow tank and hanging under both of those a long black cashmere T.

They picked up the colors in her tweed skirt with its full unpressed pleats and asymmetrical hemline.

It was a funky design and she'd thought she looked pretty

cool when Charles had given it a pleasantly surprised glance. She might work for him, but her personal style was her own.

"I'd rather be a kingfisher than a mouse, so I'll put that down as a compliment, though I'm not the sort of person who fishes for them…."

She paused as he laughed at her play on words. Crinkles fanned out round his fascinating gold eyes.

On the whole, his description of her was pretty accurate. She loved color.

"I guess in your—" she hesitated, searching for the right word "—chosen profession not many fashion magazines come your way. Believe me, this is cutting-edge fashion, though not what you'd find in girlie magazines or calendars."

He smiled again, and she was getting more than a little annoyed that he found her information funny.

"Well, I should know. I designed the outfit myself. It's what I do. I'm an intern with Charles Fortier. You know, the couturier."

This last earned her a surprised lift of his brown eyebrows and a patronizing nod. "I have heard of him, and no, I don't go in for girlie magazines."

He ran his gaze over her from the tip of her boots to the top of her head. "I'm not a voyeur. I prefer my women in the flesh, not paper. But don't worry, you wear your cover well, Roxie, I'll give you that."

She experienced hot and cold flashes of confusion while trying to make up her mind whether he'd given her a compliment or a warning of intent. "I don't suppose I'm up to your standard, though."

"Not many are," he agreed.

She jerked back as he brushed past her and reached over to turn on the shower. Not the response she'd expected.

Roxie had discovered to her cost that she wasn't any good at reading certain men. And men of Mac's stature she usually tried to avoid for all the looking up gave her a crick in the neck.

His close proximity swamped her in feelings of claustrophobia, and as the water pipes clanked and rattled, she edged toward the door, desperate to get out of there, yet nervous that he'd find something to object to.

"Okay, the noise of the shower will stop us being overheard better than the basin faucet, so you can cut out the act. I know it wasn't any coincidence that you turned up when you did."

"What? No, I was sent, but I didn't know you lived there," she explained truthfully.

She would have added more but he leapt in. "Who sent you?"

"What difference does that make?" she countered. "If you must know, Charles Fortier sent me to see a Madam Billaud, but I got the wrong apartment."

The bright gold flash of annoyance in his eyes was tempered by a heave of his massive shoulders in a demonstration of supreme control. "All right, have it your way. I guess I should have known you wouldn't give out."

The expression tickled her funny bone.

Her offbeat humor had a reputation for springing to life at the most inappropriate moments. "Not on the first date, anyway," she told him pertly.

"Yeah, you're right. Why should you? We both have our secrets and it's best we keep them to ourselves for now."

Secrets? What were his?

She was annoyed by the notion that Mac hadn't believed a word she'd said, and that being the case, who had he decided she was?

Mac wasn't bothered by her silence. Hell, he hadn't exactly used thumbscrews. Besides, he had his own way of discovering whom she worked for.

That entire story she'd given him about working for Fortier?

She'd put it over reasonably well. Maybe she wasn't the virgin agent he'd taken her for, but she was still pretty green.

Whichever outfit she worked for, its sources weren't as good as IBIS's or they would have known IBIS was on the job and left the field to its agents, instead of interfering.

He couldn't help the smug feeling in his chest, knowing that when he'd said yes to Jason Hart he'd taken a big step up.

From the Office of Naval Intelligence to a much higher life-form growing on the same family tree.

Mac saw no reason to let Roxie in on the miniature cell phone Thierry had slipped him in secret. It had only taken a quick look to know his fellow agent hadn't failed him.

The cell phone was a secure digital one, and he had every intention of putting it to good use once Roxie fell asleep.

Not only that, the device could also screen the room for bugs. Listening devices had to be his next priority. But he had to find them in a way that left Roxie unaware of how he'd managed it.

Of course he only wanted to *know* where the listening devices were hidden. To remove them would be like playing hide-and-seek, then standing up and giving the game away.

Where would be the fun in that?

Though he'd have enjoyed seeing Zukah's expression.

Face it, he really enjoyed his work, and would have reveled in the situation but for his latest problem.

The problem of his libido doing an about-face where Roxie was concerned. Her stripping off that coat was as mind-blowing as when a butterfly shucked its cocoon. And much more destructive.

No one could have been more surprised than him to feel the quickening in his groin.

He'd been thinking that at least he wouldn't have to take cold showers. Now, if Roxie could be talked into sharing the bed, chances were he'd need one. Or, maybe a few.

He would have liked to blame his reactions to the way the steam softened her round the edges, making her look more appealing than at first sight.

Take her eyes. Right now they looked misty and vulnerable.

Too much more of that and he'd end up believing the cover story she was using.

"Shall I leave you to it, then?"

"Uh-uh," he told her, "not before we have a chance to talk."

"But we just talked." She reached for the handle, her head turning away from him.

"There are rules to be set."

Her eyes snapped open as she lifted her head to glare, eyes cool as steel. "Rules!" she protested. "What rules?"

Mac stepped closer and held a finger to her lips. "Shush…"

He bent closer, his lips almost touching her ear, his hand on her shoulder. Without the covering of her coat, Roxie's bones felt fragile, easily broken.

A surge of regret foreshadowed the emotion of that event coming to pass. For all he'd been rough on her earlier, and carried scars both bodily and mental from Lucia, he couldn't bring himself to physically hurt Roxie.

No, not him. But Zukah's men—now, there was a different breed of animal all together.

He tried to shrug off the thought. Such sentiments on his part were dangerous, the price so high he couldn't afford to pay it.

Better to remember this was simply an act they'd begun to save her life. "Don't say anything you wouldn't say in front of Zukah and his crew, especially out there," he warned her, voice pitched to add a hard edge to the words.

"The bathroom looks clear, but chances are the other room has been bugged."

She gave him another of her wide-eyed stares and mouthed one word. "Bugged."

What had she expected? Hadn't they taught her the basics? She closed her eyes as if trying to get her head around the notion.

"Look, they believe we're lovers and that's the way we have to play it, okay?"

Beneath his palm, he felt a shiver accompany the nod she gave in reply. "*Chérie,* you're freezing. Why don't you take a shower while I look to see if they've provided anything useful apart from the bed? There doesn't appear to be much in the way of heating so we'll just have to cuddle up."

There was only one bed.

Of course, Roxie understood that Mac's suggestion was for the Algerian's benefit, but she had to clamp her teeth down on a nervous stutter. "W-we'll, what?"

Mac raised a warm smile and she knew why; he expected her to share that bed with him.

She wanted to ask, "What kind of illegal deal are you brokering that warrants us being threatened with guns and knives as well as taken prisoner?"

But that was obviously one of the secrets he'd mentioned so she saved her breath. She wasn't completely stupid.

Mac was probably from the Russian mafia buying weapons from…

Her thoughts faltered. She could feel Mac's large, strong hand on her shoulder, strong enough to kill her with one blow.

Darn, she needed to find a scenario that wasn't so scary, but she couldn't get it out of her mind and panic surfaced at the speed of light.

Her chest expanded as she looked from his hand to him, and a scream built in her lungs.

Mac cut it off with a kiss, and for a minute she couldn't breathe never mind think. The kiss deepened, and before she knew what had happened she began to enjoy it. This wasn't good.

No. This was very bad.

Her head was still spinning when he lifted his lips from hers. She'd just discovered what it meant to become putty in someone's hands, but she wished they hadn't belonged to Mac.

"Better now?" His voice was gentle, as was the hand rubbing her back. Soft. Gentle. Sexy. "Believe me, you'll get used to it in time."

She nodded, ignoring an urgent desire to melt into his arms and throw every particle of moral decency she believed in out of the window.

"All you have to remember is no matter what I do or say, play along. They think we're lovers. We have only to keep up the charade and everything will be okay."

As his breath grazed her cheek, she was struck by the absurdity of them standing so close, when he'd said they could speak freely without being overheard.

Yet, she stayed where she was, steam billowing like sea fog round an island, hiding them from the rest of the world. "You really believe that we'll get out of this with our skins?"

"Yes, and you better believe it, too. So far, you've handled it like a pro. Be proud of that."

In a way he was correct. It was one thing letting him know she was frightened, but she had hidden it from the others. Mac aside, that's what had kept her alive. "I'll try."

He patted her shoulder, an action that ought to have reassured her. "Have that shower now," he said, "and try to get warm while I check the rest of the attic. If I find a bug we'll put it to good use."

"You mean misinformation?"

"Exactly. And by the way, while I'm gone, get used to the idea of sharing the bed."

So much for him treating her like a niece.

She spluttered, but he didn't give her a chance to object.

"I've no intention of freezing my butt on the floor, so we share the bed and the warmth and that's all. However, if I find any bugs next door we might have to do a little pretending. Make the bed squeak and moan a little. Put on a show to stop arousing their suspicions."

Mac left before she could let rip. *Put on a show?* She hadn't signed up for this. In fact, she hadn't signed up for being intimidated by Mac, or being taken hostage.

And she definitely hadn't signed up for sharing a bed with a man she'd known less than six hours.

Chapter 4

Mac sent up a silent *thank-you* to his Maker that he discovered the camera on top of the armoire before starting his search.

Guess they hadn't counted on him being so tall.

His second piece of luck was in knowing the make and model. It recorded in monochrome and was triggered by movement, but it didn't have a facility for sound.

It irritated him to know that if his mind had been on the job, instead of worrying about Roxie, he would have anticipated its presence.

It made sense that Zukah wouldn't expect him to go around talking to himself. That didn't mean he could discount them having placed listening devices.

The camera meant he needed to take a much more subtle approach to searching for the little beasties.

On leaving the bathroom, the first place he'd checked had been behind the armoire. The woodwork was badly scarred and it was too heavy to move without making a noise.

He'd run his fingers down the small gap between it and the wall next to the bathroom door and found nothing. But the armoire wasn't as high as the bar he used to do chin-ups.

As soon as he raised his head above the contoured wooden ledge, he'd noticed where the dust had been disturbed.

Then again, the wire leading from the miniature camera was a complete giveaway. What bothered him most about the setup was the camera angle. It hit the bed square on.

Roxie was going to give him problems, or maybe not. Maybe the camera had solved that one for him.

His mind raced ahead, planning.

Content with his decision, he took off his jacket, folded it and laid it on the floor by the side of the immense piece of furniture, all this done without moving in front of the camera.

Roxie had to be in the shower by now and the plastic curtain ought to give the illusion she was safe from prying eyes.

Clouds of steam engulfed him when he opened the door. Once inside, he saw a neat pile of folded clothes on the white marble counter surrounding the basin, while her black boots sat on the floor.

Behind the opaque white plastic her shape was a pink blur, an enticing blur. Too bad that the time, the place, the woman and the moment were all wrong.

It hadn't occurred to him that she might not have heard him enter as he called out, "Roxie?"

She let out a whoop of surprise and for a moment looked as though she might slip. He stepped forward to catch her, but all that happened was the plastic curtain ballooned, then resettled.

Rosy-cheeked, her head appeared around the edge of the shower curtain.

He hadn't the heart to tell her that the plastic she was clinging to for protection showed the perfect curve of her breasts with their dusky centers as clearly as if it had been fashioned from glass.

"What are you doing here? Can't I have a shower in private?"

"This is urgent or I wouldn't have intruded. There's a camera...."

"What, in here?" The hem of the curtain skidded across the metal bath as she wrapped it closer. Close enough for him to tell that the hair guarding the apex of her thighs was as brown as the damp strands curling against her cheeks.

"No. It's on top of the armoire and aimed straight at the bed." While he watched her take in the information, he kept his eyes fixed on her face. Her panic would only escalate if she looked down and saw the view he had of her nude figure.

"Wonderful, we have a permanent Peeping Tom in the bedroom. We'll never get away with pretending to be lovers."

"Yes we will." He needed to persuade her it was imperative they make the show convincing.

"Look, I'm not saying it will be easy. This bathroom is the only place we can let down our guard. But once they suspect that we're playacting..."

He paused, wondering how he could put it without alarming her more than he already had. "Wouldn't you enjoy fooling them?"

Her wet eyelashes were clumped together by small droplets that fell as she nodded emphatically. "I'd like that very much."

From where she stood their eyes were level at last, but it only served to emphasize how tiny she really was, and make him wonder once more what had made her go into the spy business.

But his momentary lapse into empathy now made him even more blunt. "I'm still the man with the money, they need me. If they discover my deception they'll probably put it down as a hero complex and laugh it off as some stupid act of valor, it's a guy thing. But you...?"

He gave it to her straight with the certainty that she wouldn't thank him for treating her like a child.

He'd been correct. She shook fear by the throat and said, "Come on, Mac, spit it out. They'll kill me, won't they?"

Reluctant to load her with more bad news, he bit the inside of his cheek, before deciding that this was one aspect of their incarceration he could share with total honesty.

Hell, she was an experienced agent; she should know the score.

Sure, he'd had a moment's aberration when he'd kissed her and gained a response, but they both knew that was a no-go area.

There was a rueful quality to the sigh that accompanied the shrug of his shoulders. "I hate to admit it, but there is every chance of them taking that way out."

Damn, since when had he become so namby-pamby? "*Chérie,* what other choice have the bad guys got? You've seen their faces."

"So have you." She did the eye-roll thing, a flash of silver that made him wish he could promise nothing would happen to her, and asked him, "Aren't you frightened they'll kill you as well?"

He didn't want to supplant the hope he saw in her eyes with disillusionment, but he had no other choice.

Once she suspected he wasn't as crooked as the others—that he was just a guy doing his damnedest to keep America and the rest of the world secure from terrorists—she might let her guard slip, and then it would indeed be curtains for Roxie.

And not the see-through shower type, still giving him an occasional glimpse of her womanly charms to stir memories of having them pressed close against him.

"The unfortunate part, *chérie*, is that I'm the other half of the deal. If they go down, so do I."

"I wouldn't dare identify you, Mac. You saved my life."

"So you say now, Roxie. You could change your mind."

He couldn't afford to forget that facet of the operation. Hell, with his training, he couldn't believe an agent would put accomplishing her mission ahead of everything they'd been taught.

Of course, Roxie could have stashed some sly tricks up her sleeve. He knew he had.

They would be just another of the many things that she wasn't about to share with the crook she believed him to be.

How could he tell? It was a like a grab bag. Some were willing to confess to anything to stay safe. And against all odds, the most mild-mannered person could turn into a hero or heroine.

Since that shared kiss, a slim thread of doubt lingered in the back of his mind. If Roxie was who she'd claimed, he was already guilty of corrupting an innocent.

Damn, after only six hours. That would be a record.

"What do you want me to do, Mac?"

"Nothing drastic. I need to discover where the bugs are, but I can't do that with that camera recording my every move."

He'd already thought the steps out. "Once you're somewhat decent, come through and slip into bed. I'll say I'm turning the light out. After that it will be easy to toss my jacket over the camera and switch the light back on so I can search for bugs."

She nodded at him, wet curls bouncing on her forehead as if this was nothing out of the ordinary. Yeah, she was an agent. The decision made him feel better.

"Look, even if I find the bugs, they'll have to stay where they are. I don't want Zukah or his lackeys suspecting anything other than that we're content to spend some time together."

She showed him a wry grimace. "Our so-called honeymoon?"

"That's it in a nutshell. Are you with me, *chérie?*"

"Of course. What choice do I have?"

"Couple of days, tops, and we should be out of here. Until then…it will have to be make and mend as we go along."

"Okay, turn your back and let me get out of the shower."

"No, hang on a minute." He pulled out his shirt and began to unfasten it.

"Are you going to have a shower after all?"

"No, I'm going to wet my hair and pretend we've shared a shower." He stripped off his shirt, then turned on the faucet.

The water had just begun to run when Roxie cried, "Ow!"

The faucet spun round in his fingers as he shut it off again. "Sorry, forgot these old-fashioned systems wouldn't have a pressure equalizer. Did I burn you?"

"Not in any way that counts. The water just turned icy. Let me get out first this time." She turned around and once more all he could see was a flesh-colored blur, but she'd left him wondering what she meant by saying, *Not in any way that counts?*

He'd just decided if anyone ended up burned by this arrangement it could be him, when she said, "Shower's off."

Mac began running hot water into the basin.

"When I leave here, I'll make a show of looking through the armoire to see if anything useful has been left in it. Just remember not to look straight at the camera. And no matter what, follow my lead. Act as if you love me."

He almost told her, *The way you did when I kissed you.* She didn't seem to have to put on an act then.

Her mouth had simply flowered under his.

In the mirror he watched his own mouth twist in an expression of grim reality. Until he had Thierry check Roxie out, she'd better believe his was simply an act to make sure they both survived.

That way, he might not only get out of this situation alive but with his honor still intact.

"What are you doing, *chéri?* Come to bed." Mac heard a sultry ring of impatience in Roxie's voice. Only the two of them knew it wasn't the sound of a hot-blooded woman anxiously awaiting her lover.

Or, that having him in bed with her was way down on her wish list, if indeed it made it at all.

"Soon as I switch off the lights."

Under cover of darkness, he threw his leather jacket over the camera, but before turning them on again there was something he needed to be sure of.

Barefoot, he padded softly toward the window. A pale gold haze bloomed behind the trees like dawn on the horizon. Since it wasn't anywhere near daybreak, it could only mean a largish town wasn't too far distant.

Interesting, but that wasn't what he needed to know. The window overlooked the dark driveway and was unbroken by patches of light.

That meant the other occupied rooms must face the back of the house, which meant it was okay to flick the switch on without anyone noticing there was light coming from the attic while the monitor showing the attic was dark.

"How many extra quilts did you pile on this bed?" Roxie's voice sounded hot and breathless, though she'd only worn her long black T-shirt to sleep in.

Her words reached out to him through the thick gloom, a reminder that the conversation was lagging.

"Only two."

"One would have done." As the light came back on she tossed off the quilts he'd found in the armoire and slipped out of bed. Her dark hair, dry now, had a tousled and sexy appeal, as if someone had just run his hands through it.

For God's sake, keep your mind on the job, Mac.

He palmed the countersurveillance gadget. Just in time, a second later, she was over at the table standing beside him shivering. "Trust me, we'll need them."

"Come under the covers and then tell me that. The sheets are cold as well."

He knelt down. Keeping his hands hidden, he ran a scan and found a bug. There were so few pieces of furniture this shouldn't take long as he'd already covered the armoire.

That left the easy chair and the bed. His concentration focused on one thing alone, and again Roxie had to fill in the conversation. "Isn't this the most uncomfortable bed we've ever slept in?"

She'd gone back to the bed and was jiggling the edge of the mattress.

"I don't remember doing much sleeping," he said from the end of the bed as he knelt to check underneath and got a faint signal.

He moved to the other side. Roxie followed by rolling across the quilts, achieving a few satisfactory squeaks of the mattress.

They were eye to eye as she inquired, "Don't you know a euphemism when you hear it?"

"You mean you'd prefer me to use a much more earthy term?" he asked, then ducked his head, quick to hide his grin. And there it was, a bug behind the antique iron frame supporting the sway-backed spring base.

Damn Zukah. That one would have to go. Somehow he'd have to make it look like an accident, so that the Algerian kept thinking he was as dumb as they were both acting at the moment.

Her voice came down to him, "Actually, I meant instead of making love."

"With you, *chérie*—" he punctuated his words with a couple of crude kissing noises "—I always make love." Then putting a finger to his lip, he pointed behind the headboard.

He had to admit she was quick on the uptake. While he turned the attic into a pool of darkness for a second time, she contrived to make smooching noises on the back of her hand.

Within two minutes he'd shed his jeans and was slipping into bed beside her.

Tonight, though it might be uncomfortable, he kept his shorts on as a concession to Roxie, the first time he'd worn a stitch to bed since junior high.

He felt her body heat seeping under the covers, calling him closer, or maybe that was the dip in the mattress.

It took him a couple of seconds to realize she had been lying there rigid from the moment he hit the sheets. Time to take up the slack before his macho reputation took a dive with whoever was listening. "*Chérie,* I want you out of those clothes."

He sat up making the bed groan and finished with "Now isn't that better?"

Better for whom, Roxie wanted to ask, but instead infused her voice with steam heat. "Much better. Come closer, I want to feel you against me," she told him, counting on his promise not to jump her bones. After all, they *were* in this together.

The gasp he uttered satisfied the devil in her, but she wondered if he felt all that kissing of the back of her hand was worth the effort he put into it.

Then all thought vanished as he moved his lips to the fine skin inside her wrist.

Her pulse raced. Darn, she knew he could feel it hiccup when his lips lingered on that particular spot before moving to the inside of her elbow.

No better. Her skin was so sensitive there that his tongue felt as rough as a cat's as he licked at it.

His breathing became labored and heavy and all too real, the sound of it making her head swim as her own breaths mimicked the noises he made.

This had to stop. He could forget trying to seduce her, she wasn't about to roll over and think of England or even France for that matter.

"Oooh, Mac," she groaned, thrusting off his hand so she could reach for a mental life raft.

Whoa, Mac told himself as he came up for air.

The sensation of her pulse jolting against his tongue was enough to tempt a saint to forget his vows.

It was a small leap from there to remembering the view he'd had through the shower curtain. Blood rushed into his groin.

Instead of sipping, Mac wanted to plunder. Wanted to feel her body under and over his, while he discovered some of the many delights Roxie had to offer.

Thank God one of them had some sense.

But it should have been him who pulled away, not Roxie.

He'd come up against some fantastic-looking women in his time. It was one of the hazards of his occupation. Damn, he couldn't count the number of bad beautiful women who worked for the enemy.

Only one had gotten past his defenses, though, and he couldn't let that happen again.

And why would he? He wasn't a fool, and he wasn't about to risk blowing his cover by sweeping Roxie into his arms and really making love to her.

Time to get back to playacting.

"How's that feel, *chérie?*"

"Wonderful." The word seemed to tremble from her lips as he moved up higher in the bed. Her breath feathered across his shoulder as the dip in the mattress threw them together. Double damn.

He pushed her away and sat up, but worse was to come. She eased up, elbow resting on her pillow and, in an impassioned whisper that rippled across the last threads of his control, said, "Oh, Mac, take me, take me now."

Thank God, he felt her shoulders shake. She was laughing.

A small miracle, but he grasped it in both hands.

Action. That's what he needed. Holding the brass headboard with one hand, he began to bounce. Desperate times called for desperate measures, the occasional grunts from his efforts would have to pass for passion.

When the headboard accidentally banged against the wall, he did it a few more times. Serve them right if he deafened the pervert listening and made Yves of the many hands go crazy with lust.

That thought led straight to another, a brilliant explanation for the bug at the head of the bed breaking.

He heard an odd hiccup from Roxie, somewhere between laughter and tears. He gave her a nudge in reply with his knee and the game was on, Mac thumping the wall while Roxie kept time.

It was he who had trouble muffling his laughter as she did the classic coffee-shop scene of exaggerated moans. And Mac's body felt exhilarated and exhausted at once, as if they'd really made love.

The headboard hit the wall another couple of times, as he yelled loud enough to deafen anyone listening. Out of breath, he slid under the covers that no longer felt cold. "Was that good for you, *chérie?*"

Roxie sounded genuinely sleepy. "Mac, you're the best. Night…" He felt her roll onto her side, facing away from him.

Too bad his performance hadn't done anything to cull his aching need. Listening to her moan had exacerbated his condition to the point of torture.

But wondering how it felt to be inside her, to be the one who made her sigh and gasp, would be more kill than cure, and his mother never raised a masochist. No sir.

True American patriots, his mother and father had served their country with diplomacy in embassies set in some of the most far-flung countries of the world.

Serving the United States had become ingrained in him from the time he was a small child. That's what had made him the man he was today, a man of honor. As for the different roles he played, the lies he told, they didn't count.

At first the pretense had simply been a way to serve his country, but after meeting Jason Hart, they had become a means of keeping the world safe from terrorism.

He turned his back to Roxie.

Sleep wouldn't find him as easily as it had her. He still had work to do, Thierry to contact. An hour passed slowly in the heavy silence.

Finally, at 3:00 a.m., he slipped from under the covers, hardly disturbing them as he left her sleeping, and dressed in his jeans and jacket, then unfastened his watch to retrieve a fine tungsten lock pick from the back of it.

Mac had checked the door to the attic earlier and been quietly pleased to discover Yves had made it easy for him by removing the key. The lock turned with hardly a sound.

Easing the door open, he slipped out onto the top landing and down the stairs, confident of being back before she even knew he was gone.

As well as contacting Thierry, there was the layout of the house to reconnoiter and an escape route to plan. This time, he would be prepared, and should another gorgeous woman chance to cross his path, he'd step aside and let her go on by.

With Roxie, he was sailing too close to the wind.

Let her believe he was a criminal. He didn't care. Nor would he let her know that no matter what he'd told her, he wouldn't stand by and watch anyone harm her.

It took him thirty minutes to reconnoiter the house and talk to Thierry. The question uppermost in his mind had been answered.

The identity of the fourth man.

IBIS had identified the owner of the house, Monsieur Victoire Sevarin, deputy minister of France's Department of Defense.

No matter how deeply some internal security agencies scrutinized the backgrounds of their employees, one rotten apple always managed to taint the whole barrel.

Sevarin's had been the hand that controlled France's biotech weapons research. Who better to acquire Green Shield than the man who was supposed to control its destruction?

One problem solved, a thousand to go.

Already aware of Sevarin, Thierry's priorities took an oblique angle. "Who was the girl?"

He gave Thierry all the information he had, which didn't include her surname. How to explain that the blood running hot in his veins had put a little thing like surnames out of his mind.

It wasn't the type of information Mac wanted to get around.

Back in the attic, Mac locked the door, with no one the wiser that he'd been gone. Quickly discarding his clothes, he padded over to the bed and slid under the pile of quilts covering Roxie.

As soon as his body hit the mattress, the extra weight sent her rolling toward him. She snuggled against him without waking. Then wrapped around him, tangling her legs with his as if they always slept that way.

It was a long night.

Roxie's head rested serenely on his chest as the sky began to turn from blue-black to gray. He hadn't slept, but that was something he was used to. It hadn't taken him long to discover she'd ditched the T-shirt she'd been wearing in the half hour he'd been gone. Now the soft swell of her lace-covered breasts presented him with a tease he didn't dare respond to.

He was totally firm about that in his mind.

His body had no such scruples.

Mac discovered when it came to Roxie, no amount of reciting times tables or logarithms could suppress the erection lying between them. It pressed into the welcoming curve of her belly as if it had a mind of its own.

As soon as the sun came up, he would leave her in bed and treat his libido to a cold shower, since that looked like being the only reprimand it understood.

Chapter 5

Bars of pale watery sunlight slipped through the bars on the window, painting stripes on the faded blue quilt covering Roxie.

Memory hit her the moment she opened her eyes and surveyed her prison. She leapt out of bed, checking her watch.

It was 8:00 a.m. and she was alone.

Roxie glanced down at the lacy camisole revealing her breasts, and from it to the little-boy short panties that matched. The T-shirt she'd gone to bed in was on the floor, and she couldn't remember taking it off, but at least she was halfway decent.

It took several moments more to recall the camera that watched her every move, and less time than that to pick up the black T-shirt and pull it over her head.

Trying not to glance the camera's way, she ran her palm across the rumpled sheets on the other side of the bed. There was still a dent in the feather pillow from Mac's head.

The sheets were still warm. Almost as warm as the memory of the act she'd put on the night before.

She could hear the shower running on the other side of the bathroom door. Hoping Mac was discreetly tucked behind its curtain as she dashed to the bathroom, with a perfunctory knock she dived through the door without waiting for a reply.

Eyes closed, Roxie leaned back against the coat she'd left hanging from the hook, to catch her breath.

It must have been Mac leaving the bed they were sharing that wakened her, since he couldn't have been showering long, for the steam still hadn't filled the bathroom.

She could see Mac's tall shape through the opaque plastic curtain, the top of his head level with the curtain rail.

Although his outline was blurred, she made out that it tapered nicely from shoulder to waist, six-pack abs but no unnecessary mass to his muscles.

Heat scored her cheekbones as she remembered curving her hand round his arm while pressing against his chest. But she had no time to dwell on the memory as Mac asked, "Come to join me?"

"No!" she snapped. "Just to get away from being peeped at."

His head appeared round the edge of the curtain and he flashed a wide grin. "I hung your panty hose over the towel rail."

"Thanks." *I think.* "At least something will be fresh."

She huffed down her nose; his sudden affability felt suspicious. Had she done more in her sleep than drape her body across a notable selection of pecs and abs?

The memory of rough hair tickling her cheek was an impression she wished she could dismiss. So instead she got stuck on their owner. "How soon do you think we'll get out of here? I mean you must be miffed that these people don't keep their word. If it were me I'd say the hell with it and let this one pass...."

"Well, you're not me and I never get miffed." Mac moved round as he spoke and a shoulder appeared on the lower right of his face.

This bald statement required no comeback. Just as well.

She was too busy comparing how bronzed his skin was to her much paler version. The shower curtain clung to his knee, to a thigh, and higher, then she realized the darker shadow was the hair surrounding his sex.

She glanced away, embarrassed, then back again, eyes sparking as she realized Mac must have seen her as clearly last night.

"You look beautiful when you're angry." His grin flashed, but to draw back or hide was obviously out of character.

"Flattery…will…get…you…nowhere." She shot each word separately, wishing they would pierce his armor. Then she sent him an incensed "You might have told me."

Mac knew it was time to put her straight again. "Even with the best intentions in the world, I'm unrepentantly human. And for my sins, exceedingly male, as well, I offer no apology. You were the most delicious sight I've seen in a long time."

He looked her up and down. "Still are, I might add."

Roxie might not be tall, but with her T-shirt barely reaching the hem of her panties her legs looked as if they went on forever.

He watched her chest rise as she sucked in moist air.

Indignation or surprised delight, at the moment he found it hard to tell which had the upper hand as she told him, "Well, I'm not used to dealing so…so personally with a stranger or sleeping with one."

Mac couldn't let her get away with that statement. "All I can say is you sure cuddled up to me as if you were."

But he wasn't done taunting her. "That curvy body you're sporting fit mine as if it were made to measure."

What was the point in pulling his punches while there was no chance of them being overheard?

"Oh, come off it," she scoffed. "I'm human, and it was cold, that's all."

"Well, just say the word. Making love to you would be a hell of a lot easier than pretending to." Too damn easy, but he didn't dare let it happen. He knew the road to purgatory lay in that direction, and as attractive as the view looked, he drew the line at thinking this business was only about the two of them.

Roxie and Mac. Mac and Roxie.

"Ooh." She marched closer. "I may not be as sophisticated as some Frenchwomen, but I never make love with a man who can't be bothered asking my name."

Well she had him there this time, he decided as his conversation with Thierry came back to haunt him.

Forgetting to discover Roxie's last name had been a mistake.

Although, from her expression, he was sure it was a mistake she was about to rectify, even if it was only with her cover name. The one she used as a supposed intern for Charles Fortier.

He looked down the length of his nose at her and filled his smile with ice as he said, "Your name is Roxie…whatever, it doesn't matter. All that counts is your connection to me. Zukah belongs to a dominant-male culture."

Roxie sniffed her defiance. How dare he take her for granted? "It matters to me." She tilted her head to look up at him. "My name is Roxie Kincaid and don't you forget it."

As if from the force of her insubordination, the curtain swayed toward Mac and clung.

Flushed to the roots of her hair, Roxie couldn't tear her eyes away even though she was uncertain whether or not such revelations were actually good for her.

He was definitely the male of the species, and a magnificent specimen at that.

Mac's amber eyes that had held her at first glance narrowed and hardened into shards of granite. "Is that what you want carved on your tombstone? Roxie Kincaid, stubborn to the bitter end?"

Mac swung the shower curtain aside, looking so fierce the clatter of the curtain rings sounded like a death knell, off key, but scary nonetheless.

Intimidated, she stepped back.

Her view widened.

And she agreed, he was exceedingly, unrepentantly male.

She was used to male models, but there was nothing pretentious in Mac's manner as he stepped out of the bath to grab a towel.

He rubbed it over his hair, his eyes never leaving hers as he ground out a warning. "How many times does it take for the message to get through? For however long we are here, all that matters is that you're *my* woman. Your life depends on it. Maybe mine as well if they discover I lied. *Understand?*"

She nodded. He'd wanted to frighten her and he'd succeeded, and not by standing unclothed in front of her. This was no sexual encounter.

He towered over her, gloriously naked, and she noticed nothing more than how strong he was. A supple strength that could snap her like a twig should he feel so inclined.

"These men downstairs are the real deal. Don't make me regret saving your life." He slung the towel round his neck and grabbed another to wrap round his waist.

Darn it, how could she have forgotten? She began to backtrack. "Don't think I'm not grateful. It's just that it seems I've wandered into someone else's bad dream, and last night…"

"Whatever it takes." His eyes narrowed and filled with ice-cold sparks as his jaw hardened. He took her chin between finger and thumb and glared down at her. Roxie shuddered. She remembered him wearing that expression in his apartment when he'd demanded she say, *"I still love you, Mac."*

His face was so fierce, she stepped back, frightened, but he didn't let go of her chin, tilting it so his face filled her vision. "Listen to me," he said, "Don't let your guard slip when dealing with Zukah. Act the way you did last night."

She began to breathe easier with another lesson to chew over. No matter what he said, she instinctively knew Mac was a more dangerous breed of animal than any of the men downstairs.

"Whatever you say, Mac, you're the expert. I'll try to follow your lead." Hard not to while he held her chin in his hard fingers.

He let her go, her apology earning a raised eyebrow as if he doubted her ability to keep her word.

The feel of his fingertips clung like a burn to her skin as she prayed that Mac believed her worth saving. "You've left the shower running," she said helpfully, and blundered again.

He shook his head. "There's a reason, remember? This is the only place we can talk. Take advantage and have another shower."

"A lot of good that would do when you've used all the towels."

"No problem. I'll bring in some clean ones once I'm dressed. And don't worry, I won't look, at least, I'll try not to," he said from the doorway, and left with a grin on his face.

Though it took a swipe at her own courage to admit it, she felt relieved. All that mattered was his white grin was once more in evidence. That person was a whole lot easier to live with than the Mac she'd just visited. Some people you just wouldn't want to run across in a dark alley.

Mac's looks were deceiving. He was handsome as the day was long and had the kind of body to turn a woman's head, but once more he'd demonstrated his lethal side.

Too bad he hadn't shown that side of his nature to Zukah when the Algerian insisted they accompany him, and then carried them off on this farce of a honeymoon.

She hadn't yet come to a conclusion, but she was positive there was more to Mac than either she, or the Algerian, realized.

"Hey, out there, open up, we're hungry." Mac hammered on the attic door with his fist, not with words as he had with Roxie, but then she'd needed a scare.

All the playacting last night had given her the wrong impression and he'd had to set her straight.

He wondered just how long her air of contrition would last. Going by what he knew of her—and he intended knowing a lot more—she'd be back to normal by the time she finished eating.

He'd lied when he said he wouldn't look when he'd taken in the towels; he hadn't been able to resist. He did, however, regret his earlier remarks about the way she'd clung to him in her sleep.

Roxie was built like a pocket Venus with all her curves in place. He could still get hard remembering the way her nipples had ignored the barriers of lace and silk piercing his male libido effortlessly, the way he'd had bullets penetrate his skin.

Yeah, he was hot for Roxie Kincaid.

But it would never happen. Mind you, his father always said that death and paying taxes were the only two sure things in life. This had to be the third.

He was never going to make love to Roxie.

His groin wasn't the only place that pained him as he thought it. The scar where Lucia had stabbed him ached as a reminder of what happened when you let your guard down.

Breakfast was on the way. That was likely to be the best news of Roxie's day. So far nothing else had pleased her.

She didn't know what to think about Mac; when someone seemed too good to be true, they usually were.

She looked at the view outside the windows. Swathes of mist rose through bare-branched trees that appeared to be fighting a losing battle against clumps of mistletoe.

The sound of the attic door opening caused her to swing around away from the window. Jean-Luc came in carrying their breakfast with Yves behind him, empty-handed. His pocket was obviously the repository for the key, but there was no way she would dare get close enough to steal that.

"I'd just about given up believing in *petit déjeuner,*" she announced. "I hope there's enough, I'm famished."

Mac caught her eye. "Make that two of us, but let's see what they've brought before going crazy with delight."

The clatter of crockery drew her attention to cups and plates as they slid across the tray Jean-Luc was carrying. "Mon Dieu, there are too many stairs for me to wait upon you," he moaned.

She ignored the look Yves gave her by bending to pull out a chair. Roxie cast her eyes over the contents of the tray, then sighed. "Oh dear, no coffee."

Jean-Luc's hands stopped rearranging the tray. "That will be here soon, I couldn't carry everything, but it's excellent coffee. I made it."

A white napkin covered the plate in the center of the tray. She was about to whisk it off, when she noticed what else they were missing. "No knives."

Mac grinned. "Well, hardly."

Her jaw dropped as she whipped away the napkin. Croissants the colour of burnt toast. "What happened? How can your *pâtisserie* sell such poor quality?"

The boast had gone out of Jean-Luc. "They were frozen," he muttered, hunching his shoulders. The others must have been served burnt offerings, as well, if the black look Yves gave his compatriot was anything to go by.

She'd rather see Jean-Luc on the receiving end rather than suffer the hungry looks Yves kept throwing her way.

There was something in his eyes that frightened her in a way that Mac—for all he'd grabbed her and kissed her twice—had never done.

An idea presented itself to Mac as if it had come on the same plate as their breakfast pastries.

If it worked, it would get them out of the damn attic.

After a long day of being with Roxie and the bed in the same room, the combination might prove too tempting.

Maybe he could save his soul and eat better as well if the story Roxie had told him about learning to cook from her grand-mother was true.

He began putting his plan into action, saying, "We're not used to eating pig swill. Tell Zukah, if this is the best he can offer, then maybe we won't hang around after all."

He flipped the napkin back over the food, hoping that Zukah was listening downstairs. "Take this mess away and fetch cof-fee."

"No, Mac, maybe I can rescue some of these if I peel away the top layers. I'm hungry enough to attempt it."

He reached across the table, took the croissant from Roxie's fingers and shoved it back on top of the others. "*Chérie,* you shouldn't have to. This is an insult to French cuisine," he said, rubbing salt into Jean-Luc's wounds.

The Frenchman didn't try to defend himself. He just picked up the plate, saying, "Maybe I'll do better next time."

Mac did an about-face from derision to empathy. "Look, don't take it so hard. It's just that Roxie is an excellent French cook. She learned at her Grandmère's knee. It's hard not to make comparisons."

If there was one thing Mac had learned about Frenchmen dur-ing his Paris sojourn, they loved good food, and if it took going hungry a little longer…well, it was in a good cause.

He watched the expressions of the Frenchmen when they met up at the door. His plan looked to be a partial success. All it needed was the Algerian's approval, and with a gut like Zukah sported, he had to love his food.

It might be enough to get them both out of the attic.

Roxie had the grace to wait till the door closed before going for Mac's throat. "What was that about? I was hungry. I could have eaten the inside layers. With a little cherry conserve the burnt taste wouldn't have been so noticeable."

Mac put a finger to his lips. His face was a mask she couldn't read as he pulled out a piece of cellophane. She recognized it as the stuff she'd stripped from the soap and tossed on the marble counter. A second later Mac rustled the paper under the table.

"Do you want to stay shut up here in this attic?" His voice was a husky whisper that she had to lean close to catch.

Roxie responded in kind. "Not particularly. I don't see how we can change that unless you have a secret weapon that will help us blast our way out of here."

Mac's eyes started to glitter the way they had the night before, but she steeled her senses not to respond to the hypnotic light that had drawn her to him when they met. "You're my secret weapon."

"Me?" Roxie flung herself back in her chair, its legs scraping the wooden floor with the force of her astonishment. Her thoughts spun. Heaven only knew what he was going to ask of her now.

It was one thing pretending to make love for an unseen audience, but it was off the other end of the scale to expect her to keep up the act 24/7.

Mac rose from the table, surreptitiously slipping the cellophane into his pocket as he grabbed her arm, pulling her out of the chair. "Don't pout, *chérie*. The caffeine fix will help."

Roxie couldn't prevent her eyes straying toward the silent observer; Mac was saying one thing but doing another. Had he forgotten the video camera? As he motioned her to follow, it dawned on her that they were moving out of the camera's line of sight.

Shut in the bathroom once more, he ran the water, then propped his hip against the marble counter. "You're not very experienced in undercover work, are you? Do you want Zukah to know what we're up to?"

"What's with the *we?* I'm not up to anything, and I object to being ordered around as if I had no mind of my own. You might be used to this cops-and-robbers stuff but I'm not, and I'm sick of being kept in the dark."

He gripped both her shoulders as if he might shake her. "You don't have to put on a show for me. We haven't long before the coffee arrives. You said you could cook. Was that true?"

Her eyes widened. He was going to put her to work. "Of course it was the truth. I don't lie."

Not if I've a choice, she qualified silently.

One of his eyebrows lifted a fraction. The man was a conundrum. He expected her trust, while he didn't give an inch.

A wave of pity for him dashed over her. Made her consider smoothing the dark stubble crowding his jawline. It must be terribly lonely when you trusted no one.

She capitulated. "Tell me what you want this time and I'll do my best to fall in with your plans."

"Oh, they won't be my plans, they'll be Zukah's. Protest a little, but I'm sure you'll enjoy this much more than staying here with me while I have nothing to do but devise ways of getting you into the sack."

She should be taken aback, surprised even, but nothing about Mac surprised her anymore. Did he think she was stupid?

Was this all part of his scheme to con her into doing exactly as he wanted? He moved toward the door and she followed. "Sorry, Mac. If your aspirations extend to receiving my cooperation for that, dream on…."

It was no big stretch for him to cup the back of her neck in his huge hand. His fingers caressed the sensitive spot behind her ear as he pulled her closer. She didn't resist, couldn't.

So much for her last boast.

His mouth mesmerized her as it came closer, so close she could taste him. She licked her lips and felt energy arc from his mouth to hers following the damp trail her tongue had left.

Lifting her eyes, she sought out his gaze, suddenly in need of reassurance they weren't about to plunge into another disaster, but his lids had already closed as if he could find her mouth by instinct, and he did.

The first touch of his lips was like a tiny spark in a forest that had only needed the correct fuel to become a conflagration.

Roxie felt like a flame in his arms.

A twist of fire and smoke that could wind its way round his body to feed off his energy and never get enough.

The seam of her lips parted under the pressure of his tongue, and once it gained entrance, teased hers to dance. To twirl, entwine and thrust as she followed it back into a mouth filled with masculine tastes and treasures that made her blood sizzle while her temperature headed for the boiling point.

She reached up to stroke the velvet stubble that heightened the sensations of his mouth moving over hers. Her other hand dug through the thick strands of his hair, clamped onto the back of his neck as she strained against the solid wall of his chest.

His hand slipped from the back of her neck, down under her sweater to her collarbone, leaving a trail of heat behind it, branding her with Mac's personal stamp. "Please," he whispered.

All that had been needed was the magic password. She groaned into his mouth at the touch of his hands on her breasts.

Breasts that ached for his rough caress.

One small step and the solid buttress of Mac's leg slid between hers. Tension gathered in his muscles as he lifted her closer, higher, to ride his thigh.

Her breath came thick and fast as denim brushed soft tender flesh that parted, aching to receive him.

The pressure felt delicious as he enveloped her in a tight embrace that allowed her to feel the burn of male flesh, pressing the softness of her belly.

It wasn't enough.

She wanted him.

Wanted Mac.

He lifted his mouth, left her head lolling on her shoulders as the ceiling spun overhead. She felt dizzy, as if she'd forgotten how to breathe.

Her heart thudded against her sternum, as if knocking to get out.

As Mac slid her down his thigh, she came to the conclusion that here was a man who could rip her heart out of her chest and she would let him.

Simply give it into his keeping though it killed her.

This wasn't good. Not good at all.

The man was a criminal, or worse, a terrorist! And she was falling for him. Why hadn't Grandmère warned her that men like this existed?

Men who could hold you in thrall and turn your life inside out without raising so much as a squeak of feminist protest.

Good grief, this *was* bad.

More, it was disastrous.

"Now do you understand? Your cooperation was a given from the start. I could take you anytime I want and it wouldn't be rape." His words provided the dash of icy water she needed as he took away the support of his hands. Left her standing before him with breasts heaving and skin pulsing with heat.

A glare wouldn't have the effect she was seeking. She needed something subtler, like the lift of an eyebrow or the curl of a lip to show her disdain for his tactics.

She gave him both.

"So, you consider seduction to be the lesser crime. I think not. I'm no match for you, haven't your experience, yet. But thanks for my first lesson. I'm a quick study, so metaphorically speaking you won't sweep me off my feet as easily next time."

He grinned as he pulled the door open, as if he knew something she didn't.

Before he left her standing on her dignity, he said, "Don't bet the bank on it, *chérie.* You have hidden fires and I just learned how to turn up the heat."

At least he didn't wait for a reply, for truthfully how could she deny she'd turned to flames in his arms. The trick would be to keep out of his arms for the duration of their incarceration.

She heard the sound of voices in the next room.

The Frenchmen were back and she still didn't know what Mac had planned for her, but as long as his scenario didn't verge into the ridiculous, she would help move it along.

Decision made, she went to join them.

Chapter 6

Roxie walked straight to the table without a sideways glance and picked up the coffeepot. No one offered help. Like Mac, everyone looked to be erring on the side of caution. Just as well. Judging from her expression, she'd slam-dunk anyone who got between her and her caffeine fix.

Turning her back on them, she stared out the window.

Mac waited, then said, "Roxie?" He recognized the danger of using the term *chérie*. He could have sworn he heard her snarl. Obviously, she wasn't feeling as human as he'd hoped. The jolt of caffeine still had a way to go.

It wasn't a revolt as such. She simply refused to respond.

"R-o-xie…" Mac coaxed. "Zukah would like a favor."

She turned, one eyebrow raised as if questioning the term *favor* and was preparing to refuse point-blank, but Mac knew he'd only put out the fire in her libido, not her sense of survival.

She spoke to Jean-Luc. "And what concessions…can I expect for this favor Monsieur Zukah wants?"

Jean-Luc was past pretending. "He said, since you're the only female around, and the closer I get to a stove the more useless I am, will you come down to the kitchen and put all of us out of our misery. You'll have the run of the kitchen…it's large."

"Now, there's a man who knows his way around a favor," she replied.

Mac didn't blink. He wasn't surprised, also he doubted if Jean-Luc caught the ring of sarcasm, but then, it wasn't aimed at him. Outwardly he was perfectly still, but his mind raced, then he got it. She was letting him stew.

His eyes held her gaze for one whole minute out of time, neither wavering as a message passed between them.

Then Mac nodded, the concession was his.

"Of course I'll help out," she said. "Just let me get another cup of coffee and I'll come down with you."

Roxie had worked out that if the kitchen were on the ground floor, then she would be three levels closer to escaping.

And at least she knew where they were. She'd recognized the hulking shape on the horizon as Château d'Angers.

No matter what Mac said about Zukah shooting her, if she saw her chance, she would take it. By now Charles was probably tearing his hair out wondering what had happened to her.

But even if she couldn't escape, downstairs there would be more chance of locating a phone.

Deep down, she felt she had failed him. He'd given her instructions and her impulse had cocked them up.

Mac's voice interrupted her schemes. "Here is the concession we want. She doesn't go downstairs unless I accompany her."

He'd baited the trap with her cooking skills and now he was about to slam it shut. "Zukah," he continued, "brought us here as a couple and that's how we stay."

Jean-Luc stuttered, "I—I don't think…"

Mac was back in power and cut Jean-Luc off with a swipe of

his sharp tongue. "I don't think you're paid to think. Yves can give my message to Zukah. Tell him it's all or nothing."

She could see her chance of escaping dissolving if Mac had gotten this wrong.

The moment Yves turned the key in the lock, she turned to Mac. "Are you out of your mind? They're not going to let you downstairs. We're going to be stuck in this attic without even as much as a decent meal to keep our strength up."

"*Chérie,* what kind of a man would I be if I left you at the mercy of three strange men?"

She wanted to blast him with the truth. That, charming kisses aside, he was every bit a stranger as the others, but just in time she remembered they were playing live downstairs. "You don't really expect Zukah to let you have a knife to peel vegetables?"

He had the nerve to laugh. "*Tiens. Chérie,* you know I'll do what I always do when you're in the kitchen. Supervise."

Mac was impossible to argue with. As long as the Algerian could hear every word they said she had no comeback. And she was wary of doing a repeat session in the bathroom simply to tear a strip off his luscious hide.

For a start she didn't trust him, and second, she didn't trust herself. She wouldn't give up trying to escape, though.

If Mac made it impossible to take off while she worked in the kitchen, she would search the drawers and cupboards for some tool she could use to pick the lock.

Now, wouldn't that surprise Mac if she could find a way to creep out of the attic while he slept?

She'd love to see his face when he woke and found no Roxie sharing the bed. Of course it would never happen.

No, because she wouldn't see his face. She'd be long gone.

The air outside the attic slid down like clear cold water and tasted of freedom. A delusion, like the overwhelming impression of grandeur that blinded the eyes at first sight. The house wasn't Versailles, Mac decided, it just wanted to be.

How long their partial release would last there was no saying, as he still only had Roxie's word that she could cook.

If she'd been tossing him a line, then he could be knee-deep in the local manure heap.

This was his first view of the house in daylight, and if he, a guy, could tell someone had spent serious money getting the house into this shape, Roxie could probably put a figure on it. Her clothes might seem over the top, but he recognized high quality in their cut.

As a spy, she wouldn't look out of place among the top echelon of France, the movers and shakers of French politics.

The kitchen was the one place he hadn't checked out last night, expecting the attic to be monitored from there, but he'd been wrong.

Though during his tour of the house, he'd discovered two occupied bedrooms on the second floor housing Zukah and Yves. Both their rooms had rung with snores, muffling his approach, but he hadn't come across the other Frenchman.

Jean-Luc had to be at the lower end of the hierarchy since he seemed to be doing all the donkeywork, like cooking and manning the listening devices at night, et cetera.

With less at stake he might be more easily turned.

Mac's speculation crashed to an abrupt halt as Roxie tugged to attract his attention. Her elegant hand looked out of place against the beaten-up black leather.

He had a flashback of her in bed that morning.

He'd wanted her then and he wanted her now, and no words to the wise were going to change her effect on him.

When it came to this woman, his conscience didn't stand a snowball's chance in hell of giving advice his libido would heed.

Roxie kept her voice deliberately low, which probably made the Frenchmen behind them think they were conspiring.

"It's been a long time," she said. And given the train of his thoughts, he immediately put the wrong connotation on her words.

He soon learned his mistake as she told him, "It's been well over a year since I saw a decent kitchen. What happens if they don't like my cooking?"

He pulled her in close to answer. And to curb any notions of their plotting from Yves's mind, he made his actions blatantly sexual by spreading the width of his hand round the curve of her derriere.

Dipping his head, he said, "Don't sweat it, *chérie.* It's been a long time for me, but I won't forget how to make love to you."

She gave him a push, looking embarrassed as she glanced over her shoulder. Mac eyed her flushed features, speculating. Roxie was either one hell of an actress or the real deal.

"It's not the same thing, at all."

"You mean, one comes naturally and the other has to be learned." He put a hand on her elbow to guide her down the last few curved steps after the banister finished.

Roxie's indignation had won the day. There was nothing kittenish in the swipe she gave his hand, but then she wasn't putting on a show of pretence.

He moved down to the flagged floor, leaving her two steps up, and turned, their faces almost level. Mere inches separated their lips, a breath away from a kiss.

The inclination to teach her how natural his instincts were passed, as her heels clicked onto the floor beside him.

For once, he didn't see the advantage of measuring six foot five. *Comme ci, comme ça.* You win some, you lose some.

Roxie was about to ask the way when Mac beat her to it. "Okay, which one of you is going to show the lady the kitchen before we all starve to death?"

The kitchen looked out on a garden at the back of the house

and shone like a new pin, and would have appeared unused if not for lingering smells of burning.

Her eyes lit up as she spied the oak-fronted cupboards. A nostalgic warmth kindled around her heart, as for a moment she was reminded of Grandmère's Dorset cottage. "Let me look round to see which ingredients are available."

The whole place was poorly stocked.

Why was she surprised? Frenchwomen prefer shopping daily. Hopefully she would find some staple foods in the pantry.

She came across milk, dried herbs, pasta and a large bowl of eggs, which wouldn't last long with four men eating them. Great! That meant they didn't expect to keep them here too long.

Hope bloomed at her fingertips. Now, if she could only lay her hands on some sort of weapon.

Mac's gut tightened into a knot. He sat down at the kitchen table on a white wrought-iron chair that looked more fragile than it was. This way he had something to lean on as the weight of the world pressed down on his shoulders.

Forearms braced on the tabletop, he watched Roxie flit from cupboard to cupboard. Would she act so cool if she really knew what the payoff with this deal was?

Knew what Sevarin was selling?

At least by tonight he'd be able to give Thierry her surname. Though Mac hoped by then that Thierry might have discovered if anyone called Roxie worked for Charles Fortier.

Mac expected his theory would prove to be the correct one. Yet, the thought didn't lift his spirits.

What if she was as innocent as she acted?

If this deal got away from him, maybe she'd have been better off if he hadn't interfered when Yves had held that pistol to her head. Maybe every one of them would be better off dead, for life as they knew it would never be the same.

If the biotech solution worked as quickly as the Algerian had intimated, that made it one helluva dangerous weapon.

Unlike Agent Orange, Green Shield wasn't your everyday household defoliant full of dioxins that killed where it touched.

No sir, it was a living organism that sucked the chlorophyll out of one plant before moving to the next. Feeding off the land, it would get larger and more unstoppable with every blade of grass or stalk of corn it sucked dry. Discovering all that had made him more determined than ever to stop the bastards in their tracks. Someone had to do it, so it might as well be him.

Pulling out one of the bottom drawers in the island unit housing the gas hob, Roxie stood on the edge of it to stretch up for an omelet pan hanging on the rack above, but she still couldn't reach.

On the way down, she glanced toward the table and caught a flash of hot amber from Mac's eyes.

She gulped down a deep breath as a thrill chased through her insides. For a moment when they'd stood at the foot of the stairs, she'd thought Mac was going to kiss her again in front of the whole world, or at least Yves and Jean-Luc.

Thank goodness she'd managed to avoid him by taking that last step into the foyer.

Last step, huh. That was a good one.

The last step would come if she kept letting him touch her. Let him kiss her, until her body was begging to be taken.

She knew in her head Mac was dangerous—the sort of guy she ought to run a thousand miles from because one mile wouldn't be enough to keep her safe—but in her heart…

His touch made her feel more alive than she had in this lifetime. When he kissed her it felt like treading air, floating.

He was an addiction she needed to fly from.

Go cold turkey.

Maybe then she wouldn't have let him coerce her into feeding this sorry bunch of criminals. "Would you mind?" Roxie asked, looking in Mac's direction. "I can't reach the rack."

"No problem, I'll get it down for you."

Mac's journey from the table to the island unit was epitomized by his slow easy way of walking. Yet, she knew he used languor to disguise the intense energy she'd felt radiating from the muscles hiding under black leather.

At first she'd been fooled, but not anymore.

Couldn't Zukah and the others tell? He'd practically let them get away with murder the night before. The only time his eyes had flashed with annoyance was when Yves had laid hands on her.

Until then, nothing appeared to faze Mac.

Which was why she wasn't convinced he'd inveigled them into the kitchen for the sake of his stomach. She'd lay odds he'd eaten a lot worse than Jean-Luc's sacrifice to the gods.

In fact, she'd bet good money on him having a cast-iron stomach and enough stamina to keep going for days on a cup of water.

It wasn't till Mac coughed that she realized she'd been staring at him. Oh, God, she hoped he didn't think…

"Which pan did you want?"

His glance bathed her in gold and amber, jolting her heart so she couldn't breathe. It was all she could do to point and say, "The omelet pan."

"Make mine with four eggs. I'm peckish."

Uh-uh, Roxie knew what Mac hungered for, and it wasn't eggs. It was Roxie Kincaid.

The thought made her stomach muscles constrict as a sharp thrill shot through them. Somehow the realization was more frightening than the rest of the situation put together.

The pan Roxie had pointed out wasn't much of a stretch for Mac. He reached up without taking his eyes off Roxie.

The copper pan wasn't weighty, though it did ring out a couple of off-key notes as it banged into the ones on either side before he'd unhooked the handle.

If he hadn't been busy seducing Roxie, letting the force of their attraction simmer, he might have heard shoes scuffing the stone floor behind him.

As it was, Roxie's eyes were his only warning.

Her startled gaze darted past Mac and he turned in time to avoid a blow from Yves. Instead of chopping the back of Mac's neck with the edge of his hand, he hit the base of the pan.

Mac winced as the force of Yves's blow sent the omelet pan hurling onto the floor. Man, that had to have hurt.

"*Imbécile!* You might have damaged the pan," Roxie snapped.

Mac had to admit it took a chunk out of his ego that Roxie was more concerned for the pan than his head, but compared to Yves, his pain wasn't bad. He'd get over it a helluva lot quicker.

Mac began to think the blow had taken Yves's breath away. But curses soon turned the air blue, signaling that the Frenchman not only had an inventive flair for invective, but that he couldn't unholster his pistol and swear at the same time.

Mac glanced over his shoulder for Jean-Luc, who had suddenly made himself scarce, so he tried, "Sorry, buddy, it was an accident. I didn't know you were there."

Didn't know you were about to attack me without warning.

And then he added, "Hey, man, do you really think this is a shooting matter? I don't think Zukah is going to be too pleased if you shoot his cash cow."

When Yves took off the safety, Mac began wishing he'd used the time to jump over the island counter where there was some protection between him and the bullet sliding into the chamber.

"Get down, *chérie.* I think he means business," he said, knowing he was going to have to take the pistol from the lunatic before someone got hurt, namely him or, worse still, Roxie.

Mac took a swift step into Yves's line of fire, a step that would make a mockery of the fact that he'd let them take him hostage and cause some speculation that he'd hoped to avoid.

Fast as he was off the mark, Roxie beat him to Yves.

Mac broke out in a cold sweat. He could only see one outcome. A yell froze in his throat as he realized what she intended.

Talk about walking into a lion's den. He didn't have half the courage Roxie displayed as she walked between Mac and the bullet and enveloped Yves's hand, pistol *et* all, in an ice-filled napkin.

"Here," she said, all false concern. "This will make your hand feel better and stop it from bruising."

Mac was the only one who caught a glimpse of her raised eyebrow and pursed lips, as if to say his contribution hadn't been at all helpful.

Yves was too busy to notice.

He looked down at his hand as if it had magically turned into a block of ice, though his expression didn't quite match the astonished expression on his face when his hand had slammed into the copper pan.

The sweat on Mac's top lip didn't get a chance to dry, as next moment she'd taken the gun from Yves's hand.

If she threw it to him, he might be forced to use it and that wasn't part of the plan. He didn't breathe easy until she placed it on the table.

He wasn't certain whether or not her actions would have been as successful if Zukah hadn't chosen that moment to rush into the kitchen with Jean-Luc on his heels, both heavily armed.

Could that have been relief Mac saw in Zukah's eyes when he found neither he nor Roxie were sporting bullet holes?

Sevarin wouldn't be too pleased to discover that the cash register could only ring up *no sale*.

Yves turned to face Zukah, scattering ice cubes as he staggered back from the fierce frown on the Algerian's face. "He had a weapon," he said by way of explanation for the kerfuffle that had broken out.

Roxie wasn't done. She picked the omelet pan off the flagstones and examined a dent in the copper base. "These are far too expensive to be thrown around the floor, but I don't suppose it will make any difference to the taste of the omelets."

Whatever the outcome of the incident between him and Yves, it had made Mac see Roxie in a new light.

It just hadn't reversed the healthy lust that swamped him whenever he got within kissing distance of her. In fact, his admiration for her daring might have made it more potent.

Only someone with nerves of steel could calmly walk up to a gunman the way she had. Yeah, that woman had more mettle than was needed by any fashion designer.

It just went to prove, he'd been correct in his assessment. She was a professional. And he could live with that, for at least the next day or so.

Or however long it took for Sevarin to arrive.

Roxie's omelets had drawn an "excellent" from Mac that she felt was tinged with relief, and a *"magnifique"* from Zukah.

Not bad, considering she'd still been shaking from her contretemps with Yves, who remained surly.

Thankfully, most of the ingredients and cooking methods were locked in her memory. She could still hear her grandmother reciting them as she worked while Roxie watched.

It was a ritual that had started while they were both grieving over the deaths of her father and mother.

Later, she'd decided this was Grandmère's way of keeping her from the dark side that had taken her parents, which in her grandmother's mind equaled danger and excitement. She'd filled her son's head with stories of her life in the Resistance, which had led to David Kincaid following in his father's footsteps and joining British Army Intelligence.

Her parents had been killed when the IRA blew up their house in Belfast where her father had been stationed.

So long ago, it had taken hindsight to figure out why Grandmère blamed herself and her stories.

Two years ago her grandmother had died.

It was as if she'd been waiting to see Roxie's ambitions firmly set on a career as a fashion designer.

Once Anastasia Perdieu Kincaid had considered her job done, she'd surrendered to death as eagerly as she had fought to escape it during the war.

Roxie looked up from her meandering. Zukah had deserted them again, leaving them to the tender mercies of Jean-Luc and Yves, neither of whom she trusted.

Yves stalked the other side of the farmhouse-style kitchen, prowling the floor like a lean gray wolf.

His attitude had put paid to any conversation, and Roxie had had to clear up the kitchen alone, since Mac had been forbidden to offer her any more assistance.

Mac sprawled at the table, his body lithe and long, legs outstretched as if he hadn't a care in the world.

Roxie knew better. She'd watched his eyes.

He was aware of every move any of them made.

"So, *chérie*," he drawled now, as if savoring the words, "what gastronomic delight are you going to concoct for dinner?"

"Something simple with chicken since the options open to me are constrained by a lack of ingredients."

Mac gave a slight nod in her direction as if acknowledging their wait at the château mightn't be overly long. "Let me know if you need help cutting up that chicken. I'm pretty handy with a knife."

"*Non!*" Yves spat out the denial emphatically. "No knives allowed, no pans for you. I've told you before, nothing that can be used as a weapon. I will help your woman."

"It just so happens I have a name. Mademoiselle Kincaid, feel free to use it…." *Or not,* she decided. His attention now focused on her instead of Mac as if she'd encouraged him.

"Lucky for me," she continued, "the chicken is already in pieces, so I don't any need help except for hanging the pan up."

She pushed the pan across the island counter, hoping he got the message, and turned her back on the rest of the kitchen.

Yves might have banned Mac from anything he considered lethal, but she was a different matter. One he didn't consider a threat, though she had noticed him counting the knives in the wooden block to make sure all the slots were filled.

That didn't mean she couldn't steal something, and she'd noticed some fine steel lacing skewers.

Not for a weapon, but maybe she could use it to pick the locks and escape while the others slept. She had yet to decide whether taking Mac with her, if she succeeded, was a good idea or not.

He had more or less admitted he was a criminal, and every bit as bad as the men he was dealing with.

Her good sense told her to get the hell away from him as soon as she was able…but there was something about him that lifted him above Zukah and his men. She hadn't come to that conclusion simply because he'd saved her life.

Something about him called to her in a way that was more than gratitude and every bit as potent as sex, but went beyond that level—higher, much higher.

She couldn't explain it.

She only knew that if she survived this, her work for Charles would change. Become more than an elegant sweep of lines with a pencil as she drew her ideas.

Yes, for all he'd said he wouldn't save her again, she trusted Mac, and she no longer trusted easily, so maybe she was losing her grip on reality.

And heaven help her, their situation had more in common with Alice and rabbit holes than real life.

* * *

Water splashed into the white butler's sink as Roxie rinsed her hands. The room and everyone in it were reflected in a window mirrored by the darkness on the outside.

The coq au vin, simmering in the oven, smelled pretty good.

From time to time she'd caught one or another of the men scenting the air like a lion with food on its mind and was sure dinner would pass the test.

What she hadn't liked was the way Yves had confiscated the bottle of wine. She'd only used one cupful to give the dish that final dash of panache, but now he was down to the last glass.

Dinner would be ready as soon as she grabbed a loaf of bread from the freezer. She'd warm it in the oven to eat with the chicken.

Picking up a towel to dry her hands, she stopped staring at the reflection in the window and turned around to a room that was suddenly in full Technicolor.

Mac had the sullen expression on his face that schoolboys affected when they were bored with a subject.

If he'd been allowed a knife he'd be carving his initials on the tabletop to pass the time.

And if someone had told her she'd feel relieved to go back to the attic, she would have denied it point-blank. Yet that's where she'd rather be now.

And from the look of him, so would Mac.

She tucked the towel over the rail and caught Yves staring at her. No, she couldn't get out of the kitchen soon enough.

Slipping into the pantry, she opened the freezer door. The choice wasn't prodigious. There was a chunk of beef that would do for roasting if they were still stuck in the château tomorrow evening and two or three loaves of crusty bread.

Roxie picked up the bag of frozen croissants and began counting. She'd run out of eggs so they were all she had for *petit déjeuner.*

She'd counted eight when she felt a hand slide over her hip. Mac, she decided, and turned with a smile on her lips.

Wrong. She was so wrong.

"You like that, *bébé?* You like Yves?"

She gulped as a cloud of wine fumes filled the air. "Keep your filthy hands to yourself, *cochon!*"

"I have seen you watching me, you want Yves, eh, *bébé*," he said boldly, not exactly drunk, but the wine had taken the edge of his inhibitions as he crowded her into the shelves of the freezer.

If she could have managed, she would have climbed inside the freezer to get away from his wandering hands.

Twisting, she sank an elbow into his ribs, but he appeared oblivious. Didn't even grunt. She'd been afraid before, but it had been manageable. Now terror surfaced.

His long, bony fingers gripped her wrists, lifting her arms above her head. The breath locked in her throat, and though her mouth opened wide, the scream she let rip was silent as his mouth dipped closer to her neck.

She thought she might faint if he kissed her.

The knowledge that if she gave in to fear he might have his way with her before anyone discovered gave her the strength to move.

She bent her knee, raising it high for greater momentum. Driven by the damp breath grazing her neck, at last her scream broke free. It went on and on, mingling with a yell of pure pain from Yves as her heel tromped hard on his instep.

The combined force of their voices rattling off the pantry walls subsided into a whimper of pain as Yves stumbled backward, rocking the jars of dried goods on the shelves.

The pantry had been crowded before Mac's arrival, so the distance to the comforting bulk of his chest was nothing.

The angry rumble of his voice swamped Yves's moans. "Bastard. What did I tell you about touching my woman? Be thankful she's already dealt with you and it wasn't left to me."

"I'll kill you!" Yves screamed his frustration, his humiliation at being beaten by a woman showing. "Just wait, I'll kill you both, but first I'll take her and make sure you watch."

With Mac's arm round her, the vitriol Yves spewed at them couldn't hurt her, so when Mac bent closer to ask, "Do you want me to take care of him now or later?" She shook her head.

"Leave him, he's not worth it."

A moment later she was out of the pantry, lifted up off the floor and held high against Mac's broad chest as he returned to his chair. "I always knew those heels of yours were lethal. Remind me to teach you a few other tricks to play with them that will do as much damage as possible."

His hand slid over the crown of her brown curls once more, soothing. She closed her eyes, letting him press her into the curve of his shoulder, unperturbed by his offer to show her how to inflict even more violence on the loathsome Frenchman.

His hand continued stroking, releasing her tension, diminishing the build-up of fear. "What you need, *chérie,* is a little TLC and I'm just the man to provide it. Jean-Luc can dish up the chicken, 'bout all he's good for."

"Oh, God, don't stir anymore. The other one just threatened to kill us. We don't need two of them after our blood."

"Don't worry, Jean-Luc knows his place in the pecking order. It probably did his heart good to hear the howl Yves let out. And he's not likely to let Yves forget it in a hurry. So stop worrying, no one is going to kill us, not yet. I reckon we're pretty safe until I've paid over the money."

"What do you mean *we're* safe? You might be, but I don't have any money, and what Yves wants, I'm not selling. I'd rather die."

Fate worse than death. The words were clichéd, but she didn't intend hanging around to find out if they were correct. The incident had reinforced her decision to escape.

It felt as though this had been inevitable from the moment she stepped over the threshold of Mac's Le Sentier apartment.

The steel skewer she'd tucked inside her sleeve felt like ice against her skin. Probably because her blood was running hot with excitement, knowing what she was going to do.

Chapter 7

Sometimes *his edge*—everything he knew that his enemy didn't—was the only weapon of value an agent had left.

And so it had been with Mac. He had a knife in his boot, a garrote hidden in a seam of his jacket, and his martial art skills. Today all of them had been redundant.

And the irony?

Twice now, Roxie had shown him up. Stepped up to the mark and put her life on the line while he, the way Mac remembered it, had been all threat and no action.

Now she lay silent on the other side of the bed. Though, he could tell from her breathing, she wasn't any more asleep than he pretended to be.

Midnight. Boredom had set in at least an hour ago.

Once you've seen one dark room you have seen them all, and not even the thought of Thierry waiting for his call could prevent his eyelids drooping.

Each time he wakened with a start he was sure it took longer than the time before to lever his eyes open.

Night was racing toward dawn at a snail's pace.

Mac's last thought morphed into a dream of Roxie where there was no holding back. They were locked in each other's arms, closer than wallpaper and paste when she dissolved and he was left holding air, his nose squashed against the feather pillow.

Senses still clouded with dreams, he reached across the mattress to return her to his embrace, but apart from him, the bed was empty.

That was the only wake-up call he needed.

He rolled onto his back and listened for the sound of running water that would explain her absence. But there wasn't a squeak from the bathroom, not even a crack of light creeping round the edges of the door.

Where was she?

He sat up.

Somewhere a mouse was gnawing on the wainscoting. He focused on the noise. That mouse had metal teeth.

What the hell was she up to?

He swept the bedcovers behind him without disrupting the tension shimmering across the distance between him and Roxie at the attic door.

He rolled off the bed, silent as a cat with its sights focused on its prey. No way could he let this naughty little mouse escape either the attic or him.

Intent on picking the lock, Roxie didn't hear him coming until he covered her mouth, suffocating her scream with one big hand while scooping her up with the other, hissing, "Silence."

Her skin felt icy cold and he cursed under his breath that it had taken him that long to realize she was gone.

Where Roxie was concerned he was off his game in more ways than one. Not only had he let her sexy body and luscious-tasting mouth get under his skin, he'd let down his defenses in daylight.

Fooled by her domestic skills and how sexy she looked

wrapped in an apron, he was damned if she hadn't crawled underneath them.

She needed to be taught a lesson.

Teeth that he preferred smiling at him clamped down on a slither of skin from the pad of his thumb.

He'd had worse, one helluva lot worse. Knives hurt like the dickens and bullets felt worse coming out than going in.

He rolled her body against his chest to ease them through the bathroom door, then heeled it shut and peeled her T-shirt up over her head, using the fine wool to clamp her arms.

The lace of her camisole twisted the hairs on his lightly furred chest as she continued to struggle and heat leapt between them.

The erection he'd been nursing when he woke sprang to life with a vengeance.

His whisper reflected his feelings. "Not one word, hear me? Not one." He took his hand from her mouth and almost slapped it back as she gasped loudly enough for it to ricochet round the hard fixtures as he dumped her on top of the counter.

Anger surged in his gut. He took it out on the faucets, twisting them both together with a lack of restraint that sent water gushing into the basin and splashing up over the side onto his bare chest and abs.

He made a grab for the towel, rubbing it over the dripping water before he dared glance Roxie's way again.

Bunching the towel in one fist, he let it hang in front of his aching flesh, hiding the power Roxie had over him.

He didn't want her getting the impression he couldn't touch her without getting a woody, even if it were true.

She had taken a chance tonight when she thought he was sleeping—dammit, he had been sleeping. What liberties might Roxie dare if she knew he only had to glance her way to want her?

Their survival could depend on his refusal to let *his* libido twist him round *her* little finger.

The only other woman who'd been able to do that really *had* stabbed him in the back.

"Okay, hand it over."

Her fingers tightened around the edge of the marble counter. "Hand what over?"

The stubborn pout tilting her mouth downward belied her question. She acted like a child who'd been caught out in mischief, but the sigh that lifted her breasts, tightening their lace covering, was all woman.

"Whatever you were poking in the lock. Let me have it or I'll take it off you by force."

Her eyes flashed silver sparks, inflicting freezer burns, cold and hot at the same time.

After his most recent demonstration she obviously didn't doubt his stated intent, since she promptly twisted her clenched hand out from under the folds of her T-shirt, opening it palm up.

The small steel skewer glistened as it rolled, coming to rest where her fingers curved. It was four inches long.

Mac's first thought was how much damage she could have done to him while he'd carted her into the bathroom. More to the point, how much damage had she done to the lock?

Damn, if she'd buggered it with that clumsy pointed steel, there went his chance of leaving the attic to contact Thierry.

He lifted it from her hand and ran his thumb over the tip. It had lost its point and now he was dying to leave her sitting there while he checked if his lock pick could do the job it was intended for.

Instead he set about convincing her that he was every bit as bad as she'd no doubt suspected. "What miracle did you think you were going to achieve with that piece of trash?" he growled.

"I thought I could unlock the door with it."

"Then what?"

She glanced to the left and he knew she was about to tell him a barefaced lie. "I was going to wake you up, then we could escape. Together."

Mac began tightening the thumbscrews. It was all she deserved after almost bringing his mission to an ignominious end. "And how were you going to get through the door downstairs? There are dead bolts top and bottom and the windows are wired."

Roxie looked down as she crossed her legs, then placed her hands on her knee. From where he was standing the view got better as her navel curved above the matching lace, little-boy shorts she wore.

She was stalling for time, but what the hell, he was going nowhere and neither was she, now.

"There's a small window in the pantry. It isn't wired."

"*Small* being the telling word. I've seen that window and I could never fit through it." But Roxie could. Only there was no way he was letting her take off alone.

He would keep it in mind, though; think of it as the escape pod science-fiction writers always built into their spaceships.

If the situation became desperate, he would shove her through the blasted window himself. Until then, she wasn't going anywhere without him.

"I could have found help. Stopped a car and had them take me to the nearest gendarmerie."

It sounded so plausible when she said it, she'd obviously put a lot of thought into the plan. The biggest problem she had now was a case of differing points of view.

"*Chérie.*" He let his tongue roll around the word, drawing it out. "You stop a car dressed like that and what you've got isn't help, it's trouble."

She tossed her head and fixed him with a stare, a big gray-eyed stare. "I'm not stupid. I was going to toss my clothes out the window first, then climb through it. It would have been easy, I know someone who escaped a house that way and let the rest of her friends out."

He read defiance in her eyes, and God help him, in a different situation he might have acted on the challenge. Instead, he tossed the towel he'd been holding on to the rail next to the basin and hitched one hip onto the other end of the counter.

Not as effective as a cold shower, but it did cool his ardor some.

"Sounds as if you've been associating with the wrong kind of people for a fashion designer. And that being the case, what makes my company so hard to take?"

"Did we just skip a page here? Or are you not the guy who managed to get me taken hostage, transported—" she hesitated "—God knows where and thrown into an attic?"

He could have told her where, but then she'd start asking how he'd discovered the location of the house.

"Since then I've been forced to share a bed with you and cook for people who have the manners of a pig."

Had it occurred to Roxie that she knew exactly how to dangle bait in front of him? Sorry specimen that he was, Mac bit.

"Hasn't it registered that my saving your life used to be on top of that list? One day and you've forgotten what I did." He felt like a jerk for laying it on the line when her actions with the ice had returned the favor and then some.

"I haven't forgotten. It's still there. How grateful I ought to be has yet to be decided." She huffed out a long breath and everything became clear to him.

Her reasons for the aborted escape attempt and the time she'd chosen to begin looking for a way out.

Sure, he'd gotten them out of the attic, but for his own ends, nothing to do with Roxie's wishes. "Yves won't hit on you again."

"You can't guarantee that. No one can. He has guns, *your guns,* I might add, and you have your bare fists. Not what I'd call an equal-opportunity scenario."

Had she been reading his mind an hour ago while he tried to wait her out? This wasn't the appropriate moment to mention he had other skills, other weapons, without making it sound like sour grapes.

They both knew he had acquitted himself lamentably in that department to date.

But only one of them knew why.

Apart from a state-of-the-art lock pick that made the skewer she'd used look pitiful, his thin-bladed knife was small but deadly. And behind the double-stitched flap running the length of the zip on his leather jacket hid a thin unbreakable wire capable of taking off a man's head.

He couldn't see any of those pieces of news making Roxie smile or feel safer.

It didn't matter that he had *still* to discover the true nature of her visit to his apartment. He only wanted to keep Roxie under his thumb, not scare her to death.

It was *too* easy to imagine her expression as he explained to her about the garrote.

Even for Mac, it was a weapon of last resort.

And should she turn out to be an MI6 agent or, God forbid, a member of a terrorist cell as he'd first suspected, he'd be a fool to reveal the location of any weapon she could turn on him.

"You coped pretty well today, but in future I'll take care of you. Or perhaps I should I say, I'll take care of Yves. The guy has fast hands but you don't have to put up with them wandering where they shouldn't. Got that?"

She nodded as he stepped in front to her.

"Good, no more escape attempts." He held out a hand to her, saying, "C'mon, stand up and go to bed. You look beat."

One foot went out from under her as he pulled her down to the floor. She landed heavily against his knee. "Oops, my leg went to sleep without me."

They both stared at her hand on his thigh. Her skin looked pale and fragile, emphasized by the small blue veins running under it. With any other woman he would have suspected her of deliberate seduction, but not Roxie.

She didn't need to seduce him. She could have him anywhere, any way, any time she wanted. One touch and he was ready. With Roxie his body didn't care if she was friend or foe.

Did, he wondered, the blood race through her delicate veins, to pump through the chambers of her heart loud enough to hear in her head, the way his did?

He cupped her nape, positioning her between his thighs. Seductress or innocent, her trust in him at that moment was paramount. Mac felt the tiny bones of her neck flex while she stretched out the kinks, unaware how easy they'd be to snap.

Even as his thought took flight, he knew he could never be the one to do it.

What the hell had come over him?

He was one of IBIS's top agents. How could he think that a knife wound in his back from this woman would be easier to live with than the guilt of having to hurt her?

Mac reminded Roxie of a big bear; he growled a lot, and might cuff her—metaphorically—round the ear occasionally, but for her own good.

So, her plan had been more impulsive than well-thought-out?

It had worked for Grandmère. And at least Roxie had given it her best shot, which incidentally, was more than could be said for Mac. There was so much he wasn't telling her.

Earning his trust could take a lifetime, and she didn't have that long.

Her head felt heavy, filled with thoughts she couldn't control. She eased onto her toes, leaning back and letting his hand support the weight of her neck when she felt she could hardly hold her head up.

How her life had changed in twenty-four hours.

When she'd left the Fortier workroom yesterday, sexually she'd been as pathetically innocent as a woman who'd only had one lover—and a cheating one at that—could be.

Unlike Mac, who'd given her nothing more than gruff assurances that he'd take care of Yves for her, her lover had showered her with flattery and protestations of love.

So how come she was as close to naked as she'd ever been with another man without being covered in blushes, or flustered by it?

Did she actually trust the guy?

What troubled her most, considering Mac played for the wrong team, was how natural it felt for him to hold her.

His hand massaged her nape as he pushed the curls away from her face with his other hand and brushed the back of his knuckles down her cheek with a tenderness she'd never thought to find in such a huge man.

A man of huge contrasts.

"Why is it," he asked, "in the midst of winter you smell like peach blossom and spring with the promise of summer to come?"

Roxie had a struggle to believe her own ears, he sounded so romantic. "Are you talking about me?"

"There's no one else here but me and you."

He turned his head toward his shoulder and sniffed. "Nope, not even a mother could compare my scent to flowers." His voice turned husky and added its power to the thumb teasing the hollow behind her ear.

Before she knew it, her camisole felt too small, its lace scratchy as it scraped her protruding nipples.

Heat built inside her until even the thin camisole felt suffocating. Lifting her head, she stared into his eyes. What she found there paralyzed her. Kept her still as a statue, frightened to move in case something compelled her to touch Mac, to feel the warmth of his skin under her fingertips.

To lose all control.

"Roxie." The timbre of his voice sank lower, sent pinpricks of tension through her nervous system. "Did it never occur to you that I might have a reason for not trying to escape?"

"I can't say that it…did." Her voice faltered on the lie.

She knew he had a *ton* of secrets she should try her best to delve into, but instead felt content to let him keep them under the pretext that what she didn't know couldn't harm her.

"I suppose it's what any rational person would do considering the situation we're in," was all she could come up with.

His abrupt laugh came back at her from a dozen directions as it ricocheted of the hard painted walls like a bullet gone wild, leaving nowhere to duck.

"You could be right, *chérie,* but no one in their right mind would play a game where if you lose, you're dead. Not unless the stakes were so high there was no getting out of it."

Roxie stayed silent, but in her heart she concurred that no sane person would associate with the Algerian or his cohorts.

It had been a mad impulse by Mac to save her life, to claim her as his own when discovery meant certain death.

She remembered the look in Yves's eyes after her heel had stabbed down on his instep. She'd seen the shock and pain and, yes, murder in them as his hands had reached for her throat.

If Mac hadn't intervened she would be dead, no question.

All the more reason for a sane person to escape.

Mac's hand swooped over the dip in her collarbone and came to rest on the curve of her shoulder, covering it like an epaulette.

She wasn't ready for the shudder of pleasure that followed, though previous experience should have taught her what to expect from the brush of his hand across her skin.

They made a great pair. Mac diving into situations without any thought for his health, and she, who couldn't stay away from him, knowing his touch drove her crazy.

For heaven's sake, she was twenty-four, way past puberty, no longer a teenager without a sensible bone in her body.

Yet she kept coming back for more.

What was sane about that?

"You're shivering. Get back to bed and this time go to sleep.

Dream about the fourth member of the quartet turning up tomorrow, so we can all return to Paris."

To her it sounded like all the more reason to escape now; she had no wish to meet *le patron*.

Then she wondered where Mac's home was. His French accent was perfect. He was as comfortable in the language as she, and it was only occasionally she noticed a Stateside twang creep in such as when he'd bawled out Yves for molesting her.

He turned her away from him, but not before she felt the hot, hard length under his shorts trail fire against her hip.

"Go on now, scoot." He patted her a couple of times on the butt to send her on her way.

"Aren't you coming?"

She looked up over her shoulder and caught the wry twist of his lips as he said, "No, I was thinking along the lines of a cold shower."

Roxie swung round to stare up at him. Without her shoes on she felt tiny, vulnerable even, dwarfed not only by Mac's height, but the massive width of his shoulders and the depth of his chest.

She knew what she would see if she followed the light hair covering on his chest downward. Even as she held her breath, an overwhelming urge cried out to be heard.

Offer to take care of it for him.

Mac was giving her an out. Sending her away from temptation. Yet part of her, most of her, didn't want to be protected from the desire that sizzled between the lines of every sentence they spoke.

The bones of his face molded into a hard mask under the harsh overhead light. She had a feeling he was waiting for her to speak, as if he knew the tug-of-war going on in her brain.

Her palms itched to smooth the pain of abstinence away.

What was she waiting for? She only had to reach out.

And then, what?

If she gave in to her sexual urges once...she would do it again. Intuition told her that Mac was a man she would never get enough of, never drink her fill.

When this was over, supposing she was still alive, would she ever get over him?

She didn't think so.

With a Gallic shrug of her shoulders she walked to the exit as if her heart wasn't pounding nineteen to the dozen, and casually managed to say, "Enjoy your shower."

Closing the door behind her, she leaned back against its cold wooden panels and heaved a sigh of relief. When her heart settled down to a more normal rhythm she skipped across the icy floor and dived into bed.

She would survive another night in the attic.

As she snuggled under the quilts she concentrated on listening for the shower to run, imagining how he'd look.

And for a long time all she could hear was the pulse of blood surging through her temple.

Separated from Mac, she filed away the knowledge that once more she'd had a close escape, though not life-threatening.

She was no match for Mac under any circumstances.

He had too much of everything she felt she lacked, not just width and height, but force of character.

The courage to say what he meant instead of pretending, like her, that she had enough courage to step in front of a gun and save someone's life.

Mac had all the qualities of her grandparents', qualities her papa had emulated and died for. All the dangerous character traits Grandmère had tried to stamp out of Roxie.

Thank God she hadn't succeeded.

Though Roxie's heart had been pounding when she stepped up and enveloped Yves's hand in the napkin filled with ice, at least he hadn't been able to shoot Mac.

Though, she doubted, acting gallant and brave, the way her

grandparents had done in the Resistance, would convince Mac he'd met his match in her.

Mac's skin was so cold it was hardly worthwhile slipping into his jeans and jacket. Only the thought of being caught outside the attic by one of the Frenchmen, particularly Yves, sent him scrambling into his clothes.

Roxie's even breathing assured him that this time she had fallen asleep. At first glance no one would think Roxie had the guts to do what she had tonight.

Stealing that metal skewer from under Yves's nose had either taken skill, or the luck of the devil.

The Frenchman had been so close to strangling Roxie.

Damn, he should have realized that Yves hadn't taken his eyes off her while she finished preparing the evening meal.

Tonight he'd take the knife in case he ran into Yves.

So far, nothing about this mission had been easy.

Mac grunted with relief that Roxie's efforts hadn't ruined the lock, and once outside, he locked the door behind him.

Last night when Thierry informed him who owned the château, he'd explained it lay in the Loire Valley, the vicinity of Angers. With any luck, Thierry would have more for him tonight, such as news about Roxie.

Mac flicked the blade open.

Made of a black alloy so it wouldn't gleam under street or moonlight, it was almost invisible in the dark.

Should he meet up with Yves, it would be no holds barred. The Frenchman would never see what sliced him, or be able to report whose hand had wielded the knife.

That was the thing about death—it was ultimately silent.

Chapter 8

If anyone was under the impression that the night belonged to lovers, Mac McBride could prove them wrong. In the wee small hours, under the cover of darkness, the Joe Citizens who were up to no good owned the world.

That's where people like Mac came in.

They policed the night.

Over the years, he had lost track of how many hours he'd racked up between midnight and dawn, when the earth's denizens came out to play.

The trick in not being frightened to embrace darkness lay in remembering that night wasn't an entity in itself, simply an absence of light.

Leaving the attic, he walked down the stairs to the floor below them and took the corridor that branched to his left, picking a room that was two floors above the kitchen and on the opposite corner of the house.

He hadn't figured out exactly where the video recorder and

listening equipment were housed, but it had to be a room on the first floor. Zukah avoided climbing stairs whenever possible.

From the bedroom window Mac had a lower view of the road that passed the end of the driveway than he had from the attic.

For all Zukah had rushed them inside when they first arrived, the highway looked to carry few if any vehicles during the night.

Mac punched in the speed-dial code for Thierry's number. As he waited for him to respond, he wondered how many country creatures he'd disturbed with the ring tone.

He counted, one, two, three…four—

"Thierry here."

"*Bon soir,* Thierry, I hope I haven't been keeping you up?"

"What happened? You're late tonight."

"My little companion had trouble falling asleep. In fact, she decided to do a little breaking and entering in reverse. Though, she assured me she would have wakened me to leave with her once she'd picked the lock."

Thierry's laughter echoed through the earpiece. "I thought a man of your considerable charms would have had her around your thumb by now. What happened?"

Mac told how he'd managed to get them out of the attic, then got down to business. "By the way, her surname is Kincaid. Were you able to get anything on her?"

"On her, I have nothing, sorry. And Sevarin looks as if he's hiding in his house, so we haven't been able to tap his phone."

Mac's mind started racing. "We need to know if he's in charge or only a tool. Have you checked out others working under him in the Defense Department?"

"We're working on it. We know he was the one who supposedly put a stop to the Green Shield trials and destroyed the weapon. Seemingly the project was his *bébé.*"

"It must have been tough to destroy something he'd had going for years. Yeah, it would be his baby. Not a disgruntled scientist selling his work as we thought. What about Sevarin's bank accounts, have we accessed them?"

"Yes. He's been spending freely over the last few months. A new mistress, one who, by the way, loves to shop at Charles Fortier's."

An icy blade of pain cut into the back of Mac's neck. He stalked the empty corner bedroom, stopping by the window. "Not…"

"No. Not named Roxie. Madeleine Saber."

Mac stared into the darkness, surprised by the relief that flooded him. He let his mind drift for a moment.

Most of the trees in the big garden had already lost their leaves. What would it be like to live in a world where the trees never had leaves again?

Where there was no spring and no autumn because Green Shield's microorganism didn't die with the plants it destroyed. It lay dormant in the ground, waiting to pounce once more.

"So, Thierry, our SAC, Cliff Eagles, is making progress?"

"He personally gave me the news."

Mac thought about it. What happened if Sevarin was taken out before the Algerian closed the deal? His and Roxie's lives would be worth a bent nickel.

"We have to get them all at one swoop, Thierry. Explain to Eagles that there's still the chance of a civilian casualty if it blows up in our face. I want to get Zukah and Sevarin in the same net," he instructed.

"I always wondered how the Algerian made such a leap up the arms-dealer rankings," Mac mused aloud. "When you think of it, who but an amateur would place their hostages in their own home?"

Then he remembered the woman he'd left sleeping in his bed. "Write up Roxie Kincaid as top priority. It's time I knew just who I'm dealing with there."

"Don't worry, Mac, as soon as we hang up, I'll be on to it.

They've already made a start. The security in the couturier's is tight. Guess they have their own kind of spies to deal with."

Mac walked to the door, opened it and looked out into the dark corridor. Nothing stirred. "Guess so, Thierry. Later today, I'll look for a way to contact you.

"I can't use the digital phone in the attic, even in the bathroom. It might interfere with the listening devices. If you don't hear from me within twenty-four hours, or if they take Sevarin in, come and get us," Mac said, then hung up.

Swapping the phone for the knife, Mac did some more exploring, looking for the listening equipment, but it was still a mystery.

He made it back without incident, and within minutes he was shedding his clothes, crawling into bed beside Roxie as the clouds filling the sky outside the window began turning the color of old pewter.

Roxie was lying on her stomach, cheeks flushed and hair tousled like an innocent child's. He propped the pillow behind his shoulder and lay there staring at her.

If the mission went awry, as some of his British counterparts called it, what would happen to her?

He groaned, thumped the pillow, stuffing it under his neck as he closed his eyes, throwing his arm across them with his elbow up in the air. Soon, it would be light enough for the camera to catch them on tape again.

Mac could hide his eyes, but he couldn't run from the thoughts in his head.

In his mind he reached out and touched Roxie as she had appeared in the bathroom. Skimpy lace pants and camisole. No bra.

She didn't need one. Her breasts were high and firm and just the right fit for his palm.

He skipped that thought and started from the beginning. How long had it taken her to lose her shyness?

Less than twenty-four hours? But, she wasn't *his* hostage, so the Stockholm syndrome didn't apply. Yet, they had this love-hate relationship going on.

In one way he was pleased she had enough spunk to attempt an escape, but he couldn't allow it.

That presented more dangers than keeping her in his bed.

He was questioning whether to tell her the truth about himself. Civilian or agent, would she give him away if the dice fell badly?

Could he trust her not to sell him out for a get-home-free pass?

Mac didn't think so.

Could he—no, should he—bind her to him emotionally?

It wouldn't be hard—they were already sleeping together, and she was attracted—but it smacked of the dirty-tricks brigade.

He'd never been one of those guys who rated their performance in bed, though he'd never had many complaints, always remembering it was ladies first, and sometimes second and third.

He'd had good manners drummed into him. McBrides do this and McBrides don't do that. There was a lot of family history riding on his back and surprisingly some of it had stuck.

Of course he had sense enough to save the pretty-pleases for the ladies. The terrorists and others he dealt with never saw that side of him. He was as hard-assed an agent as any around.

That came with the territory.

The problem with Roxie was, he still hadn't decided which category she fell under.

She had this annoying trend he hadn't come up against before. Roxie could turn his loins hard with a touch or drive him crazy to possess her with a look.

In Mac's books, that made her a dangerous proposition.

Yeah, he was more than heavily into lust, he was entrenched in it. Which could make things awkward if Thierry discovered the Roxie she'd told him about didn't exist.

* * *

Did it make Roxie Kincaid a pathetic case because she was happy Mac was still sleeping beside her when she woke up?

She'd been dreaming about him.

One of those dreams where the person you were trying to catch took off on a bus or a train before you could board it. But now she was awake and *he* was still here.

She rolled onto her back before he could wake up and catch her gawping at him. When she thought through her escape attempt, she felt humiliated that it had been so poorly done.

A better plan was needed. One she could present to Mac for his approval before putting it into action.

For a few minutes she thought of Grandmère. Such a long stretch of time had passed since her grandmother's day. Wars were simpler then. The electronic age had taken the excitement out of close escapes and stealing people away from under the noses of the Gestapo.

Her grandparents' adventures seemed mixed with the innocence of youth—Grandmère had been fifteen when the British Army Intelligence sent her grandfather to France.

These were harsher, more complicated times where you wouldn't recognize your enemy if you saw him on the street.

If only she knew what was behind Mac's reluctance to leave.

Her thoughts darted around, unable to settle. She had no idea of the time. With no sun in the sky, it was impossible to guess how far into another dull, gray day they had progressed.

Mac's left arm came up across his eyes.

He was wearing his watch. If she sat up she could read the large face and see whether it was closer to nine than noon.

Pulling the sheet with her to cover her body, she pushed up on one arm, leaning over to check Mac's watch.

Almost eleven. That's what happened when half the night had been spent in an abortive attempt to pick a lock.

"Hey, how you holding up?" Mac's arm slid away and his

gaze held her hers. His eyes were plain amber this morning, sleepy, bracketed by laughter lines at the corners, and too darn sexy for his own good.

"Phew." A sigh echoed in her head. It looked like he wasn't holding a grudge over her abortive effort to fly the coop.

Roxie lifted his wrist. "According to your watch I slept well. Breakfast time has come and gone."

A smile teased his mouth, which made her insides thrill and shortened her breath. "Looks like we'll be doing brunch today."

So this was what it would feel like to wake up in bed with a lover. It seemed the most natural thing in the world to lean over and brush his lips with hers, and she made it halfway there and back again when she remembered.

This wasn't her lover.

She flicked her aberration off with a slick remark. "Or maybe I'll do a Marie Antoinette and tell them to eat cake."

Mac's hand shot out to cup her neck, destroying the fragile balance she'd achieved on one arm.

His breath grazed her cheek, then her ear as she tumbled on top of his chest. Her weight wasn't enough to make him flinch, and she wished she could summon up the same kind of nonchalance Mac exuded.

Heat radiated through the lace of her camisole. Against her crushed breasts, she felt the thud of his heart, slow, steady, strong, a powerhouse driving the blood through his veins.

Her heart raced to catch up before he left her behind.

There was an intimacy to being this close to him that went beyond sexual.

Her breath locked in her throat as his lips brushed the tender skin behind the curve of her jaw, then his teeth pinched her earlobe. It wasn't pain that brought her back to reality.

It was Mac's whisper. "Once more for the cameras."

Roxie's mind knew it was just an act when his mouth covered hers, but it forgot to tell her heart.

His lips were urgent, compelling. They slipped past her guard without raising a whimper in protest, opening the way for his tongue to forage.

What that man could do with an instrument designed for eating and speaking was out of this world.

Her body felt enervated. She lay on top of him like a lax lump of clay he could fashion at will, hardly able to crack open her heavy eyelids once he deprived her of his mouth. He was breathing harder, as if he, too, had gotten caught up in their game.

The glitter appeared in his gold irises. This close she recognized it as the hard glint of bullion, not the molten metal.

An icy sheen of inflexibility spilled into his words, sharp enough to score the small space of air between them as if it were made of glass. "Wanna take a shower with me, *chérie?*"

She drew a harsh breath through her nose, trapping her true feelings behind her teeth until she could speak without showing them. "Not today, *chéri.* I don't feel like sharing this morning."

The whole weight of her body was behind the thrust that pushed her to her knees and out of bed onto the cold, bare floorboards.

She was halfway across the floor, wearing nothing but what she'd slept in, when she realized she was putting on a show for the boys downstairs.

It was all she could do not to poke a face at the camera in her rush for the safety of the bathroom.

It wasn't until hot jets of water pummeled her head and neck that she was able to stop analyzing every wrong move she'd made.

So she'd gotten carried away, she was only human.

Only someone who had been on the receiving end of one of Mac's kisses could know how invasive the sensations his mouth evoked could be.

She would be foolish to let her conscience drag her over the coals for falling under his spell.

Roxie Kincaid wouldn't be the first female to be swayed by his silent powers of persuasion.

What hurt her most of all was the belief that she wouldn't be the last.

The mood in the kitchen wasn't conducive to cooking quality food. If Roxie had been preparing soufflés they would have come out pancakes.

Mac's sullen expression made her stomach sink: He'd spent the day grumbling to Zukah about *le patron* not showing up.

Then when the Algerian disappeared, Mac grabbed a bottle of wine from the rack, his dark, ominous glowers daring anyone to question his right to it.

The farther the wine sank in the bottle, the heavier the atmosphere in the kitchen became.

Yves prowled, alternatively casting if-looks-could-kill scowls from under his black brows in the direction of her or Mac.

The least little noise either of them made appeared to provoke his disapproval.

Jean-Luc seemed the only one oblivious to the gathering storm. She felt as if she'd been sucked into a weather front, forming a low depression filled with ominous black clouds.

After discovering the cupboards were practically bare, she chopped up what steak and vegetables she could find, intending to make *Boeuf bourguignon.* To make something out of nothing.

With five to feed, the last two loaves she'd pulled from the freezer weren't going to stretch far.

Hearing the clink of glass, she looked over her shoulder in time to see Mac pour another glass of red wine.

It ticked her off to think she was slaving away over the clichéd hot stove, browning the meat, while he was drinking his way toward salvation in the bottom of a glass.

And he would still expect to share her bed.

That did it.

Roxie marched up to the kitchen table, filled with enough righteous indignation to swamp all thoughts of self-preservation.

She snatched up the neck of the dark-green bottle, ending up in a tug-of-war over it as Mac wrapped his fist round the other end. Red wine sloshed around the punt in the bottom of the bottle in a way that should have shown Mac there wasn't enough left in the vessel worth fighting for.

"Who said you could have a glass?" Mac's demand was surly, but the gleam in his eye as she tugged the bottle away made her wonder if the alcohol had made a dent in his sobriety.

"I want it for the sauce. You can't make *Boeuf bourguignon* without red wine."

"Have it, then." Mac released his firm grip.

The bottle was all hers, but as the bottle recoiled she had to step backward to maintain her balance.

Mac wasn't looking.

The legs of his chair scraped across the flagstones as he pushed it back. "Hey, Yves, where's the nearest little boy's room? I need to use the john."

As if by way of demonstration, Mac staggered a little, leaning both palms flat on the table to stop swaying.

He might have fooled Yves, but not Roxie.

"Jean-Luc will show you. There's a cloakroom off the foyer."

Mac was up to something. And it had to be something important if Mac was willing to leave her alone with Yves. She only hoped it wasn't dangerous.

She didn't fancy being left alone in the kitchen with Yves.

To complete the recipe, she needed a heavy iron Dutch oven to transfer the meat into while she browned the vegetables and made the sauce.

She'd noticed one on a shelf in the pantry sitting below the high window she'd considered climbing through.

Yves's gaze was fixed on Mac and Jean-Luc as they left.

She'd feel safer if Zukah was in the kitchen, but she took the opportunity to tuck the small vegetable knife inside her sleeve.

She ducked into the deep pantry before Yves could turn around.

The person who had arranged the shelves had to be taller than Roxie. Even in her heels she couldn't easily reach the double-handled pot, so she dragged out an old wooden crate, carefully checking if it would take her weight before standing on it.

At full stretch she had just enough height to lift the Dutch oven with both hands.

Fingers curling round the loops that served as handles, she raised it a few inches above her head.

Something touched her calf.

She went dead still. No, it wasn't her imagination, something was sliding up the inside of her knee. Higher. Something warm.

Higher.

Roxie screamed. The Dutch oven glanced off her shoulder as it fell and all hell broke loose.

Mac had a harder head for wine than he'd made out.

He kept up the act as Jean-Luc accompanied him into the foyer and pointed out the cloakroom Mac had discovered on his first nighttime reconnaissance.

The door Jean-Luc had directed him to lay to the left of the entrance, with the toilet facilities through a second door.

The hand basin and mirror came first, but neither room featured windows. As soon as the lights came on a fan took care of recirculating the air.

Grabbing the door handle, Mac shouldered his way clumsily through the first of the doors, turning as he reached the second to see Jean-Luc behind him.

Mac had calculated that problem into his plans when he'd thought of a way to call Thierry on his secure cell phone.

It had taken most of the afternoon to make a well-thought-out opportunity seem like a natural occurrence.

The wine in the rack had been a godsend, but knocking off a whole bottle in one fell swoop was too boorish to be realistic, so he'd sipped, taking his time, instead of gulping too fast.

Pretending to be a melancholy drunk had been entertaining. Boy, had it set Yves's teeth on edge to watch a slob consume one of the most expensive wines in the rack.

There wasn't room for two men in the small cloakroom, but getting angry about it wasn't the way to get rid of Jean-Luc.

With the other door half open behind him, Mac looked Jean-Luc up and down and smiled in a way that challenged the Frenchman's manhood. "You coming to hold my hand?"

Jean-Luc's hand went to his pocket, but Mac wasn't worried. He knew that's where the guy kept the dark cigarettes that Zukah had forbidden him to smoke inside.

The Frenchman pulled a soft crumpled pack of cigarettes from his pocket; they were vaguely reminiscent of the first smokes Mac had tried as a kid, before he knew better.

"I'll be right outside the entrance taking a smoke. Don't try anything stupid."

"Don't worry, I'm not going anywhere," he drawled. *Just to make an important phone call.*

After that morning's close call in bed, Mac knew he was near breaking point when it came to Roxie. He had to be certain of her identity before crossing a line that might damn him for a fool the rest of his life.

She was getting through to him. He wanted her the way he'd wanted his first car, a red Mustang.

He'd lusted after that car for two years.

He had less patience now and less available time.

Roxie was either a saint or a sinner, or somewhere in between the two—another agent. He'd take either the first or the last; anything in the middle he'd throw to the wolves.

The scream echoed along the corridor from the kitchen before he could close the door on Jean-Luc. It was followed by an almighty crash that made the hairs of his neck stand on end.

Roxie!

Jean-Luc had a head start, but Mac was faster, shouldering him out the way. At first glance, the kitchen looked empty and he imagined her carted off over Yves's shoulder.

A growl came from the pantry. A low female growl, dragged from the throat he'd kissed that morning.

"Cochon! Crapaud!" The names were delivered with loathing.

Mac dived for the pantry, Jean-Luc's footsteps on his heels. He thrust aside the door, bouncing it off the wall.

The second time he set the barrier aside with more deliberation and took in the scene. Yves clutched Mac's own gun, the Makarov.

Damn, did the guy realize how sensitive its trigger was? Mac thought as he noticed a tremor in the hand holding the gun aimed at Roxie's head.

She knelt on the floor, surrounded by a welter of pots and broken dishes, defending what Mac presumed was her honor with a small knife.

For a second that lasted a lifetime, Mac hesitated.

Then he did exactly what he'd sworn never to do. He stepped between Roxie and the gun.

Chapter 9

The Makarov dropped to the floor, firing when it hit, missing Mac's leg by inches and slamming into the doorjamb.

Mac's mouth twisted in contempt as Yves yelped. Satisfied that until he recovered from the paralyzing grip he'd put on the Frenchman's wrist, Yves wouldn't be pointing a gun at Roxie again anytime soon.

As his ears stopping ringing, he heard Roxie moan, but he had no time to check. First he needed to clear the place of Zukah's wiseguys.

Putting all his strength behind the blow, he slashed the edge of his hand across Yves's throat as he began reaching for a knife. In Mac's book, two cents of prevention was better than a dollar's worth of cure, any day.

The guy crumpled without making a sound.

In one continuous movement, Mac relieved him of the knife, then whirled to face Jean-Luc.

It was easily seen why Yves had been left in charge. Quick thinking didn't appear to be part of Jean-Luc's repertoire.

The only thing the other Frenchman had in his hands was the pack of cigarettes he'd pulled when Mac ushered him from the cloakroom.

Mac threw Jean-Luc the same smile that had intimidated him then, but cut it with a lethal edge, flashing the blade of the knife he'd retrieved from Yves. "Are you up for it, *mon ami?*"

"I don't want trouble, Monsieur. I have no quarrel with you."

Jean-Luc backed away as he spoke, hands open to show he wasn't armed. "Yves talks big but he was stupid. He let your woman get under his skin because she made him lose face. Last night all he spoke of was what he'd like to do to her. Now he knows she is as hard to handle as you."

Mac threw a quick glance over his shoulder. "How you holding up, *chérie?*"

"Just peachy fine, *chéri.* I wondered when you would be interested."

Her voice came from behind him, curling round his senses like a hot woman. His body stirred and he laughed. "Oh, I'm interested, all right. I just had to take care of a few bad guys first, but you might say my interest is riding high and hard. Pass me that gun up from the floor, *chérie.*"

Her hand reached between his feet and picked up the gun.

"Hold it real carefully now," he told her. "We don't want it going off again."

He had the Makarov back in his fist where it belonged by the time Zukah puffed onto the scene. "What is going on?"

Mac touched the spring and closed the knife. It went into his pocket. He was certain Yves wasn't carrying the Glock as well, but it would do no harm to check.

"Is he carrying anything else dangerous and noisy?" he asked as he reached down to pull Roxie to her feet. She came up easily, placing her hand round his waist.

He could feel her tremble, but she was braving it out. She flicked Yves's jacket open with the toe of her boot, but there was no sign of a shoulder holster.

Flattening her mouth against her teeth as if in distaste, she rolled the man on the floor over with an upward thrust of her foot under his shoulder then tromped on the small of his back.

"No gun, only this," she said grimly, picking up the key off the floor.

Her voice was low and slightly shaky, without its earlier bravado, as she looked up at him to whisper, "Mac, he touched me."

A low growl let loose from the back of Mac's throat. Zukah backed away, giving as wide a berth to the fire in Mac's eyes as he did the pistol in his hand, as he and Roxie stepped over Yves.

"You ought to choose your friends with more care, Monsieur Zukah. Yves has been putting his hands where he shouldn't. Trying to get into the cookie jar, if you get my meaning."

Flustered, the Algerian began blowing hot air, "I assure you I had no idea…."

"Can it, no excuses. For you the fun part is now over. Come on, *chérie,* let's get out of here." Mac swung her up into his arms, for the second day in a row, achieving his goal without losing his grip on the pistol.

Zukah went pale, and for him that was saying something. "You are leaving?" he asked cautiously.

"No, Zukah. I'm not leaving till I get what I came for, but this little game is definitely over. No more cameras. No more bugged beds to put ideas into crazy Yves's head. We'll keep the same room, but we won't be locked in and Roxie won't cook unless I'm hungry, got it?"

Zukah nodded. "Understood."

"I still don't know who your patron is," he lied, "but tell him from me he needs to hire better help. We could have been out of here the night we arrived. Would have, if you didn't have something I want."

He glanced down at Roxie and caught her eye, taking the warm look she gave him deep inside and holding it close to his heart.

He wanted her out of here, even if it was only to the attic. "Tell *le patron* I've been patient long enough. I give him thirty-six hours, after that just let me say, my people will find another less civilized way to gain what we're after."

Carrying Roxie in his arms, Mac strode to the foot of the first flight of stairs. He could feel her shaking and it really pissed him off.

But the aftershocks of her experience faded as he put his foot on the first step. She looked up at him as if he'd lost all his marbles. "You're not really considering carrying me up all those stairs."

He squinted up at them as if counting. "I see what you mean, I could be seriously winded before I reach the top."

Truth be told, Roxie felt light as a feather in his arms. He could carry her up a thousand such flights if she promised him he'd never have to listen to her scream like that again.

Panic had crowded in on him from the walls of the small cloakroom, and ice had swum in his veins at the thought of reaching her too late.

Mac was taking no more chances. He wanted the living, breathing woman in his arms, and he'd almost left it too late. Thank God the woman had guts.

He didn't know what kind of crazy revenge he'd have enacted if, when he dived into that pantry, he'd found her lying dead on the floor.

He swung around and faced the way he'd come. The Algerian and Jean-Luc were watching from the end of the corridor. Neither of them had thought to check up on Yves.

The guy had just lost his mana. Whenever they looked at him now, they would see a loser. Too bad, so sad, never mind, eh?

Tongue in cheek, he told her, "Maybe I should have asked them for a better room."

"No! No, don't. We're fine where we are."

He started up the stairs. "We could do better."

She stared at him, a misty-gray clouding her eyes with puzzlement or mistrust. "How do you know?"

"*Chérie*, look at this place, we could do better. You always can." He wasn't particularly winded by the top of the first flight so he threw caution to the wind and carried on.

By the time he reached the second landing, Zukah and Jean-Luc had come to the foot of the stairs and were looking up at him.

Neither of them appeared to be on the offensive, so he took that as a good sign and called down to them, "We're going to catch up on that trial honeymoon you promised us, so we don't want to be disturbed."

Outside the attic, Roxie asked, "Did you really mean that?"

"What, about a trial honeymoon?"

"No, the part when you said you could have got us out of this place whenever you were good and ready."

"*Chérie*…have you never played poker?" She shook her head.

"Well it's like this. In the words of an old song, you have to learn when to show your cards and know when to fold them away. It's like life, just one big bluff. This time it worked."

He laid Roxie gently on top of the quilts and stepped back reluctantly. There were a few matters he had to attend to before he thought about himself. First the miniscule listening devices.

He stomped on them.

The camera was stubborn. The lead from it went down behind the armoire, and when he put his shoulder against the walnut paneling on the side of the unit it began to swivel away from the wall.

Now he could see what was holding up the proceedings. The wires went through the top edge of a door. To cut a long job short, he sliced through the wires.

He'd like to know where that door led, though.

He wrapped what was left of the wire around the camera and

marched onto the landing, then called, "Look out below," and tossed the lot over.

The microphones probably reached the ground floor, but the cable managed to wrap itself around the chandelier, where it spun like a piñata on a string.

That taken care of, Mac shut the attic door behind him, walked over to the bed and stood looking down at Roxie.

Her eyes were half closed, the lower lids tinged with blue shadows that added a vulnerable quality to her features. Four times in the last few days, her life had been seriously at risk and it was starting to show.

He sat down on the edge of the bed. "Okay, woman, what's it to be, your innocence or your life?"

His quip drew a smile from her lips. "Take my innocence, I owe my life to this guy I know, two—three times over."

She struggled up to rest on her elbows and a wince flashed across her features then disappeared. Whoever she turned out to be, the woman was gutsy.

But now, the way she was positioned on the bed thrust out her breasts, and she no longer looked defenseless, just sexy as hell.

"Your innocence it is. But first, show me where it hurts."

Of course she denied it. "Nowhere. I'm okay."

His voice was rougher than he'd meant. "Don't lie to me. Remember, I saw you sitting among a jumble of broken crockery. You didn't escape that crash unscathed."

She looked away, but it didn't hide the tears welling in her eyes. He lifted her chin and, turning her face up to him, said, "Tell me."

Roxie fixed her fingers around his arm and pulled herself closer. He hadn't been wrong, the tears were for real. Her bottom lip trembled. "I thought he was going to rape me. You should have seen the bloodlust in his eyes."

"Ah, *chérie,* no wonder you called him a pig and a toad." He sighed and pulled her closer. "Don't think about him."

Her head nestled in the curve of his shoulder, muffling her

voice. "He was so angry when he pulled out that gun. I thought I was dead for sure. That it would happen just like you said. He would shoot me like a dog."

"Did I really tell you that? I must have been trying to frighten you, I'm sorry. I'm a bad man." He kissed the top of her head. "Tell me, what were you going to do with that knife?"

Her shoulders shook and he heard a bona fide giggle bounce off the sleeve of his leather jacket. "I thought maybe to castrate him, so he couldn't rape me."

Mac shuddered. He took hold of her shoulders and pushed her away from him so he could watch her reactions. "*Chérie,* you are one vicious woman, but you always manage to make me laugh. I just hope that knife was sharp."

"Oh, well, it doesn't matter now. You've killed him."

He had to tell her the truth, about that, anyway. "Sorry, but no. He'll probably have a bit of trouble talking for a while, but I didn't hit him hard enough to kill him."

He pushed the hair from her eyes. "Don't worry, though. I won't let him near you again. We can put a chair up against the door handle so he can't get to us while we're sleeping."

"No need." She felt behind her. "I still have the key. You can lock the door from inside."

Roxie was learning quickly, maybe too quickly. He just wished he'd had time to call Thierry before all hell had erupted in the kitchen.

"Thanks for the key. I'll lock the door right now so you feel safer. Tell you what. You could have a bath tonight instead of a shower. Soak your aches away while I investigate. Come and see what I've found."

Mac locked the door and left the key in it, positioned so it couldn't be knocked out, which is what Yves should have done instead of carrying the key around with him.

Roxie slid down from the bed and joined him as Mac pulled the armoire around to reveal the door.

"What do you think?" he asked her as he pulled the latch undone and dragged the door open to reveal ancient stairs.

"I think I should explore it with you, it looks horribly dark. What happens if you should fall?" she asked.

"In that case, I definitely won't take you with me. You go run a bath. This won't take long. I think these stairs were the way that the servants moved unobtrusively about the house. There's probably a door leading out onto each floor."

She clung to his arm. "I don't like it. You need some sort of light before you take these stairs on." He could tell she was serious. Her face fell and twisted as if she might cry again.

"Hey, Roxie, don't worry about me. Haven't you noticed I have cat's eyes? I can see in the dark."

"I can believe it. Just the same, promise to be careful."

Mac wasn't sure if the thought of ending up alone with Zukah and his men prompted her concern, or if she was anxious about his health.

Either way he intended carrying out his plan before Yves came round. "It can't be too dangerous," he said. "Someone used the stairwell to run the video camera cable."

He wasn't quite as certain about the possibility of Zukah forgetting the hidden stairs' existence. Therefore he needed his inspection over and done before the others dropped out of their trance and realized he'd practically performed a coup on their headquarters.

The room they were watching them from had to be at the other end of these stairs.

For Roxie's sake he'd take them carefully. He should have known the moment their paths crossed that he would end up doing some damage to his person to keep her safe.

As if she could read his mind, Roxie shuddered.

"Off you go." He turned her round. "Go run the bath and forget about what I'm up to. I'll be back before you know it to scrub your back."

The light from the attic aided his descent into the gloomy stairs, and the second flight wasn't insurmountable once he got used to the distance between steps.

The wire led him to a room on the second floor where Zukah and the others had bedrooms.

How could he have missed this one when he searched?

For several moments he stood, hardly moving, holding his breath before turning the handle. No sound broke the thick silence gathering around him. Mac turned the handle.

Standing in front of the mirror, Roxie stripped off her clothes. A button was missing, lost in her struggle with Yves.

Her appearance looked sadly the worse for wear after three days in the same clothes. Charles would shudder in his highly polished shoes when she told him. If she ever got a chance.

Thinking of the couturier kept her mind off Yves.

But not for long. The bruise where the Dutch oven had glanced off her shoulder was dark red. Soon it would turn black and blue.

Shivers racked her as she relived the moment. Yves hand, sliding up her leg, then higher, under her skirt, leaving her in no doubt of what lay in his mind.

What could she have done to change the outcome?

Even now she could feel the small knife in her hand, holding the wooden handle tight, its imprint on her palm.

Mac had laughed at its size, but she'd been ready to use it on Yves.

Had Grandmère turned in her grave, knowing Roxie was as ready to kill as *she* had been all those years ago and in almost the same cause? And did she hate that all the feminine skills she'd taught Roxie counted for nothing when the chips were down?

Though, now Roxie thanked God for the hours of ballet lessons she'd taken. They'd served to help her build strong, flexible muscles, and she still used the exercises to keep in shape.

Sure, by the time it was over she'd felt drained, as if she had withdrawal symptoms, because the adrenaline had stopped pumping through her veins like a high-priced designer drug.

She pulled the lace camisole over her head. The silk froufrous made her look like the woman her grandmother had invested her all in—on the surface. But inside, Roxie knew the genes of her French ancestors were running hot and strong.

She pulled the zipper on her skirt open and let it pool round her feet. Stepping out, too tired to be bothered, she tossed the garment onto the chair she'd dragged with her into the bathroom. Only her boots and little-boy panties left to remove.

She stopped her hands on her hips.

It had all happened in a flash.

Happened so quickly, she hadn't had time to ponder why Mac hadn't used his skill in martial arts to escape Zukah, until now.

Naked, Roxie examined the nicks and scratches that came from sitting among the breakages littering the pantry floor.

She had yet to discover what *le patron* was selling that Mac was willing to pay millions for. What would make a man like him suffer the humiliation of being taken hostage?

The stakes had to be high.

By now, Zukah had to have come to the same conclusion. Which meant all Mac's threats probably weren't worth a hill of beans.

She turned off the faucets and dipped her hand into the bathwater to test the temperature. Satisfied, she sank up to her neck in warm water and waited for Mac's return.

One of the faucets dripped. Each drop reminded her that they were sitting on a time bomb and that it might go off at any second of the thirty-six-hour deadline that Mac had given Zukah.

The door opened silently, slowly—Mac wasn't pressing his luck. There was a lamp burning in the room, but the overhead light was off and the room was empty.

He went inside. Like the attic bathroom, its curved walls were part of a corner tower.

Two monitors and recording equipment sat on shelves next to an open door leading to a bedroom.

Covered in wallpaper, the door would be practically invisible from the other room when shut, which was the first thing Mac did.

Zukah had left in a hurry, and the reason why soon became obvious. One of the screens was blank—Mac's work. The other showed the Algerian and Yves arguing in the kitchen.

Even without sound, Mac had a fair suspicion what the quarrel was about. That explained how Zukah had known to come running when the fight started.

An oak desk took up most of the space. On it, the lamp sat next to a laptop. He switched it on and, while it loaded, examined the rest of the equipment.

By now, Zukah would be laying down the law, informing Yves, who was shaking his head, what his seduction technique had cost them. Being Arabic, maybe he was warning Yves that any more such attempts would cost him his hand, not just the use of it for a couple of hours.

Soon they would be arming up, determined not to be caught napping again.

Their complacency had come in handy. Saved Mac from showing his hand too soon. But what else was a guy to do when a moron threatened his woman's life?

His woman?

Mac shook his head to loosen the mental aberration.

He'd repeated the words so often to pound it into Zukah and his cohorts' heads, they had become lodged in his own synapses.

Sure, Roxie was attractive, but she was still an unknown entity, something he ought to correct before he went back upstairs by calling Thierry.

The day might come when he took a woman for keeps, but for his parents' sake, she'd have to come from the right kind of family. An American blue blood like himself and all the generations of McBrides that had gone before him since they'd exchanged Scotland and its English king for freedom in the colonies.

He punched the button that would get him Thierry while he pulled open a filing cabinet that matched the desk. The top drawer slid open easily, which usually meant there was nothing anyone wanted to hide.

Mac flicked through the files as Thierry came on the line.

The date on the first file was ancient. So old, in fact, that he doubted the person's name on it was still alive.

"What did you get me on Roxie?"

"She is an intern with Charles Fortier. The big surprise is, no one seems concerned that she hasn't turned up for work. They think she's on holiday."

Thierry hardly stopped for breath. "I'm waiting to hear from our English bureau about MI6, though I get the feeling you don't have to worry. She doesn't sound like she'll cause much trouble."

With a laugh, Mac walked over to the laptop. "That's your considered opinion, is it, Thierry? Maybe you'll change it when you see her wielding a knife."

"What happened? How did she get a knife?"

Mac laughed softly under his breath. "Well, it went down like this…."

The sound of the armoire being pushed back into place vibrated through the floorboards. Mac had returned safely.

Roxie released a sigh and let her chin touch the water as she sank lower. At last the bathroom door opened.

Roxie placed both arms on the rolled rim of the bath, pushing up to turn her head and look over her shoulder.

Since he never said a word, she was forced to inquire, "Everything go okay?"

His leather jacket was already hanging on the back of the door, and as she watched he unbuttoned the cuffs of his shirt, revealing his muscular forearms.

"At the moment every little thing is hunky-dory. Perfect." His fingers started on the buttons fastening the front of his shirt as he said, "Long may it last."

She ought to be used to seeing his bare chest, yet she still experienced a thrill as she watched his shirt slide off his shoulders. It flew through the air and landed on the chair, covering her clothes, setting her nerves jangling.

She wanted his body to cover hers the same way.

She must be insane.

She'd only just escaped being raped by Yves, yet if anyone could push that memory aside it would be Mac.

He'd promised to scrub her back, but right now she needed more than the pleasure of his hands on her back.

She held her breath as he walked up and stood beside the bath, and she released it in a rush as she watched him unfasten the waist of his jeans. "Did you want to share my bath?"

"Well, that will do for a start, but be warned, I want more, much more." His voice ran roughshod over her emotions.

She tensed as heat bloomed between thighs already pink from the hot water. It was going to happen!

Roxie drew up her knees to make room for him, making the water slop back and forth over her breasts, and Mac's eyes lingered on them.

Roxie couldn't remember when her breasts had felt so full, so heavy. The tips tightened into hard, serrated berries as if Mac had physically caressed them.

Her mouth went dry.

Mac's jeans and shorts slid down in one practiced movement, but that wasn't what had robbed her of saliva.

Her eyes widened and she swallowed in nervous reaction. The fact that he was a large man hadn't escaped her.

She'd even seen him naked, knew he was comfortable in his own skin. But it wasn't quite the same as her view from the bath.

He leaned over to touch the bruise on her shoulder. "Poor baby, he clipped you a good one."

"Actually, the pot I was holding fell when he put his hand on my leg."

"Same difference." His voice grumbled in her ear as his fingers advanced to the nape of her neck. "Now, there's a man who doesn't know how to take no for an answer."

She wanted to fall into that sensation, to fall into Mac, but she still wasn't sure. "And you do?"

"Affirmative. Does that mean that you're telling me no?"

She twisted round so she could look into his eyes. Had to see if he wanted her with more than his body. Then, satisfied, she said, "I'm telling you yes, so come join me."

"Scoot farther down to let me behind you, *chérie.* I promised to scrub your back, and I'm a man of my word."

A man of his word. Now, there was an ambiguous statement. A liar could make the same announcement with equal fervor.

However, Roxie wasn't going to let doubts cloud her enjoyment. Something told her Mac could be an experience it would be a shame to miss.

Chapter 10

Water overflowed the bath as Mac's body proved Archimedes's law of displacement. Not that he gave a damn about theories or laws or anything that took his mind off the awesome sensation of Roxie's naked body in his arms.

Her narrow rib cage pressed against his chest, sending his heart on a slow roll. Control. He needed control.

Her legs felt like satin, silky, feminine and sexy, instead of roughened with coarse hair like his.

Roxie trembled under his big hands. He spread the width of his palms across her breasts and looked down, feeling more, much more than the usual *sexsational* urges from having a woman between his thighs.

The burgeoning weight of his sex was ripe and full, almost too heavy to go the distance. Roxie got to him like no other woman. Thankfully, when Zukah searched his wallet, he hadn't tossed out his condoms.

Mac felt moisture break out across his forehead. He was sweating and not from the water temperature being too high.

No way. Beads of sweat were breaking out because of the strain he'd put on his control. He wanted to be inside Roxie, thrusting fast and deep.

If someone could bottle this tense, breathless feeling of being on the verge of an out-of-body experience, he'd fast become an addict. Mac wanted the way he felt now to last forever, but knew nothing ever did.

He stroked his gaze down to his right shoulder. Her head was cradled against its curve, damp curls framing her face. It shook him how slight she looked in comparison to his broad frame.

His heart beat faster, for he'd never intentionally hurt a woman. Even in the heat of passion it couldn't be excused.

Twice today Roxie had demonstrated her courage.

The first time when she'd stood up to Yves with a tiny knife, the second when she trusted him enough to let him sit behind her, virtually placing her slim neck in his powerful hands.

That's why he intended to take *real* good care of her now, to make sure her pleasure came before his own, and to erase the memory of Yves's loathsome touch from her mind.

Warm runnels of water spilled over the backs of his hands as they explored the curves and hollows of her tender woman's body, which had the added advantage of making Roxie writhe against his.

She sighed her approval as his hands shaped her waist, her palms sweeping down his hairy thighs.

The contrasts between male and female were unmistakable.

As she arched her hips in supplication, Mac's finger slipped between her thighs. Her sighs held him balanced precariously on the edge of his unwillingness to let her spin into freefall.

Instead, he took her higher and higher still. Determined that when she eventually flew, he would take off with her.

Distracting her attention, he slid his fingers into warmth that would have been hot and damp without the tubful of water.

Roxie gasped as the feel of his hand breeching her feminine core caused her breath to quicken. He pushed farther, deeper, until her muscles tightened round him.

"You feeling okay, *chérie?*"

Her head twisted, rocked against his shoulder. "Oh ye-e-s, better than okay," she moaned in pleasure.

He dipped his head, covering her lips with his own, needing to capture her next groan with his mouth. To take her expelled breath deep inside where his heart pounded.

Her lips clung as his tongue mimicked the journey his fingers took her on. The bathwater surged over them as she made waves. Pushing with her feet against the end of the bath, until she gradually rode higher against his erection.

Suddenly the soft, rounded cleft of her buttocks felt too damn good. Too much like the real thing.

With a shudder, he sucked on her bottom lip. Nipping, licking till it grew red and full from the attention. He couldn't get enough of her taste, or the urgent drag of her tongue on his.

He felt her body tighten as the first tentative tremor rippled through her. No time to waste.

Roxie was trembling on the brink and he didn't want it to crumble before he joined her.

Words were redundant, but he'd been brought up to ask, not take, so keeping his honor intact he growled in her ear, "Tell me you want me. This is your last chance to say no."

Her nails dug into his thighs as she crushed his fingers with another muscle spasm. "You needed to *ask?* I want all of you, Mac. I want you inside me, now, before I explode without you."

"You got it, *chérie.*"

Roxie twisted as if to climb into his lap. He stopped her. "No, don't move. Leave everything to me. I guarantee you won't be sorry."

"Hurry. I need you."

Her limbs squirmed in agitation until he had to clamp a hand round one of her water-slick hips to hold her. "Lie still, *chérie*. Let me do all the work."

Swiftly, he lifted her legs to overlap his, then pulled her up higher against his chest.

Groin on fire, he felt the blunt tip of his erection probe the warmth his fingers had prepared for it. They came together naturally, easier than he could have imagined.

Exhaling a long, deep breath, Roxie slid down his tensed stomach, letting her weight carry her, sinking down his length as he thrust upward to meet her.

Heaven and hell encompassed a moment of time.

Enfolded in heat, Mac could hardly breathe as her female flesh surrounded him, teasing his erection with subtle movements. One more thrust, one more lift of his pelvis, and he filled her.

Gripping the sides of the bath, Roxie lifted her shoulders away from his chest close enough for his mouth to find the cord that ran down the side of her neck.

Eyes closed in the agony of passion, he alternately nipped then soothed while seeking command of his body, slowing the race to completion down. His control was short-lived.

Mac felt he might drown in tension as she moved against him.

This was the last place for second thoughts, for guilt. Yet, he couldn't shift the feeling that he was the big bad wolf with his teeth at her throat.

Downstairs they'd had too many foxes in the henhouse and only one chicken. But as usual, he'd managed to twist it to his advantage.

What kind of a bastard did that make him?

Annoyed by the direction of his thoughts, he snapped his eyes open, stunned with the erotic intimacy of the view.

He could see as well as feel his erection fill Roxie to the hilt. Saw her lying open and vulnerable, awaiting his touch, his exploration. Saw how she trusted him.

If he'd been a better, more compassionate man, he might have taken less from her, but he wasn't.

He was case-hardened and he needed her.

Maybe she would save his soul.

He reached lower.

The hard tip of his finger circled nerve endings so sensitive he felt his caress make them sing.

Roxie's hips flexed, bowed, moved on him as supple as a piece of clay fashioned by his touch. Rocking in time with her movements, he felt his erection expand as she took him deeper.

Shuddering against him, Roxie emitted a low sound from her throat that called to the animal in him.

Mac's heart jolted.

The hair at the back of his neck rose and his chest swelled with an emotion he'd never experienced before, or expected to again, urging him to roar, "Mine!"

The next moment, Roxie stiffened, as if scared by the fall that was coming. "Let go, *chérie,* let go. It's okay, I'm here to catch you."

He slid one arm under her breasts, holding her close even as his touch egged her higher, higher, no turning back.

Make the leap!

Mac's last caress sent her over, his mouth catching her screams, swallowing them, tasting their fervor as she trembled through her climax, contracting around him.

Until, suddenly, there was no more time, no more control, his equilibrium exploded in a million pieces and raced to catch up with hers.

For long moments neither moved.

Mac lay, eyes shut, unwilling to spoil the intensity of the moment with words. He simply breathed her in.

As her scent seeped inside his skull, Mac knew making love with her was something he'd never forget. Yet, it was probably the biggest mistake he'd ever made, for her flavors, her passion, would haunt him for a lifetime.

Too bad it didn't account for his knowing that if they got out of this alive, nothing, but nothing, was going to stop him making the same mistake over and over, loving her like this again.

The sun was shining when Roxie woke the next morning, as if making love with Mac had changed everything, including the weather.

His warm body lay along her back and his shoulder pillowed her head. She wished she didn't have to move. Wished *they* didn't have to face Zukah and the others, but as Mac had explained during the night, they were fresh out of alternatives.

She felt the palm of his hand rubbing her hip as his erection nudged her. "You awake?" The rough morning sound of his voice dampened her neck and the stubble on his face tickled.

"If I wasn't before I am now."

He drew her up hard against him as if making certain she knew of his condition. "I've been thinking."

Roxie dragged her instep slowly over his shin. "Oh, is that what they call it?"

"Sorry, that's not what I meant…not that I'd say no." He patted her hip. "Though, I was wondering what we ought to do when *le patron* gets here. And it would be better if you don't meet. If this deal goes crazy, I want you safe, away from the fireworks."

"That's the worst of the two ideas you've come up with today," she taunted, rolling in his arms, wishing there was something, anything she could say to persuade Mac to abandon the deal he'd been working on.

It didn't matter that she knew he lived outside the law, or as the saying went, there was no honor among thieves.

She sensed that whether he knew it or not, there was a deep core of honor in Mac, and she couldn't just walk away and let him be taken down by the jackals downstairs.

Tentatively, she told him, "But it will be four against one. I could even the odds…slightly."

His chest shook. "What with? A vegetable knife?"

Yet she saw no sign of laughter as his hands clamped on her shoulders. His amber eyes crackled with an intensity that diminished the bruising pain of his grasp. "Look, things are going to go off here either today or tomorrow. When Sev—"

She drew in a quick breath as he stopped mid-sentence. "Who? I thought you didn't know his name."

He didn't look her in the eye as he said, "I'm guessing, and it won't do you any good to know if I'm wrong."

Mac was lying. She'd been as close to him as two people could get, and although he'd kept quiet about the group he worked for, she had been certain he'd never deliberately lied to her before.

She huffed through her nose. "All right, don't tell me. I can live with that, but as for me hiding while your life is under threat, that's a coward's way out."

He threw back the covers and leapt out of bed, unequivocally naked, and mad as hell. "Can't you get it through your head that the danger lies in you being there? I can't look after you while making sure Zukah doesn't back out on the deal. Get it?"

"I should think the whole neighborhood got it." Roxie leapt out the other side, dragging the sheet, no longer comfortable to flaunt her nude body in front of a man who thought her help would get him killed.

She stared at his erection. "It would seem *that's* not the only thing you get up with in the morning. I suggest two aspirins for your sore head."

The rueful twist of his lips made an appearance for less than a second as he shrugged. "Low blood sugar, I'm hungry. We never got round to eating last night."

It wasn't much of an apology, but she'd take it at face value.

"I meant to tell you that since we're almost out of food, they must be expecting *le patron* soon. There was only enough for a couple of days."

"Well, that's good news. Here's what I want you to do."

He began pacing. "You keep the door key with you at all times. If we get wind of the headman arriving, I want you to come upstairs and lock the attic door."

"But I could be stuck here," she protested.

"Not if you go down the backstairs to the study I told you about. They won't expect it, and they won't feel the need to watch the kitchen while I'm there with them. Any questions?"

Just one, she thought. When do I have to salute?

She hitched up her sheet and said primly, "I think you've made it perfectly clear that you don't need my help."

"Good, let's get cleaned up and see if they'll send Jean-Luc out to buy more food."

But when they got downstairs, they discovered *le patron* had sent word he'd arrive the next day.

Jean-Luc had already been sent to buy food. And Roxie stopped pretending she was unhappy to be left on the sidelines.

Her worst fears were confirmed later when she unloaded the bag of produce and found part of that morning's newspaper, *Le Figaro,* a weighty, intelligent paper with tightly packed columns.

Without making it too obvious, she quickly scanned the front page. What she read made the blood drain from her face.

Mac had bitten back the word that morning, but she'd heard enough. She'd guessed all along he was waiting for Victoire Sevarin.

It had begun with that glimpse of a famous château she'd recognized in the distance. When she'd added the coincidence of being kept in an old house with a single tower on the left-hand corner she'd been almost certain.

Grandmère had driven her past Sevarin's house one holiday when she was young, pointing out *this* place as the home of their enemy. And during fittings, Madeleine Saber, his mistress, had gushed about all the money Victoire Sevarin was spending on his country home—*for her,* so she'd thought, poor fool.

Sevarin. Roxie would as soon clasp an asp to her chest as trust anyone of that name. Should she tell Mac?

The deputy minister of defense would recognize her just as easily as she would him, since he'd visited the House of Fortier frequently with Madeleine.

Roxie moved the vegetables around on the newsprint, surreptitiously reading more, then wishing she hadn't as everything fell into place. Sevarin had resigned and a scientist at the research establishment he oversaw had committed suicide after it was discovered that a biotech weapon, supposedly destroyed, had disappeared.

The whole idea of the weapon Mac was set on buying scared her to death. How could she have fallen for a man who dealt in that kind of destruction?

By late that night, Mac was sure the change in Roxie was obvious only to him. You couldn't become as close as they had been the past three days without sensing when something was up.

Yves hadn't been near her all day, so it wasn't that.

If anyone was in the doghouse, his name was Mac.

Once, when he'd caught her eye, he'd felt that if he touched her right then, he'd get frostbite.

The glance she'd swung his way had been *that* cold.

Something had happened, but what?

He'd counted off the hours, three since they'd come to bed, and still she tossed around, unable to sleep.

And it couldn't be because she had a hard lump of a gun under her pillow the way he did.

Sevarin would be here tomorrow.

This could be their last night together, and she had turned her back on him. It was enough to make the meal she'd cooked turn to acid in his stomach.

After a bright clear day, the moon was riding high in a deep, midnight-blue sky and shone into the attic window, silvering her with moonlight. Needing to get to the root of her problem, he reached across to touch the cold shoulder she'd been giving him.

She jumped like a scalded cat.

"Whoa, *chérie,* you're like a bundle of nerves that have been wired wrong. What happened today?"

She ignored him. Grabbing the blue quilt, she huddled on the edge of the bed and pulled the cover over her head.

If there was one thing Mac couldn't stand it was the silent treatment. How could he fix things if she wouldn't tell him what he'd done wrong?

"Is it still Yves? If you want me to tear him limb from limb, just say the word, *chérie,* and it's done."

His throat tightened, roughening his voice, "The thought of him laying a hand on you drives me crazy. The idea of another man touching you does my head in. So, put me out my misery here and tell me what's wrong."

His pulse beat loud and heavy in his temple as his imagination raced ahead of his words. This time he got a reaction.

Roxie flung the covers off and jumped out of bed.

It wasn't the result he'd expected, but at least she was facing him at last. Any reaction was better than nothing.

As his father always said, "Women think men are mind readers, when all they really want is pointing in the right direction."

"That's better. Tell me what he did. If he put a hand out of place I'll break all his fingers."

She threw up her hands and shouted, "Pah, men! Only two things get through to you, sex and violence."

Next minute she'd pulled the quilt off the bed and stomped over to the table in front of the window.

The chair she dragged out seemed to punctuate her feelings with the screech of its legs being pulled across bare boards.

Mac followed, wearing only his shorts.

Cold air shivered across his skin, but it was the glare she hit him with that made the hair on his arms shoot upright.

Straight-backed, wrapped in the quilt and bathed in moonlight, she cut him to the quick with a glance that was ice cold.

A glance that told him he was on the wrong track.

It wasn't Yves who had stepped out of line, it was Mac McBride, last scion of the Philadelphia McBrides, who never usually put a foot wrong where women were concerned.

Who had always been able to smooth-talk until they were once more wrapped around his little finger, his mama included.

Yet this time, when it mattered most, he didn't know how to fix things and Roxie wasn't tossing him any clues.

"If I've done anything to offe—"

"Oooh," she snapped, "Don't be preposterous. What good is an apology? You haven't enough skin on your knees to get down and apologize to the whole world for what you want to do."

She leaned a bare elbow on the table and thrust her chin toward him. "You may have thought you fooled me, Mac whatever your name is. But I'm here to tell you that you're wrong. Dead wrong! I know what you're up to."

So, it was no accident that Thierry hadn't been able to find anything on her. Damn, now he felt ridiculous. He had fallen for the tricks of another agent.

The question now being, which side was she on?

Then for the second time since he'd sat down at the table, she caught him off guard.

"Did you know Sevarin had resigned?"

Chapter 11

Roxie only had to watch Mac's face to know she'd hit the jack-pot. Myriad expressions flitted over his features, ranging from genuine surprise to black anger.

So, it *was* Sevarin he was dealing with.

But did Mac know the false nature of the man? Did he know the name was synonymous with treachery and deceit or that the Sevarin family constantly played both ends against the middle?

At last he stopped looking at her as if she was something disgusting that had crawled out of a drain, and asked, "Okay, out with it. Tell me who you're working for."

Damn, she thought they'd settled this. She scrunched up her eyes as if in disbelief. "What do you mean who am I working for? I told you. Charles Fortier."

"Yeah, that's likely. What interest does a couturier have in Green Shield?"

Roxie blinked. "So that's its name."

Le Figaro had concluded that the reason for Sevarin's resignation was the disappearance of a biotech weapon, but such things had never come within her scope before. "And before you go on about Charles, I doubt if he's heard the name either."

His hand splayed over the tabletop with a quiet yet sharp bang, like five fingers pointing accusingly at her. "But you do. So what group, slash agency, slash cell do you work for? Is it MI6?"

MI6? As if. "You crack me up. Because I'm English, you've added two and two and made five and come to the conclusion I work for MI6."

Roxie rolled her eyes incredulously, then shrugged, letting the slippery quilt slide off her shoulders. "I'm also part French. I don't think they'd have me."

She watched his stare drop lower, to her breasts stretching the lace as the brush of cold air flowed over them.

He looked away quickly.

Too late. The touch of his gaze hardened her nipples into tight points. Did he think she was trying to tempt him with the memory of his hands shaping her breasts, or the taste of her as he'd sucked her into his mouth?

This was not a good moment to become aroused.

She hitched up the quilt, but it wouldn't stay put.

"I told you the truth," she said. "I'm a fashion designer. Me being at your apartment was a mistake, and before you think of putting a dent in my windpipe like you did Yves, I'm telling you we should escape while we can."

His taut, muscular forearms rested on the table as he leaned forward, hands clenched, his face no more than eighteen inches away. "So, you think I should walk away and leave the field open to you? In your dreams, *bébé,* you need me. Tell you what, though. Give me the name of the agency running you and maybe we can make a deal."

She deliberately misunderstood him. "I don't have an agent yet. Maybe one day when my name becomes known."

Holding the edges of the quilt in her hands, she closed the distance separating them by letting her forearms rest on the edge of the tabletop. Her breast brushed against the lace as she heaved a sigh. "The fashion industry can be fickle. I might never make it that high."

"I get it. You're scared of what will happen if you talk. What if I guaranteed your protection?" He reached over and touched her wrist. Heat blossomed.

God, did he really think she was such a pushover?

"The only person I'm frightened of is Sevarin. You don't know him…." *He might kill you.*

"And you do?" His whisper was harsh, urgent, and surged into action with his fingers tightening round her wrist.

She winced and pulled away, her heart plummeting. "You didn't have to do that. We both know you're stronger than I am. You don't have to prove it."

She made a point of rubbing her wrist. Yes, she was weaker, but she had other skills. It might take all of them to persuade him to leave now, *tonight, before it's too late.*

If only Mac would understand. "I was trying to tell you, I know Sevarin's family history. And people don't change—it runs in their blood."

Mac didn't believe her.

Look at the difference between him and his father. Joshua McBride Senior reached his goals by diplomacy, Mac with cunning and a little necessary force. His father would never have grabbed a woman hard enough to break her wrist.

He watched Roxie's fingers rub where he'd held her. Without a cloud in the sky, the pale watery light from the moon was clear enough for him to see she was going to sport another bruise.

"If that's so, whom do you take after?" Mac asked.

She blinked in surprise, and he was struck by how the moonlight glanced through the curve of her eyes and turned them luminous.

"You know, until a couple of years ago I would have said my mother. She loved pretty clothes, yet look at me now."

She ran her fingers through her tousled curls, and he wondered again if the slip of the quilt was deliberate.

"But now I'm sure I take after my grandmother. Grandmère was in the French Resistance and a leader by the age of sixteen."

She stopped playing with her hair as a smile played around her lips. "My grandfather said she wouldn't take lip from anyone, including him. He came over from England to work undercover in 1942, just before the rest of France was overrun by the Nazis."

God, she could be so annoying. What was about her that made him want her so much? He cleared his throat and asked, "What's that got to do with anything? Stick to the subject."

She looked irritated. He wasn't the pushover she expected. "But I am. Grandmère had to contend with Sevarin's father, Michel. He was a traitor to France and its people, yet he managed to walk away without even a slap on the wrist."

This time she reached out to him, her fingers threading through his. "Please don't let history repeat itself."

He had to close his heart to her touch, her warmth. He shook his head to clear it.

Poor kid, it looked as if Roxie's grandmother had done a number on her—how she could have won the war if it hadn't been for the big bad man.

He'd heard those stories before from older agents and put them down as excuses.

"Listen to me, *chérie.* You're talking ancient history, long gone. What happened then has no bearing on my deal."

"Don't be too sure. Sevarin started as a small cog in the Vichy government, but he had big ambitions, so he moved to Paris. Just like his son." Her other hand covered the one she was already holding.

Trapped.

"He claimed," she continued, "to want to help the Resistance and got a job working in Gestapo headquarters so he could warn them of raids."

Mac tried to butt in, to redirect the conversation.

She halted him with a peremptory wave of her hand.

"Uh-uh, let me finish. Sevarin was passing the information both ways, and a lot of loyal Frenchmen and women died because of him…I don't want you to die because of his son."

Her voice caught as she turned to face the room, hiding her expression in shadow.

He wasn't buying it. It hurt to admit, but he'd been conned by a better artist than Roxie and it had nearly cost him his life.

Though Lucia's beauty had been more blatant than Roxie's subtle sexiness, he knew which had shattered his notion that Mac McBride could move from one sexual experience to another without breaking a sweat.

He'd never forget Roxie. Never be able to replace what he felt as he thrust inside her, or for that matter, lay quietly holding her in his arms.

But he'd be an idiot to let a woman fool him again because she had his hormones in a twist.

"And how do you—" his drawl bordered on the sarcastic, but Roxie didn't seem to notice "—think we can get away from this place, walk? They'd soon catch up with us on foot."

"I know of this place. It's near the Loire. We could find a boat or steal a car."

A boat? Even for Roxie that was a stretch of the imagination. "Supposing we get away without getting shot. How would we start a car? You gonna hotwire it, *chérie?*"

He was being a typical male, but she couldn't let that stop her from saving his life as he'd saved hers. "You're the criminal, I thought you would know how to do all that stuff."

His eyes lit with laughter. She could see he didn't believe a word she'd said. Give Mac his due, at least he hadn't pegged her as *another* terrorist. What else could he be if he wanted Green Shield? And she could get shot for even thinking of helping him.

"Give it up, Roxie. I'm not leaving here without getting what I came for, and no amount of persuasion will change my mind. You can make up all the tales you want, about Sevarin and your grandmother, they aren't going to work."

He leaned back in the chair and folded his arms. "Do you really think I believed you turning up at my apartment was a coincidence? You were following Zukah. Come on, admit it."

Smug and a know-it-all. He made her so mad. Why did men have to be so stubborn? So suspicious?

She was trying to save his life!

Her frustration doubled, trebled as she fed the flames with more fuel aimed at men in general and Mac in particular. Then it came to her. Why hadn't she thought of it before?

She would trap him at his own game.

"All right, you've got me. I work for MI6. We've been watching Sevarin since he made moves to hire Zukah. That's why I was following the Algerian, to discover who his meeting was with."

She pushed her hair back behind her ear and straightened in her chair. "We knew something was in the wind, that he had set up a meeting, but I was expecting to follow him to a café, not your apartment."

"La Grappe d'Orgueil?"

"Yes."

"Son of a—" He slapped his palm on his thigh, expressing his delight. "I knew it the moment you turned up."

He had the cheek to wink at her as he said, "You have flair and style in the way you dress, and that sexy walk was just made to turn men's heads. What gave you away was how easily you slotted into the role of my *petite amie*. Any ordinary woman would have given herself away right then."

"You're right," she agreed. "I was just too good and that's what gave me away. You must admit it's been fun, though."

"More than fun." His smile turned knowing as if at a memory.

He confirmed it a moment later. "I have to say, you had me going when you let me go all the way. It takes guts to sleep with the enemy."

Her heart turned over and dived for the floor. It shattered in too many pieces to recover them all. Now there would always be a part missing to prove how stupid she'd been.

As if to press home her mistake, she asked him, "Now you know who I am and the agency I work for, what about you, where do you call home?"

Mac stood up. "I was born in the States, but most of my adult life I've called Chechnya home."

It was worse than she'd thought.

She felt giddy, as if the floor had come up to hit her, but she couldn't let him see that. "That's not a place I've ever fancied visiting."

"Who could blame you? With your looks you'd never escape attention. But in Paris?" He gave an almost pure Gallic shrug, as if to say in Paris women like her were ten a penny.

This time she was at a loss for words. To think she'd wanted to give that man her heart.

"Don't think that because we're on opposite sides it changes anything. I won't give you up to them. You've come in useful. My mother always said, Find a woman who can cook."

He squeezed her shoulder and it took an effort not to flinch.

"We stick to my original plan. You go down the stairs to the study and I'll do the deal with Sevarin." He picked up his jeans from the end of the bed and slid his feet into them, zipping them up across his hard, flat stomach.

"If anything goes wrong, it will be good to know your agency will come in and pick up the pieces." After he grabbed his leather jacket, he walked back to her and gave her shoulder another squeeze. She supposed it was meant to be reassuring.

It didn't work.

She'd have one more try to save him. "If you think I meant to hand you over after we escaped, you're wrong. I wouldn't do that."

He shrugged the jacket over his wide shoulders, saying, "For God's sake, don't tell anyone else that. I don't want to have saved you to face a firing squad. They'll throw the book at you."

"I'd deserve it."

"Look, lets not get morbid. I meant what I promised. I'll protect you from Sevarin and the others. Just do as I say."

He walked toward the armoire and swung it back. "I'm going to take another look downstairs and see if there's some way you can lock the office door from the inside."

Just when she thought he was gone, Mac reappeared at the top of the dark stairwell. "Here's something to think on. When you get back to England, I'd learn some martial arts."

Though he was almost invisible, she could detect the grin in his advice, and to turn the thumbscrews tighter he finished with "It will make life easier than depending on your looks."

Her first impulse was to swing the armoire back in place and lock him and his smug grin out. But what was the point? She dragged the quilt back to the bed, which it seemed she'd made for herself and would now have to lie upon.

Grandmère would be so disappointed in her.

Roxie threw herself onto the bed.

She just couldn't leave it at that. There had to be some way she could prevent Mac handing the Green Shield weapon over to the Chechen rebel forces.

Perhaps if she slept on it, an idea would come to her in the night. An idea to make her forget how she'd let her temper get the better of her and claimed to be something she wasn't.

But Mac had had the last laugh.

And that's what hurt the most.

* * *

Mac needed to contact Thierry, urgently. Was he the only person in the world who hadn't known Sevarin's government job had blown up in his face?

If Sevarin failed to show, the biotech weapon that the French Defense Department had supposedly destroyed could disappear into the woodwork and surface years later, God knows where.

The only thing keeping his hopes alive was that Sevarin must now need money badly and would still show tomorrow.

When Thierry came on the secure line Mac didn't bother with formalities. "What's this about Sevarin resigning?"

"Jason Hart gave the okay to pass the word about Sevarin and Green Shield on to the French government, but someone there jumped the gun."

Mac didn't like what he was hearing. He wished he hadn't dragged Roxie deeper into the affair than she had obviously intended. Hell, she hadn't even been armed when she'd blundered into his apartment.

But Thierry's story wasn't finished. "They went down to the secure facility and began questioning the scientists. The upshot is that one of them blew his brains out in the men's room."

"Great work. So, am I wasting my time here? Have they picked up Sevarin?" Mac waited on tenterhooks for the reply.

He'd lived with this mission for more than a month, and just as the finish line came into sight some overzealous nitwit had tripped him up.

"No. Sevarin did resign, but it wasn't because he'd been accused of anything. He reckoned that the French Internal Security Agency had impugned the integrity of his department and he had no other choice but to resign."

"Thank God for that. Now I'm simply back to waiting. Zukah reckons Sevarin will show tomorrow. He still thinks I don't know who *le patron* is."

"Won't he be surprised? Oh, by the way, I got you the rest of that info on Roxie."

"That's okay, I managed to get it out of her myself tonight. No force necessary." Mac smiled to himself when he thought of the merry dance she had led him.

He'd felt quite upbeat, but he couldn't trust her with his own identity, not till all this was over. For all her protests, he didn't trust her not to give him away if she was tortured.

"I've seen her picture."

Yeah," Mac drawled, "the lady's got great genes."

Thierry wasn't done. "*Oui*. French Internal Security must have taken her on because her grandmother was one of our legendary heroes of the Second World War. De Gaulle himself presented her with the Legion of Honor."

Mac felt his good mood take a nosedive. He'd been so sure of himself, and his efforts had cost him more than he could ever imagine. His hand shook as he said, "Yeah, I guess I lucked out."

She'd conned him again and he'd let it happen.

Jason Hart wasn't going to be overimpressed if he let anything happen to the granddaughter of one of France's legendary Resistance heroes.

"*Oui*, a lucky dog," Thierry agreed.

Lucky? He wished.

"Her job with Charles Fortier is real. Fortier's mama worked for the Resistance as well. That's how they met."

For most of his Paris assignment he'd lived from one moment to the next, and unlike Roxie his work wasn't personal. But like her, he was proud of his family history and he never forgot he was a McBride, no matter which name he was using at the time.

"Is that it, Thierry?"

"*Non*. Though she did receive some training, it seems the most Mademoiselle Kincaid has done until now is pass on information. The rich, famous and politically unscrupulous feel at ease behind the salon's doors. Sevarin's mistress shops there."

"Where are the FIS when she needs them? What if I'd really been Jeirgif Makjzajev?" The thought of anything happening to Roxie made his gut roll over.

When she'd come out with that lie, all he'd felt was relief. If she worked for MI6, any relationship between them was banned. The bureau might cooperate with the British agency upon occasion, but both agencies frowned on the secrets that could be passed during pillow talk between agents.

But, if she only worked for FIS on the side…pillow talk might be the only way out from the rock and the hard place his overconfidence had landed him in.

No way could he explain how he knew she'd lied about MI6.

On the other hand, he couldn't apologize for belittling her story of Grandmère's life in the Resistance.

After his reactions, an apology just wasn't going to cut it.

Dawn wasn't that far behind him as he slipped back into the attic. Outside, the moon had set and his view of dark blue velvet sky had grown a fringe of palest pink.

Roxie was asleep on top of the quilt. Her limbs outspread as if completely relaxed. Her satiny skin was the same color as daybreak, and the blue quilt echoed the sky.

Just looking at her made him hard.

He wanted her again. Wanted her one last time.

Mac removed his jacket before stripping off his two remaining layers of clothing and lying down on the bed beside her.

Easing closer, he ran the palm of one hand over the arm next to him. Her skin felt cold, icy, in fact, and she instinctively turned into his warmth without waking.

He pulled her close. She said his name, "Mac." And a sigh as soft as butter brushed his neck.

He placed a kiss on her forehead, then whispered, "I'm sorry for doubting you, *chérie*. You're a great Internal Security agent."

The reply was so quiet he almost didn't catch it as she sleepily mumbled, "I didn't want to fail" into the hollow of his shoulder.

It was all the confirmation he needed, and Roxie would probably never remember telling him.

His hands swept up under her lace camisole in a swift movement that left only one of them wearing a stitch of clothing as he tugged the lace over her head.

She clung to him as his mouth did a taste exploration of her skin from neck and shoulders, traveling down to breasts and navel. Mac worked his way down, savoring every part, enjoying the smooth softness inside her thighs as she assisted him to remove the tangle of panties from her suddenly restless legs.

And while she might still be in that state between sleep and reality, her fingers tunneled through his hair as he took one long, last intimate kiss and heard her cry out his name in pleasure.

Chapter 12

To begin with, Roxie's dream was familiar. Rushing onto an empty platform at Gare du Nord, the train ready to depart, and Mac at the far end about to board.

Leaving her behind.

She ran. All at once the platform was crowded. People left and right, everywhere, holding her back while she fought her way through the tight crush.

For a change, though, the train didn't leave her standing alone and bereft on the platform. She rushed into Mac's arms and they embraced, their clothes melting away as he sank to his knees before her, worshiping her body.

But Roxie was very much awake now, her heart pounding like a mad thing under breasts that had surrendered to Mac's hands.

She lay gasping for air, fingers tangled in his hair unable to move in the aftermath of the climax Mac had wrought with his mouth and tongue.

Shivering, she came back into her body, her skin hot and damp while the air around it was chill by comparison.

Before her heart could finish its race, Mac's big body covered hers, sharing his heat. She'd have to be dead not to be aware that his needs hadn't been fulfilled and the simple act of reflecting on them made her womb spasm with aftershocks.

He was so large, she should have felt suffocated, but neither his body nor his intensely male personality intimidated her anymore. This man had saved her life twice in three days.

In a way, they were the stereotypical couple, which drove the plots of romantic movies, the offspring of feuding families, or the lovers on opposing sides in a war.

She slipped her arms around his neck confident he would never hurt her, even if his stubborn streak prevented him separating truth from fiction.

Mac took one of her hands in his, placing a kiss in the heart of her palm. He circled it with the tip of his tongue as if to remind her how skillful he had been.

"I was dreaming," she told him.

"About me?" he laughed, as if at the obvious.

The sound of his laughter echoed through her chest and rocked against her heart. "How did you guess?" she asked once her lungs released the breath she'd been holding.

"*Chérie,* you might have been dreaming but you weren't asleep.

"Shall I tell you how many ways you called my name?"

"Don't bother, I have a good imagination."

Too good for her peace of mind.

There was never any need to fake it with Mac, no need to repeat her efforts of their first night in this old bed when her moans had been for the benefit of their concealed audience.

Mac's fingers trailed down her cheeks, a caress that made her want to cry for some reason.

Mac put it into words. "You realize this may be our last night together. After Sevarin turns up to complete the deal, we'll both be going our separate ways."

His words reverberated in her mind.

"Separate ways" meaning her going back to Paris and Mac traveling to Chechnya.

"I know," she agreed, but not for the obvious reason.

If he was intent on buying Green Shield, she had no option but to stop him even if it killed her. "I don't want to think about never seeing you again, not yet."

Although he stood for everything her grandparents had put their lives on the line to fight against, she couldn't wish Mac dead.

But, unlike Mac, she didn't trust Sevarin to let him walk away with Green Shield, unless it was in a lead-lined coffin. She knew it killed plants, but what did it do to people? Agent Orange had been responsible for hordes of genetic defects.

Mac nuzzled under her chin. The brush of his beard felt softer than that first time he kissed her. When she'd been certain she was about to die. What a little coward she'd been.

Some things were worth dying for.

Did he remember the moment he'd claimed her as his lover in front of Zukah and the Frenchmen? Who could have known that his words would come true?

"We should make the most of the time we have left, then." He sighed the words against her neck, then went on. "The sky is getting lighter, dawn can't be far away, and who knows when Sevarin will arrive with Green Shield?"

She dragged her fingers through his hair, lighter now that he wasn't incessantly wetting it to slick it back. It made him look younger. She tilted his face up so he couldn't hide the truth.

The look in his eyes was as old as time. His irises burned a deep gold, and behind them she read the knowledge that he wasn't taking the dangers of their situation lightly.

His was the expression of a man eager to do battle, yet reluctant to say goodbye to his woman. A look that made her want to cling and press all she had, all that she was, in her heart and mind, against him and say, "Take me one last time."

Her sigh spanned time, whispering the answer women always gave in the circumstances, "We'd be foolish to waste it, then."

He pulled her closer, tighter, heart to heart, breast to breast, and the groan he made sounded as if something inside him had broken. "In this at least, we are of one mind, *chérie.*"

She felt as if he poured everything into his kiss.

Tasting pure emotion, her head spun with the sheer wonder of what he said with his touch that he didn't dare voice.

His hands were everywhere, as were hers. Skimming his back, shaping the muscles of his arms as they took the strain.

Dawn coated his skin with pale apricot, glancing off the planes of his face and deepening the shadows in the hollows till the dimple centering his chin was pronounced.

He slipped his fingers through hers, holding her hands above her head while he feasted on her breasts as she writhed under him. Legs wrapped around his back, she centered his hard length between her thighs.

Inside, it felt as if she were expanding. Creating a hollow only Mac could fill, and the pressure only made her need stronger. "*Chéri,* I'm empty without you. Fill me, fill me up now."

He could give her all the climaxes in the world with hands or mouth; they meant nothing without feeling him inside her.

"There's nothing I want more, *chérie.*"

He tilted his hips until she felt the tip of his sex brush her swollen folds and, holding her breath, she waited for his first thrust.

It never came.

Instead, he eased inside slowly, cautiously, as if it was the first time for both of them.

Roxie's temperature rose. Her breath came fast until she

thought her heart and lungs would explode from an experience that was exhilarating and frustrating at once. She closed her eyes.

Mac stopped, as did her breathing as the tension became too much to bear.

"Open your eyes." The command was gruff round the edges. "I want to see them darken as passion overtakes you."

She did as he said, but thought she ought to mention, "Mac... you're killing me here."

"Not yet, but soon. I want that small sweet death to find us at the same moment. I want it to be something you never forget," he said, inching forward a little more, then he drew back.

"No!" She wrapped him in the tight bands of her limbs, but he was too strong and drew back all the way.

His next thrust took her deeper before he drew back. He repeated the action over and over, gaining speed and depth till she felt a quivering mass of nerves about to die of pleasure.

Eyes open as he'd asked, she held his gaze, his intense concentration almost as arousing as the building rhythm, deep, fast. Roxie had no experience to compare it with.

Every movement of his gleaming muscles worked to a sensual rhythm. Beads of sweat gleamed on his forehead as the sun rose, and the colors of daybreak highlighted their erotic dance.

The first ripple tugged inside her.

Mac's eyes glittered topaz in the light, and his pleased grin acknowledged his expertise. But at the very second she came apart, Roxie realized he'd never smile at her just that way again....

Then all thought was lost as a powerful spasm rocked her, amplifying the quivers rippling across her skin.

Her head rolled back and forth on the pillow, her lower lip aching as she bit back the scream building in her throat.

"Look at me," he demanded in a tone that brooked no refusal. She did.

It was the last thing she remembered, the last thing she could put a name to as Mac's thrusts lifted her off the mattress and her vision went black.

His mouth clamped over hers, swallowing the noise of her climax as if to keep it private, personal, *secret*.

Then as the waves rolled over her, his big body froze, muscles rigid, as he spilled his seed.

Filling her with the matter that all life springs from, he called out her name.

Later that morning, Roxie was just ahead of Mac on the stairs, when he heard the crunch of tires ripping the red-gravel driveway. Though the vehicle hadn't yet come in sight, he took hold of her shoulders and turned her round. "Quickly now, back upstairs."

Patting her derriere to make her climb faster, he reminded her, "Once you're inside lock the attic, then go down the backstairs. You'll be able to watch what's happening on the monitor. But if you hear anyone coming, duck back and hide on the stairs."

"What about you?"

"I'll be okay. They want money and nothing is likely to happen to me until they have that."

She halted, her feet one step from the second landing. "Mac, you shouldn't have to do this alone."

"Damn it, Roxie, keep moving. Don't you realize having you there increases the threat to me? I can't chance it."

Her lips trembled and her tears added brilliance to her eyes as she asked, "Because you're not indestructible after all? Because this time you'd have to let them shoot me?"

God, had he done a number on her when he'd conned her into believing he was a Chechen rebel.

Instead of her remembering how he'd poured his heart and soul into their lovemaking, she couldn't forget the lies he'd told.

He experienced a sudden urge to get out of the spy business.

It had already taken part of his honor, and if he left it too late the secrets and lies would eat up the man he'd once believed himself to be.

"No matter what I told you in the beginning, the danger to me will come from *not* being able to let them shoot you. Did you ever think maybe I'm not as bad as I painted myself?"

She swallowed hard and brushed away the tears with her hands. "I've always been an optimistic kind of woman."

He took her hand away from her eyes and kissed it, tasted the salty residue of her sorrow. "Good. Maybe later we'll discover your optimism wasn't in vain."

Mac pressed the coil of wire he'd attached to two small metal bars into her hand. He'd had it stuck in his pocket for more than a day.

"What's this?" Roxie stared hard at the weapon in her hand.

"A weapon of last resort."

She pushed it away, her expression distasteful. "I don't think it's necessary"

"Look, I'll need my knife if they confiscate my gun. At least this will slightly adjust the odds in your favor."

He heard heavy footsteps on the flagstones below. "Scoot, now. I want to be at the foot of the stairs when Sevarin arrives."

Before he could move away, Roxie flung an arm around his neck and kissed him hard on the lips. "Take care," she said, "Extreme care. I've an awful feeling I'll never see you again."

Mac kissed her hard. Tongue and teeth coming into play as he realized he never wanted to let her go. "You'll see me again. We're meant to be together, trust me."

Trust me. Easy to say, not so easy to carry through.

Roxie hurried to the attic. She wanted to be able to trust him, and she would, with her life. But the men he was dealing with? Never. And if Sevarin kept his word for once, how could she let Mac walk away with Green Shield?

She would have to turn him in.

Roxie felt that Mac now knew to be on his guard with Severin. But nothing she'd said had persuaded him to escape with her while they had a chance.

Voices drifted up from below as she dived across the landing. Once she'd turned the key in the lock, she breathed easier.

As she leaned her back on the door, her eyes darted around the attic. She hadn't brought much, but she intended taking it all with her when she left.

The euros in her purse would probably come in handy.

Hurrying, she thrust her arms into her coatsleeves and dashed over to the armoire. It would take every bit of her strength to swivel it out from the wall.

She turned and looked back at the unmade bed, at the tangle of quilts and covers. Her life had changed in that bed.

Not when Mac had made love to her, momentous and earth-shattering as it had been. No, it was that first night when he'd thrown himself into the pretence of having sex with her.

She'd known then that no matter which cause he followed, Mac wasn't a bad guy at heart.

Attraction had already been simmering between them, and a look or a sigh then could have set the sexual time bomb off.

But he hadn't taken advantage of knowing her protests for what they were. Words. *Hot air.*

Conversation had been glaring by its absence this morning, as if the lack of a condom wasn't worth mentioning. The fact would loom large in the next couple of weeks.

Not because she was frightened that she'd become pregnant.

Deep in her mind where her greatest fears lived, the thought of never seeing Mac again haunted her. But, if he'd left her with one small piece of himself...

She turned and fled down the stairs, oblivious to the spiderwebs floating in the darkness, as she finally admitted she'd fallen in love with a man determined to stand in harm's way.

* * *

Sevarin didn't look nearly as large as the publicity he'd always courted suggested. The long pearl-gray coat hanging from the older man's shoulders, as well as the white scarf and tan leather gloves, gave him a foppish air at odds with the liquid death he was selling.

Silver-haired Sevarin had been playing elder statesman in French politics for many years, but always on the fringes, never quite reaching the heights he aspired to.

Just as well, decided Mac.

What he, as well as most French citizens, had taken for polish came off as oiliness this morning. It dripped from the smile Sevarin assumed as he offered to shake Mac's hand.

The Makarov Mac clutched in his right fist was as good an excuse as any to refuse contact, considering both Zukah and Yves were armed. Sevarin turned away with typical French nonchalance.

Mac on the other hand went straight for the throat. "You've taken your own good time about getting here, Sevarin. I'd just made up my mind to leave, today."

Victoire Sevarin parried, "Without what you came for, I think not, Monsieur Makjzajev."

"Some things come at too high a price," quipped Mac.

And so the verbal cut and thrust went on in the foyer without a winner until Mac asked, "I hope you came here prepared to give me a demonstration."

"Since you insisted, yes. That's what took the extra time, but I trust you'll be satisfied by the efforts I've gone to." Sevarin abruptly swung around to face the entrance. The hem of his coat sliced the air in a semicircle.

As Mac watched, a man wearing a chauffeur's cap assisted Jean-Luc to carry what looked like a large glass aquarium up the broad outside steps.

Sevarin looked at the Algerian. "Ahmed, there's a tray of plants in the trunk, be so good as to bring them in."

Zukah hesitated and threw a glance at Yves, who was still showing signs of the beating Mac had given him. "But…"

A look passed between Sevarin and Yves that boded ill for Zukah. The old order changeth, thought Mac as the hairs on the back of his neck rose, a warning of what was to come.

"Take that through to the kitchen. We'll retire there for the demonstration," instructed Sevarin.

Mac had a feeling if Sevarin said, "Jump," the others would say, "How high?"

The only mistake Mac made was entering the kitchen before discovering the chauffeur hadn't been the only other person in the car with Sevarin.

The new guy announced his presence by pushing the muzzle of a pistol between Mac's ribs around heart level.

The gun felt big enough to make a good-size hole in the back of Mac's leather jacket.

Concerned as he was for his own safety, he felt a certain reluctance to be shot down with Roxie watching on the monitor. "This isn't in the manual on good business practices."

"That depends entirely on the edition," said Sevarin.

He reached over and removed the Makarov from Mac's hand, then tested the weight of it. "Very nice. The Russians know how to make a solid piece of killing machinery. I take it being Chechen this fact doesn't offend you, since it's your weapon of choice. I know how if feels…." Sevarin exhaled a long-drawn-out sigh.

What did he expect from Mac, violins?

"I, too, have had to make certain decisions that go against the grain, but then a man must live, mustn't he, Makjzajev?"

"If you say so, Sevarin, though some us aren't only in it for the money." Slick runnels of sweat coated Mac's back.

He was grateful it didn't show.

"Obnoxious to the bitter end, Makjzajev." Sevarin twisted his words into a sneer as he looked beyond Mac's shoulder into the entrance hall.

But he hadn't finished with Mac. "You have proved a nuisance from the first. Disrupting a perfectly good plan and obliging me to take into my own hands certain matters that are abhorrent to a man of my refined sensibilities."

Sevarin stared Mac straight in the eye as he fired.

Roxie stood at the foot of the hidden stairs, her heart jolting from the loud report that echoed through the old house.

The reason she hadn't entered the room was simple. She hadn't decided whether the quiet in the study meant it was empty or if someone was sitting in silence watching the monitor.

Now, frightened for Mac's safety, she flung the door open. It took less than a second to confirm no one was there.

She rushed to look at the monitor. For a breathless couple of moments she stared at the screen. As if it were a still life painting, no one moved. Half hidden, behind a crowd of shoulders and backs, she saw someone's trouser legs from the knee down.

To her intense horror, she realized a dark pool was growing ever larger on the flagstones. *Blood.* She slapped a hand over her mouth to silence the scream erupting from her throat.

"Oh, Mac," she sobbed into her palm. "Mac, we should have escaped while we had the chance."

Chapter 13

Would Mac be next? Roxie shuddered as the light-colored suiting turned dark with blood. Then, the men who had appeared rooted the floor hurriedly went into action. With the kind of expression that usually accompanied finding a fly floating in the soup, Sevarin looked down on Zukah.

No need to search for a smoking gun; Sevarin still held the weapon.

Tears she couldn't control welled in her eyes.

Not for the Algerian, but because logic made her acknowledge that if Sevarin could cold-bloodedly kill one of his partners, he could take out Mac without a second thought.

There had to be something she could do.

Some incident she could create to give Mac a chance to escape.

So far, her lover's hands weren't tied, but the guy pressing a gun to his back unquestionably meant business. "Dear God," she prayed aloud, "please don't let it end this way."

Solutions darted into Roxie's mind.

Flashes of foolhardiness she immediately discarded.

It was no good. She was too frazzled to think clearly. She needed to be calm and rational to get her brain to function.

Concentrating on the screen, she tried to make out what was going on without benefit of sound.

Even so, it was obvious Sevarin had taken charge and was issuing orders, but what orders?

The kitchen had become as busy as the Gare du Nord. She counted two men heaving Zukah around, grappling with feet and shoulders, and another three hovering in Mac's vicinity.

Vaguely, as she watched, Roxie wondered where they were taking the body and what they would do with it.

Mac hadn't been far off the mark when he'd said they would shoot her like a dog. Sevarin would kill her without compunction the moment he recognized her and put two and two together.

Then Yves moved into the frame, and she realized a quick death might not be the worst that could happen to her.

Mac suffered no illusions that Sevarin would let him go when this was over. He simply hoped that his rescuers, in the form of Thierry and the other IBIS agents, were already inside the gates. His men had to have noticed the black chauffeur-driven Mercedes pull up outside.

What was really doing his mind in was knowing he had done Roxie a disservice by not getting her out of here before the crap hit the fan.

It stung to realize he'd been so absolutely focused on his goal that the peripherals had become blurred.

Sure, Green Shield threatened thousands of peoples' lives and would put a dent in many more having a fulfilling future, but he knew none of them the way he did Roxie.

Intimately. *Biblically.*

Now, at the wrong moment, he realized that no one on earth was as important to his sense of well-being as Roxie, not even his parents.

Her scent was imprinted on his synapses. He could recognize every curve, every hollow of her body blindfolded. Her touch was like no other, thrilled like no other.

Damn, the discovery of how much she meant to him had arrived too late. She would never forgive him for misleading her.

The irony turned out to be that he hadn't been lying when he claimed her as his *petite amie* in front of the heavy-handed goons invading the apartment.

He'd been foretelling the future.

What was it his mother used to say when he was little about the first time she'd looked at his face? The heart knows.

It was time he started listening to his heart instead of letting his suspicious mind rule.

For all she'd tried to put one over on him with the MI6 lie, Roxie really didn't have a scheming bone in her body.

Mac's back was to the camera, his face hidden to Roxie, but the others? Not a flicker of emotion showed as they carried Zukah out. She couldn't let that happen to Mac.

Not now that the message of how much he meant to her had sunk in.

She began to pace, catching glimpses of the screen each time she turned. But, just staring at it wouldn't save Mac's life.

The exercise did help, though.

An idea occurred to her out of the blue. She would create some sort of distraction, but she couldn't go downstairs unarmed; first she needed a weapon.

Without a second thought, she opened the top desk drawer, then skipped through them all from top to bottom. They were empty apart from a few pieces of yellowing stationery.

Frustration simmered through every cell, an emotion that

made her want to slam the last drawer shut and break the silence she'd been careful to preserve.

If she didn't find anything here, she'd have to search through the bedrooms Mac had told her were on this floor.

With only two pieces of furniture in the room, her chance of finding what she needed immediately halved. Only the filing cabinets remained, and she didn't hold any great hope of finding anything that might constitute a threat to the men she'd been watching.

Sure, the garrote in her pocket was a silent killer, but only if she got up close and personal.

The thought made her shudder.

A fire would prove an excellent diversion if she had matches. But since only Jean-Luc smoked and an electric spark was used to light the gas hobs in the kitchen, that idea was dead in the water.

Dead... She took a quick glance at the screen.

The word was a nudge to work faster.

An empty glass on the desktop brought up a picture of her grandfather to mind. He used to keep a whiskey bottle tucked behind his files, where Grandmère couldn't see it.

Neither she nor Grandmère had disillusioned him.

She discovered the stash in the bottom drawer.

At first glance it looked no different from the others, then she realized...it didn't open quite as far.

Tipping a few tightly packed files out onto the floor, she reached back into the drawer where her fingers touched the catch.

It was old, so she held her breath until she heard it click.

The false panel tilted, giving her room to reach inside, but not enough light to see what, if anything, hid behind it.

Excitement shimmered at her fingertips. The sensation that inside here hid a secret that no one was meant to find.

Not her. Not anyone.

She reached farther and touched something cold.

* * *

With a jerk of his head, Sevarin requested Mac join him at the other end of the table from the aquarium. "We might as well be comfortable while we wait for the demonstration you were so insistent upon seeing."

Mac grimaced. Did he have to harp on about his dogged determination? It showed that he couldn't have had many previous dealings with terrorist groups if he imagined they would buy a pig in a poke.

Sevarin leaned an elbow on the table, the Makarov beside it on the pale wood as if to say, "Go ahead, try it."

Mac sat at the end of the table, followed by the man who had become his shadow. Although he could no longer feel the gun pressing against his spine, he was very much aware of its existence and of the man with his finger on its trigger.

Sevarin must have panicked when Zukah told him what had happened. That's why he'd brought extra backup.

Zukah had been dead from the moment he reported in. Now Yves was sniffing around for a promotion. Funny how the seat Sevarin had indicated to Mac had the best view of the dark stained flagstones.

The metallic odor of blood invaded the air they breathed. So much had poured out of Zukah, the shot couldn't have killed him straight off. No, the guy had bled out while everyone stood around and watched.

Sevarin saw the direction of his gaze and smiled.

"I can see you think I was hasty in getting rid of my lieutenant," he said. "But failure is unacceptable and it would have been mine if I'd allowed Ahmed's incompetence the slightest degree of latitude."

He raised his faded blue eyes to the man standing behind Mac holding the gun. "Men like these need to know that, isn't that right, Javier?"

"Whatever you say, *mon patron*."

Mac waited for the man behind his chair to click his heels, sure that if he'd been a dog he'd be wagging his tail.

In contrast, Mac kept his mouth shut and his features blank.

But though Sevarin was in a chatty mood, it seemed he had no real expectation of being answered while he carried on a one-sided conversation.

"What do you think of my home, it is beautiful, yes?" he said, answering his own question.

"There have been Sevarins living here from the days of Louis XVI. I'm descended in a direct line from the Marquis de Sevarin, but not through marriage, you understand. This was the house he gave his mistress."

The smile playing round Sevarin's lips as he looked into the past made Mac's stomach curl.

This was one weird dude.

"My ancestor killed his brother here, the one who inherited the title. It was a duel. Over a woman, you understand. And then, *poof,* France had the Revolution and there were no more Sevarins who could *legally* inherit the title."

Clasping his long, thin fingers together, he continued. "We Sevarins have always guarded what we considered ours, by any means that came to hand. We have served kings, emperors and, yes, even fascist dictators, but this house has never gone out of my line of the family."

Was there a son now, Mac wondered, another greedy Sevarin male trying to put his stamp on the world?

"After the demonstration I will show you the salon. It is the most beautiful reception room of the château. I've had the laptop set up in there for when we conduct the transfer of the money."

To Mac's way of thinking, Sevarin's high-flown notions only served to confirm that the politician was blinded by what he considered his aristocratic heritage.

He *actually* thought this small château was something special.

The house had probably started life as a dower house before the then marquis's mistress got her greedy claws on it.

Mac was caught in the middle of these speculations when Jean-Luc and the chauffeur returned minus the body.

Sevarin scraped his chair across the floor, as he pushed back from the table. "Ah, just in time, Jean-Luc," Then he turned to the chauffeur. "Gustav, you and Jean-Luc fill the tank with plants."

Mac knew he had been right to distrust that smile as Sevarin turned it in his direction.

"We can begin our little demonstration while Yves persuades your little companion to join us. I should be sorry not to meet her. Yves tells me she is quite the little hellcat."

Mac cursed aloud, then inwardly, knowing he'd given his feelings for Roxie away. "Leave her alone! She has nothing to do with our deal."

"I'm sorry, I do not think I could forgo meeting such a one as Yves has described to me. You are not the only man of good taste, Monsieur Makjzajev." Sevarin moistened his lips. "I'm considered quite the ladies' man."

As Yves hurried to do Sevarin's bidding, Mac leapt to his feet, crashing the wrought-iron chair he'd been sitting on to the floor.

Sevarin's hand reached for the Makarov.

Mac ignored the move. Instead, he turned in place, as though to watch Yves progress.

Javier had jumped back out of the chair's way; now he bent to pick it up. There was no one to notice Mac look up at the camera.

Hoping Roxie was keeping abreast of the situation, he mouthed, "Go! Get out of there. Go now!"

An unrelenting cold seeped into Roxie's palm as it curled round the pistol grip. In her hands lay the means to save Mac.

Looking over her shoulder, she checked the screen. The situation looked contained for the moment.

Her grandfather had owned a gun like this, a German Luger he'd captured during the war. It only took a flick of her thumb for the magazine to slide out of the striated wooden butt.

Six, she counted six 9 mm bullets, more than enough.

If she got two shots fired off before getting hit, she'd be lucky. But if they were enough to sidetrack Mac's captors, it might give him time to escape. Her heart turned over as she wondered if she'd actually be able to pull the trigger.

A quick glimpse at the screen confirmed Mac was still at the table. Sevarin appeared to be doing all the talking.

With the 9 mm magazine back in the pistol, she remembered what the politician was selling. When the time came she would shoot.

A man so loathsome oughtn't to be allowed to succeed.

If only there was some way she could save Mac from himself as well as help him escape. Placing the gun on the floor beside her, she reached back inside the secret compartment.

The notebook had been lying under the gun as if protected.

It was tiny, thin, bound in leather. So small, someone in a hurry and satisfied by discovering the Luger might have overlooked it.

The leather held the bloom of neglect. It rubbed off on her fingertips while she turned it and she could almost smell its age.

Her stomach constricted as she smeared her thumb over the bottom right-hand corner, certain now of the initials it would reveal.

M. S. Michel Sevarin.

It wasn't a diary, just pages of names and comments. A line had been drawn through dozens of the names heading the pages and the comments below them made her hand tremble. She felt sick.

The man had been vile.

Yet, she couldn't stop reading.

Her fingers turned the pages more quickly after she recognized the name of one of Grandmère's Resistance friends.

Her best friend, Amelie Dutetre, had disappeared and no one knew what had happened to her…until now.

She hadn't died easily.

On the next page, Roxie read her grandmother's name and on the one facing it, the French name her grandfather had been given while he worked undercover.

Roxie sprang to her feet, desperate to tell someone of her discovery. Mac!

Sevarin was speaking to Yves, and as the man walked away Mac leapt up. His chair toppled behind him, then as the man guarding him bent to pick up the chair, Mac stared up toward the camera, his gaze darkened by the intensity of his soul.

Even in multiple shades of gray she could tell his eyes glittered with warning.

She saw his lips move. "Go!"

She was in danger.

Yves was coming for her.

Thrusting the notebook in one pocket and the Luger in the other, she slung the handle of her purse over her shoulder as she rushed back to the hidden staircase.

The wooden stair treads led her down farther to the ground floor and for now appeared to be the only way to escape the château.

She left the door linking the study and bedroom next door open, thinking it might throw Yves off her scent if he thought she'd escaped through the main house.

Once the attic door gave way, Yves would see the armoire no longer sat flush to the wall; he'd realize where she'd gone.

Mac simmered with frustration. Another ten minutes and it wouldn't matter an iota if Sevarin wanted to meet Roxie. Thierry would have had the signal to come in with force and given Mac some backup.

The moment Yves disappeared, Mac turned to Sevarin. "Let's

get on with the show. I like to keep business and pleasure separate."

He turned around to see green plants gradually filling the base of the fish tank as Jean-Luc followed Sevarin's directions.

Ordinarily, Mac might have taken a cheap shot at their safety measures, but he wanted this over without delay.

Sevarin removed a vial from a foam-lined metal box with... Mac quickly counted ten spaces. "It that all there is?" He forced a laugh of disdain as he looked at the cloudy liquid. "You expect us to pay millions of dollars for that? It's not even a drop in the bucket where Russia is concerned. It won't be enough."

"You'll soon see how little it takes. Remember, it's a living organism. It will grow as it feeds on the chlorophyll."

Somehow Mac didn't find Sevarin's reply particularly reassuring. "In that case, if needs be, how can we kill it?"

"Fire. But it must reach a very high temperature. It is like a double-edged sword. To kill Green Shield, you must destroy what you wish to save."

Thunderation and damn Sevarin all to hell!

If he didn't manage to retrieve Green Shield and the organism got loose, only the fires of damnation would save the world.

He had suspected it all along, but now Mac knew for sure he was dealing with a madman.

The staircase opened into a vestibule at the ground level. A passageway faced Roxie. Beside the stairs was a door that must lead to another tower room at the front corner of the house.

Since the kitchen was at the rear, she opted for the passage and heaved a sigh of relief when it opened into a room Yves had prevented her entering when she'd explored the kitchen.

Once it must have been a scullery with deep sinks. Now it looked more like a potting shed. Spades and rakes leaned precariously against the wall, while flowerpots had toppled to the floor, scattering dirt and shards of terracotta.

But it was the door alongside the window that caught her eye. It led outside.

Someone had dumped hessian sacking on the floor, blocking the door, but not for long. With enthusiasm, she bent to drag the sacks out of her way and revealed a dead man's face. Zukah.

Roxie barely managed to squelch her scream.

This was the closest she'd been to him since the night he ordered her into the van at Le Sentier. No one had had the simple decency to close his staring eyes, but if she forced herself to do it and they returned to bury him too soon…?

She couldn't give them an excuse to look for her here.

Stomach roiling, she threw off the sacks and went to his feet. It was all in the mind-set. She must simply look at swinging Zukah round out of the way as one more step toward freedom. Her last task was to re-cover him with the dusty sacking.

Outside at last, she leaned back against the door she'd closed on the Algerian and took deep gulps of fresh air.

It wasn't until taking her bearings that she realized this was a walled garden. With no way out apart from a ten-foot climb.

She'd have to go back the way she'd come, through the château.

Her chin sank to her chest in despair. Then, scattered on the gravel path, she noticed dark cigarettes stubs.

This must be where Jean-Luc had gone to smoke, but he hadn't left via the kitchen door to the scullery. There had to be another way, another door.

Mac watched as Jean-Luc barely dipped the base of a fragile glass pipette into the fluid in the vial. Next moment, he dropped the narrow glass pipe inside the tank and closed the lid.

It was impossible for Mac to put a name to the decimation, or claim to have expected to see what came next.

Every plant in the fish tank died within three minutes.

Aghast by what he had witnessed, and to disguise his true

feelings, Mac raised a suspicious eyebrow in the politician's direction and said, "This has to be a trick."

Sevarin bared his teeth. "No trickery needed. Once we are finished the aquarium and plants will be placed in a furnace hot enough to melt glass."

The gravity of the situation was almost more than he wanted to comprehend. If Green Shield ever got out, containing it would mean instituting a scorched-earth policy.

How had he thought he could handle this alone?

There was too much at stake for one lone man to handle.

Taming a momentary flash of panic, Mac showed a calm front, "What if this gets away from us? What happens to France?"

"Measures will be put in place." Sevarin's smile was anything but altruistic. At a guess, the bastard had thought of a way to make more money.

As if he had said too much, Sevarin concluded, "Frost and snow won't kill the organism, but it will hibernate. Make sure you release it in the Russian spring for the optimum results."

Mac knew right then that the microorganism couldn't leave the château. If putting it on ice wouldn't kill Green Shield, then Mac would have to think of another way.

Maybe even burn the château down.

He had to make sure this scientific nightmare never got free.

Not a micron of warmth touched the smile he gave the politician.

As skilled as Mac had become at acting, he was having a hard time playing the role.

All he could think of was the chaos that would occur if Thierry didn't show up and *he* died—as Mac was certain Sevarin intended. No one would know how to deal with a monster that could eat the Earth.

Underneath all his other fears was the one that Roxie had been recaptured. But as much as he loved her, Green Shield had to take precedence. He had no other choice.

Pain sliced at him as he thought of never seeing her again.

It was all he could do to put that aside and do the business. "Okay Sevarin, let's close the deal."

"The laptop is ready, you have only to put through the transaction. Follow me." Sevarin turned on his heel to lead the way. They had barely reached the kitchen door when Yves interrupted their progress.

"*La femme,* she has escaped! The door to the stairs was open, but I couldn't find her in the study or any of the other rooms."

Mac tried not to let his relief show. "Damn, if that isn't like a woman, she's skipped out on me."

He glared at Yves. "Maybe she didn't like the company I was keeping. Yves had a hard time keeping his hands off her and she was mad as fire about that."

Sevarin's face was a mask of fury. "Find her. Search until you do, she can't have escaped. Javier, you stay with Makjzajev until the transaction goes through. You others search the house. She can't have got far, the door is locked. She must be hiding."

It was difficult to remain calm, knowing they'd gone after Roxie. His fault. He should have been more precise, ordered her to try pulling the armoire across behind her.

As he followed Sevarin into a salon at the front of the house, in his mind's eye he saw Roxie as she'd been in bed that morning.

Tender and loving.

Something deep in his gut told him that had been their last time together. Either he would die, or Roxie would. And if he survived Roxie, would life ever be worth living again?

Chapter 14

Stunned, Roxie let the ivy-covered wall cushion her weight.

She couldn't believe the senseless destruction of plants she'd just seen through the kitchen window, or the speed at which it had taken place.

No more holding back, she had to act.

Though it broke her heart to do this to the man she'd fallen in love with, she couldn't let Mac, or the organization he was in league with, release Green Shield on the world.

She had to find a phone and get FIS down here, *vite!*

The scratchy vine rustled against her shoulder as she ducked below the level of the sill. Then she heard Yves. "*La femme,* she has escaped!"

The danger she was in had just tripled.

Now they'd all be looking for her.

She dared one more look. All the men, Mac included, hurriedly departed the kitchen. Although, she appreciated that with a gun shoved in his back Mac didn't have much choice.

A sensation akin to grief flooded her as she watched Mac disappear. This might well be her last sight of him before he came to trial.

"I love you." She whispered the words she could never say in his hearing, words he would never believe once she gave him up to the FIS. She huffed out a long breath to strengthen her resolve.

Time to do the work she was paid for.

Leaping out of her crouched position, she reached the French windows leading to the morning room in four strides.

"Ye-e-s!" They were open.

It actually took very little effort to log on to the Internet. But somehow Mac had to spin it out, giving Roxie as well as Thierry a few more minutes of time.

Roxie needed a chance to escape, and Thierry the extra advantage of getting the other agents into position.

Sevarin prowled restlessly in front of the table with the Makarov in his fist while Javier stood to one side, his weapon aimed at Mac. Boxing him in.

Simply for show, Mac drummed his fingertips on the antique table where the laptop had been set up.

Sevarin's patent annoyance as he glanced down at Mac's fingers made the subterfuge worthwhile.

"Do you mind?" Mac snarled as Sevarin made to come around the table to stand beside him. "You don't need to know where the money is coming from, only where it's going."

Sevarin stopped in his tracks.

Though Mac could tell he was uneasy, now the politician was minutes away from millions of Swiss francs, he wasn't about to do anything to slow up the transfer.

Seemed as though losing money was the only thing likely to get under the bastard's paper-thin skin.

Mac caught the old guy's eye as he took the return trip in front of the table from the left to the right. "We should have done this in Paris. My ISP is much faster."

Sevarin had an answer to that. "But then, we are conducting this business to suit me, not you. I am much more comfortable in my own home." The look of disbelief Mac gave him was involuntary.

Not so the curl he put on his lip as he asked Sevarin, "Paris get too hot for you, then?"

"No such thing. I will return there tomorrow to console a widow on the suicide of her husband." Sevarin gave Mac a thin smile. "One of the scientists who worked on Green Shield was overcome by remorse yesterday. I believe the note he left behind will satisfy the Minister of Defense."

The politician's smile broadened. "It was heartrending to dictate such a letter, it almost brought me to tears."

The black cloud at the back of Mac's mind loomed larger. It floated level with the muzzle of Javier's gun.

Mac and Roxie. He already thought of themselves as a couple. But not for long; only one of them was likely to get out of this alive.

And just about now, fate was probably only accepting short odds-on, cash bets that it would be Mac McBride.

He couldn't put it off any longer. He tapped a few keys and said, "Okay, Sevarin, type in your account number."

The heavens were smiling on her. The first thing she noticed as she snuck through the French windows was the phone. It sat on a small end table placed next to a pale green love seat that took its color from the floral wallpaper.

But the open door into the entrance hall meant she had no cover. She couldn't just stand there in full view making a call.

It took less than a second to decide, twice that to dive down behind the love seat, which angled away from the wall. Dragging the phone with her she began to punch in the numbers for FIS.

She was breathing hard, her nerves on edge, as she listened to the ring tone of Dumont's phone in his Paris office. "*C'est moi*, Roxie Kincaid. I'm on Deputy Minister Sevarin's estate near Angers. He is about to sell the Green Shield weapon to Chechen rebels…."

The line crackled and squawked. Someone had cut her off by logging on to the Internet. She'd done what she could, but would it be enough to save her or Green Shield?

The gauzy white curtains at the window began fluttering in the draught as if, somewhere, another outside door had been opened.

She hoped the breeze wasn't strong enough to slam the French doors shut; if anything attracted attention, it would be that.

Roxie held her breath as the worst happened and one of the glass-paned doors banged, then swung wide again.

Brisk footsteps sounded on the flagstones, coming closer.

The blood in her veins thickened as she heard Yves's triumphant "I have you now, Mademoiselle Kincaid," just seconds after she replaced the phone.

"She has gone outside," he called. "You others make sure she hasn't got over the wall."

Roxie crumpled her body into a small tight ball as he rushed passed the love seat without bothering to look behind it, then dashed out the open door.

The moment she heard his footsteps crunching across the gravel path, Roxie peered over the love seat in time to see Jean-Luc and the man wearing the chauffeur's cap descend the front steps.

The way to freedom was free and almost clear.

She'd imagined herself scurrying outside and hiding among the shrubbery. But she would get nowhere fast if Yves returned too quickly. Then she remembered the weapon Mac had given her.

It was the work of less than a minute to fasten the garrote across the opening at shin level, then dash to the morning room door. A quick look informed her the other searchers were well out of sight.

Once she got outside, she would fire the pistol in the air, and hopefully that would give Mac a chance to get away. She didn't think he would hang around to collect Green Shield if he thought there was a chance of being captured by armed federal agents.

Screwing up her courage, she bolted, but the clatter of her heels gave her away. Roxie was halfway to freedom when Yves saw her and yelled for the others to look out. *"Regarder dehors!"*

Thankfully he was blind to the trip wire. But with no time to look back, she heard rather than saw the fall that gained her five more paces.

Moments later the red-gravel driveway spread across the base of the outside steps.

"Halte! La femme is getting away."

Roxie didn't hang around to hear more, she ran for her life.

Mac slapped a mental high-five as the old guy's concentration was broken by a shout from Yves. Roxie had done it.

She'd gotten away. His heart thundered as he realized how much that meant to him. The *L* word had clipped him a good one.

Damn it, that wasn't supposed to happen. Not to him.

Transfer forgotten, Sevarin strode to the open door of the salon. Mac and Javier followed as with much hand waving Sevarin shouted orders to Yves to catch her on pain of death.

What goes around comes around—to Mac as well.

He hadn't done right by Roxie.

Silently, Mac swore on his mother's life that if they both got out of this situation, he would make it up to Roxie somehow.

If she would still have anything to do with him, that is.

As an added precaution, he prayed that Roxie was every bit as resourceful as her heroine grandmother and would get well away.

A spike of pain he'd never experienced before shot through his chest at the thought of never feeling her touch again, never kissing her lips or releasing his seed inside her.

Let the punishment fit the crime.

He hadn't trusted her. And dammit, if they both got out alive he'd probably be paid back in spades for acting the hard man the secret world of spies expected.

Roxie glanced over her shoulder for a second. Sevarin and Yves had reached the steps. The driveway curved, red gravel cutting a crescent out of green lawn.

Too late to try hiding now; all she could do was run like a virgin sacrifice with a fire-breathing dragon at her heels.

A loud, anger-filled shout reached her ears.

It sounded like Mac, but she had no time to make sure. Her sights were set on reaching the roadway without delay. Maybe a passing car…

Head down, she placed one foot in front of the other.

Each breath seared her throat. She tried not to think of what would happen next. Besting Sevarin fueled her race to liberty.

Her palm sweated round the butt of the Luger, reminding her she also had the evidence in her pocket, a weapon that could turn back on the old guy and bite him where it hurt most, his pride.

Yes, Grandmère would be proud of her.

She would bring Sevarin down.

The space of time between Roxie hearing the report of the gun, and the bullet hitting her was indistinguishable.

For his age Sevarin was quick on his feet, but desperation will have that effect on anyone. The older guy was ahead of Mac with Yves by his side.

Two paces behind, Javier wasn't ready for Mac to turn and

lash out. "Always expect the unexpected," he said, as Javier fell at his feet gasping for air.

But this time he finished the job, knocking the guy cold with a tap from the butt of his own gun.

One down, two more to go.

Mac ran down the broad entrance steps behind Sevarin.

Even from behind, the politician's fury was palpable. It shimmered above him like heat off tar-sealed pavement. Yves had reached the drive, his arm outstretched, aiming at Roxie's back.

As if down the wrong end of a telescope, Mac watched Roxie's heels kick up small puffs of red dust off the gravel.

"Shoot!" Sevarin yelled.

And Mac did. He shot Yves.

A snarling Sevarin raised the Makarov, determined not to be foiled and aimed at Roxie.

The report of the shot hammered in Mac's brain, repeating painfully over and over as he felt his life disintegrate.

Then Roxie took a few more steps onto the grass and his heart began to beat again, but not for long.

When Roxie fell it was daintily, like everything about her.

To Mac it appeared as if she did it in slow motion.

His speed reached the other end of the scale. Aiming at Sevarin, his feet hit the gravel as he fired, taking the politician down before he could get off another shot at Roxie.

She lay so still Mac's heart contracted, turning over in his chest in a way that cut off his breath.

He had lost her. Lost her before she'd really been his or knew who he really was.

Mac saw the pistol in her hand before he reached her.

A Luger, *trust Roxie*. The words echoed in his mind, chased by eons of regrets. Mac's problem was he hadn't trusted her, and now he was paying for that mistake.

He sank to his knees beside the woman he had lost his heart to in less time than he'd ever thought possible....

Maybe Sevarin had missed. Maybe she'd only tripped.

His arms circled her as he pulled her into them, the better to see her face. "*Chérie,* can you hear me?"

Though her eyes opened and lifted to him, they were blurred. "Mac, is that you? You have to get away."

The color drained from his face. It must have been as white as Roxie's, as the hand touching her coat came away damp and sticky.

He moved her and more dark red blood surged through the hole in the cloth. Yes, she was alive, her heart still pumping, but not for long unless he did something fast that would save her.

For a second that lasted an eternity all his triage training deserted him. Never before had it been so important that he succeed. He *must* keep her alive.

Cold air licked at his body as he ripped off the tail of his shirt, folded it into a pad and pressed it inside her coat onto the wound, holding it down hard.

An agonized grunt made him turn.

Sevarin wasn't dead. Eyes red as flames burned in his face.

Walking awkwardly, he lurched toward them like a zombie from a horror movie. The kind of monster no bullet could stop.

Yet, Mac's did.

The rescue copter—owned by IBIS—that Mac had called up to transport Roxie was less than ten minutes away.

It had taken both he and Thierry to contain the bleeding. And though he hated to do it, he put Roxie in Thierry's care.

Mac had some mopping up to do in the château.

Jean-Luc and the chauffeur had surrendered to Thierry and the waiting agents. Had given up without a murmur, so he'd been told. But no one had seen Javier since he ran back into the château.

It didn't take Mac long to discover the results of his failure to make sure Javier didn't escape.

Two vials were missing. The metal box itself had been too

heavy for a man on the run, but now…even if they caught up with Javier the orders would have to be, "Don't shoot."

The plants inside the glass tank appeared even worse than when he saw them last, slushy and soggy, as if they had gone into a meltdown that formed condensation inside the glass.

In less time than it took him to think of the idea, Mac knew what he had to do. It was a makeshift plan but it *would* work.

Carefully, he removed the vials from their container one by one. He laid them on top of the gas hobs, then did a quick search of the cupboards until he caught sight of what he needed to make a bomb. One can of fly spray and another of air freshener.

He popped the aerosols inside the microwave oven. Not knowing how long it would take, he set the timer for thirty minutes, then turned on all the stovetop knobs on full. The room quickly began to fill with gas.

To make sure the flames would reach the plants, he lifted the cover off the glass aquarium. The stench of rotting vegetation was awful.

He shuddered to think of a whole country filled with such corruption. What the hell happened if there were no plants to make oxygen?

At the rate the microorganisms sucked up chlorophyll, they could kill the world's ecosystem in no time flat. Mac couldn't let that happen. He pressed the start button on the microwave.

Picking up one of the wrought-iron chairs, he smashed the fish tank knowing that when this gig was over he would have a lot of explaining to do. Then he ran out of the château.

Jason Hart wasn't going to be happy with this result.

He'd barely reached Roxie and Thierry when he heard the first thump as the gas propellant inside the cans exploded and caught fire as it blew up the microwave.

"Get down!" he shouted to the others.

He threw himself over Roxie's small frame to protect her from flying glass just as the windows of the château blew out.

A minute later the helicopter arrived.

It was early, but, thank God, not early enough to be blown out of the sky by the blast.

In the hour before dawn, Paris no longer looked a City of Lights.

Though it had stopped raining, Mac felt as if an ice storm brewed side him, freezing all his emotions as he awaited news.

Roxie had been through surgery, they'd removed the bullet and she was now in intensive care.

But since he wasn't related, they wouldn't tell him her condition. His IBIS ID card hadn't cut any ice with the critical-care nurse on duty.

Not after Charles Fortier and Pierre Dumont, one of Paris's top FIS officers, had shouldered him aside.

As usual he had underestimated Roxie.

She'd gotten a message out to the FIS before she'd made a break for it. According to Thierry, whom Mac had asked to report in for him, Roxie's superiors weren't any more pleased with him than Jason Hart had been.

The last piece of news had come to Mac secondhand, in a call from his fellow agent. Although he'd been expecting his career to crash like a house of cards after his escapades, the news still cut him up.

He'd decided to save Jason the trouble of firing him by writing his resignation as soon as he returned to the Paris headquarters.

He would miss being an IBIS agent.

It had become his life since Jason had drafted him out of the Naval Intelligence. But those were the breaks.

He'd done the deed, now he'd live with the consequences.

It was 7:00 a.m. when the night nurse came looking for him. "Could you be the Mac whom Mademoiselle Kincaid is calling for?"

Chapter 15

The effort to raise her eyelids was almost too much, Roxie wasn't in pain, she simply felt as if she'd run a marathon or gone fifteen rounds with a world heavyweight champ.

Last time she'd opened her eyes it had been dark, the room dimly lit around floor level, but the light seeping through her lashes was brighter, much brighter, and she didn't know if she could bear to let it in.

She'd been dreaming of Mac.

This time the train at Gare du Nord had taken him away. She had a miserable, sinking feeling that meant he was dead. Her chest shuddered over the dull, leaden lump of her heart.

Tears she couldn't hold back slid down her cheeks.

A touch on her face startled her, made her blink. Made her see. Dear heavens, was she delusional?

Mac was here, beside the bed. "You're alive."

He grinned. "Yeah, want to pinch me to make sure?"

The relief was stupendous, made her feel dizzy. Made her experience emotions too big to share with anyone, even Mac. Yet, she couldn't remember feeling so vulnerable before.

It took all her powers of deception to say, "Don't make me laugh, I'm already in stitches."

Mentioning her wound grounded her in reality and panic surfaced. "You shouldn't be here, Mac, they'll take you in."

Weakness seemed to have diminished yesterday's resolve to hand him over to FIS. "I was going to inform on you, but I can't do it. Go! Go away before I change my mind."

Mac leaned closer and she saw weariness bracketing his eyes. "That's not very professional for an FIS agent," he said, his voice sounding rusty, as if his throat were closed.

Then she understood. "You know?"

"That you don't work for MI6?" he asked, dark eyebrows straddling his forehead in a frown that faded almost as soon as it was born.

Mac took her hand, hooked her fingers round his thumb and squeezed gently. "Yes, I know." He sighed. "You weren't very honest with me, but I can't complain. I wasn't completely honest myself. My name isn't Makjzajev, it's McBride."

"But…?" She felt too exhausted to take the facts in.

He had lied.

"I was working undercover, and I couldn't take the chance that you would give me away. For all I knew you could have belonged to a real terrorist organization trying to move in on the deal." His thumb rubbed against her palm as he waited for her to speak.

And waited…

Then, "But you still saved my life…." She gasped faintly, her head buzzing, as she tried to patch in the latest addition to the bewildering equation that explained their relationship.

"I'm hoping that will count in my favor."

His favor!

Roxie's breathing became erratic, as if she couldn't catch up with it. Her pulse racing, she pronounced her dismay. "But, you…you slept with me!"

"Not until the third night."

"And you expect me to commend you on your control?"

His features contracted. "Why not? I wanted to take you to bed and make love to you the moment I saw you."

Just what had that been, an excuse or a protest?

She wanted to weep again, but she wouldn't give him the satisfaction. Instead she fisted the bedcovers in her free hand.

"And just exactly who do you work for?" she asked through tight lips.

"IBIS."

"Never heard of them," she replied primly. This man had been closer to her than any other human being. She'd done things with him, for him, to him that she'd done for no other, and embarrassment, absent at the time, now made its presence known.

"Not many people have. Being covert, we like it that way. The Intelligence Bureau for International Security is a worldwide organization, yet few people know we exist."

She pulled her hand away so he couldn't tell she was shaking.

The anger surging through her couldn't be good for her blood pressure, but she was past caring. "Some of us wish we still didn't know, that we had never met you."

"I know you don't mean that. You're hurt. It will get better."

That was all he knew; she had a wound deep inside that would never heal, and it wasn't the result of the bullet she'd taken in the back.

She had let down her guard, broken her oath of silence as much as she'd dared and he'd never even hinted he was more than he claimed. Hadn't reciprocated.

The pain struck so fiercely she couldn't voice her emotions.

She'd fallen in love with a man in whose eyes she was no more than a convenient female body. A cook, a lover, but never a confidante.

Mac knew he'd gone about it all wrong. He needed to make amends fast. "Listen to me, *chérie,* please," he pleaded. "I never dreamed you'd really get hurt. I was hoping to avoid that scenario. I even prayed about it."

Exasperation over letting her down surfaced. "Dammit, I had backup on call outside all the time. I just needed to get my hands on Green Shield before calling them in."

Roxie didn't take the news too well. "You mean we could have gotten out of the château… whenever we wanted?"

He took a deep breath and tried another tack. "Yes. *Chérie*…sweetheart, if you had seen the results of Green Shield's work you would realize why it was vital."

She nodded. "I did see it, through the kitchen window before I escaped from Yves. The garrote came in useful, it tripped him."

Once again her courage stunned him. Her small stature belied her abilities. "You did well, *chérie.* You make me proud."

Her eyes snapped open, their gray depths accusing as if he'd taken credit for her efforts. He moved on quickly. "Yves won't bother you anymore, he's dead."

"You killed him?"

"It was either you or Yves, not what you'd call a choice. I did what I had to." Mac held his breath. He'd just confessed to killing a man. Would she be able to look at him without seeing blood on his hands?

"What? Do you expect me to berate you?" A twisted half smile shaped her lips. "I'm not a *bébé*. I know this is war, undeclared, yet the battle goes on. In this age, terrorism is the monster we face. And Sevarin?" She whispered the question.

"Sevarin died at the scene and Jean-Luc and the chauffeur are locked up."

After all she'd gone through, the next piece of news would be the kicker. "Javier escaped. He took a couple of vials of Green Shield with him. We're on to it, though."

"Javier!" his name was more like a cry of pain as Roxie tried to sit up. He pressed her back against the pillow.

"Take it easy," he told her. "We'll get him."

"Didn't you know? He's Sevarin's son, head of security at the unit where Green Shield was evolved. If you hadn't been so secretive I would have told you that while we were at the château."

She looked away from him for a few seconds, her bottom lip clenched in her teeth. He nearly asked if she was in pain but thought better of it. The mood Roxie was in she wouldn't thank him for being oversolicitous.

He'd gone about everything back to front, and it didn't look like it was going to be an easy fix.

Fatigue framed Roxie's eyes when she looked his way once more and forced out the words, "I may not be a high-flying spy like you, but I do know my facts. That's why I had to escape. Sevarin would have recognized me. He visited the House of Fortier many times with Madeleine Saber, his mistress."

Her smile was ironic. "Sevarin put too much trust in her. Not only did she like spending money, she also liked to talk…."

"You could have told me, I would have made sure you were safe…." His voice faded away. They both knew he hadn't been able to keep her safe, had he? She was lucky to be alive.

It was a hard fact to swallow, but if the bullet had hit an inch lower they wouldn't be having this conversation.

"I would have given anything to make sure you never had to go through this, anything." He knew it sounded like begging, and it was, dammit!

How the mighty had fallen.

Fallen in love.

The silence in the hospital room stretched until he couldn't bear it any longer. "Dammit, *chérie,* I'm in love with you!"

Her eyes widened. She covered her mouth with her hand as if to stifle a cough…God help him if she was laughing.

Finally, she said, "How can you love me? You don't even trust me. If you'd told me this yesterday I would have been over the moon, but most of the luster has rubbed off the glow I felt."

He lifted her hand to his lips but stopped when he saw how weary she was. "Yeah, I know, my timing stinks, but that doesn't mean I'll give up."

"Go find a woman to love whom you can trust. That isn't me." Mac didn't have time to reply.

"What are you doing here, McBride?" The growl from Pierre Dumont interrupted their conversation. "I left instructions you weren't allowed in to see Roxie."

"Instructions with whom?" Mac demanded. "If you'd had a guard on her door like you're supposed to, I wouldn't have been able to get in."

Dumont's face went red as he fluffed metaphoric feathers. "A guard would only attract unnecessary attention."

Mac called his bluff. "Javier Sevarin is still on the loose. I think Roxie deserves that attention, and if you won't put a guard on her door, I will."

"Javier knows nothing about me, I'll be all right." Roxie's voice, though weak, was enough to stop the quarrel.

"We can't take that for granted, *chérie.*"

"A guard will be put on your door. It will be worth it to stop this fellow bothering you," Dumont snapped in a tone that brooked no argument, and appeared full of confidence that he'd fixed Mac. In fact he'd done exactly as Mac wanted.

Kissing the back of her hand again, Mac took his farewell, *"À bientôt, chérie."*

And for her ears only, "We *will* we meet again." Then Mac withdrew to the corridor to await the arrival of her guard.

Two hours later he showed up at IBIS headquarters, knowing he had a dressing-down to face and a resignation to write.

"There are some questions I need to ask," said Dumont, drawing a chair up beside Roxie's bed, as if his height looming over the bed might intimidate her, when actually it didn't matter to her one way or the other.

For fifteen minutes he asked questions and she answered, or hoped she'd given him the correct one.

Her mind was elsewhere.

Mac loved her.

Was it true, or was that his way of easing his guilty conscience?

"How did you become involved in this? Your mission was simply to follow Zukah and discover whom he was meeting. Did you not understand?"

"I understood *parfaitement*. I followed him to what I now know was the apartment of Monsieur McBride. They went inside, but as I could not see through the door, I did the next best thing. I entered the apartment, pretending I thought it belonged to someone else."

"You could have been shot. Did that not occur to you?"

"I *was* shot, but no, at the time I thought I was carrying out my assignment to the best of my ability. I took a risk and it paid off. Mac would not let them harm me."

Had he really wanted her the moment she walked into his apartment? God, she had been dumb with fright, hardly able to speak....

And Mac, he was the ultimate professional...very little got in his way. Not even so-called love.

"Very well, I want to know all you learned. I don't trust this IBIS agency to tell us everything."

Roxie lost track of time. She was weary and reduced her replies to monosyllabic answers: "Yes" and "No."

The nurse was her savior. "The fifteen minutes is up, Monsieur Dumont." She bustled around to the opposite side of the bed. "My patient is tired, and once I've changed her dressings she will sleep."

Was sleep the answer? Only if she didn't dream of Mac. She was already confused. Memories of sleeping in his arms would hardly break the spell of loving him.

Mac was halfway across the threadbare foyer of the Hôtel Margeaux when it occurred to him that maybe it was time to change his address. He'd gotten used to the privacy afforded by the *faux* living quarters IBIS had found him.

Certainly, the old girl had seen better days, but then who hadn't? Built in the 1920's, in its heyday the Margeaux had been a triumph of art nouveau.

The black-and-gold metal elevator doors, framed by arching bird of paradise tails, swung out to let him enter instead of gliding silently into the wall.

The decor was something he'd appreciated, thanks to his mother, an avid fan and collector of art-nouveau pieces. That's what had drawn him to the hotel. It had a familiar feel to it.

He gave a quick nod to Gaspard, who manned the reception desk, and clanged the elevator door shut behind him.

His thoughts turned to Roxie as the elevator creaked its way to the sixth floor. He could see now she was extremely passionate about what she did. She wouldn't have risked her life otherwise.

How would the resignation letter he'd sent in the diplomatic pouch to Washington look to her? Like cowardice, or exactly what he deserved?

Her opinion assumed an importance he'd allowed no other, not even his parents. Not even Jason Hart, who would be in Paris within days, hours…

Mac's suite was at the far end of a wide but poorly lit corridor near the fire exit. During the day the window on the end wall helped dispel the gloom, but on a rainy November evening it didn't stand a chance.

To cap it off, the flame-shaped glass sconce closest to his door had burned out again. He'd just begun to blame the colder weather when his scalp began to prickle.

Mac had been playing the smoke-and-mirrors game long enough to trust his senses. He shortened his stride, slowing his pace without making it obvious.

A shape in the darkness of the far corner began to unfold like a vision in a bank of charging thunderheads. Javier!

His fingers closed round the butt of the gun in his shoulder holster as the figure emerged from the gloom.

Backing into the closest doorway, Mac drew the gun.

The stranger was wearing a long black trench coat, and had shoulders that took up most of the red-carpeted corridor. The look was intimidating, at odds with the slight edge of humor in his voice when he said, "You can put that away, Josh."

Josh?

No one but his parents and schoolteachers ever called him Josh. And though the guy spoke English, Mac had trouble making out the accent.

"That is you, isn't it?" he asked, "Joshua S. McBride?"

"That middle initial doesn't stand for *stupid*."

"Look, I don't want trouble. I'm not armed. I just want a few minutes of your time, then I'll be on my way."

Unarmed? As if Mac was dumb enough to fall for that. Mac voiced the question that was on his mind. "Did Javier Sevarin send you?"

Palms open, the man held his hands out from his sides. "Never heard of the guy."

Still unconvinced, Mac stepped out the doorway and brought his Glock 9 mm into the open. "Keep your hands where they are. As you've already gathered, I *am* armed."

Edging closer, he signaled the guy to move back to the wall

with a couple of flicks of the gun barrel. "Who the hell are you and what do you want?"

Even with his hands up and his back to the wall while staring down the muzzle of a loaded firearm, the stranger didn't appear to be fazed. "I have some information you're going to want to hear."

Keeping his eyes and gun trained on the stranger, Mac slipped his room key from his pocket and edged closer to his suite door. "I'm not in the market for information tonight. And if it's money you're after, I only carry pocket change."

Mac reached behind and slotted his key in the lock. A second later he swung the door open and reached for the light switch.

"I don't want your money, and the information is free. You see…I'm your brother."

With the light switch at his fingertips Mac hesitated then barked out a course laugh. "Hah, you've got the wrong Josh McBride. I don't have any brothers…or sisters."

Light flooded the dark corridor as clicked the switch. "Well it so happens, you actually have four brothers and a *sister,* all of them dying to meet you."

Now he could see him properly, Mac was thankful he was armed.

The guy was big, broad shouldered, around the same size as his own six feet five. Still, maybe the Glock wouldn't stop an elephant, but he knew it *would* take this guy down.

The long trench coat he wore added to the impression of bulk. Mac noticed it was wet on the shoulders. Obviously he hadn't been hanging around long enough for impatience to bite him, which explained the easy attitude.

The guy's dark hair was a thousand times darker than his own reddish-brown mane, and his eyes were almost black compared to Mac's dark gold. But with the subject under discussion, the dimple on the stranger's chin appeared far too familiar and gave him a moment's pause for reflection.

Then Mac remembered. It had been more than a year since they'd met in Nepal, when Mac had gone to collect IBIS translator Chelsea Tedman after her adventure on Everest, so it had taken a moment to recognize the guy's face. Kurt Jellic.

"Now I know you. We met in the Himalayas, at Namche Bazaar." He was a mountaineer who had married Chelsea Tedman after helping recover her sister's body from Mount Everest.

"You're Kurt Jellic." Mac relaxed his hold on the Glock, letting his arm fall to his side. A short harsh laugh ricocheted from his throat. "What *is* all this crap?"

Mac looked over his shoulder. "Did Chelsea send you up first to play a trick on me?" He and Chelsea had been good friends until she left IBIS to sort out the mess left by the murder of her sister and brother-in-law on the mountain. But he'd thought she'd settled for a quiet life in New Zealand.

The man claiming to be Mac's brother shook his head. "No, sorry, mate, you've got it wrong."

"So where is she? I didn't see her as I passed through the lobby." He'd had other things on his mind—namely Roxie and resignations. And now this…

It didn't take the guy long to set the mistake straight. "I'm not Kurt. I'm his twin Kel. I wasn't aware you knew him *or* Chelsea. But I'm definitely your brother, and so is Kurt. Mind if I come in and explain?"

Still suspicious that it was some sort of trick, Mac waved him through the door. "After you."

"Don't mind if I do. Can't say this is the most redolent hallway I've ever waited in," Kel said, as if hanging around in hallways was something he did regularly.

"But all told, I was glad to come in out of the rain. Paris looks pretty miserable after San Francisco." That said, Kel Jellic stepped through the door without hesitation, as if the gun at his back was of no consequence.

Showed how little he knew.

Mac was finding it hard to suspend disbelief. Gun by his side, he followed Jellic as if untroubled. As if his heart wasn't beating rapidly.

But hiding his feelings was key in his business, and he was a professional.

Closing the door behind them, he promised Kel, "If nothing else it will give my parents a laugh when I tell them they have five other children they know nothing about."

At least, Mac hoped it would.

After Kel left, Mac decided to do nothing until he could speak to his parents, face-to-face. He wished he could dismiss the information Kel had given him as a fairy tale, but there had been a ring of truth to the story he related.

The story of a cop called Milo Jellic, a widower, who had fallen for the wife of some guy named Magnuson, a vicious criminal he'd had sent down for ten to fifteen years. That woman was supposedly his birth mother.

Mac's stomach had roiled in protest at that piece of news. She sounded so far removed from who and what he was, or had believed himself to be.

A McBride, of the Philadelphia McBrides.

Then, to learn that his birth mother's legal spouse had reached out from prison and had Milo Jellic murdered…? All of this while blackening his name, and branding him a bent cop and drug dealer, and making his death look like suicide.

Mac didn't feel he could be blamed for wondering if the story came from a movie scenario.

From the way Kel told it, Mac had had the better deal.

Milo had been dead before Mac was even born, and to protect him from Magnuson, his mother had arranged a private adoption to an American couple, through a lawyer.

Though Kel didn't belabor it, after Milo's death the family must have struggled, as much from their father's bad reputation as from a lack of funds.

But they'd managed, and if it turned out he *was* related to them, Mac knew it would be something to be proud of.

Jo, the only daughter, was the youngest, hardly more than two years older than Mac. She'd been the one to discover Mac's existence.

A detective sergeant of police at Auckland Central, Jo had never believed the lies told about her father, and for a wedding present her husband, Rowan McQuaid Stanhope, had promised to put all his resources and connections at her disposal to discover how her father had really died.

It helped that the guy was one of New Zealand's richest men.

Mac hadn't been surprised to find that Kel worked in a similar line of business to himself—the GDEA, Global Drug Enforcement Agency. Kel had that look about him.

He had a tougher edge than Mac remembered on Kurt, his twin—though that guy had taken out an assassin on Everest and saved Chelsea's life.

It had been Kel who'd tracked Mac to IBIS and Paris. All too easily, it seemed to Mac, considering IBIS's existence was an closely guarded secret.

As for the rest of his so-called brothers, Franc was an entrepreneur and electronics whiz, while Drago, the eldest brother, was a master of wine and traveled the world judging wines and writing articles on them.

Of all the brothers, only Drago wasn't married. That said, they all sounded very successful and happy for a family that must have had to claw its way up by its fingernails.

Yeah, just like a fairy tale.

Almost too good to be true.

It was the last Mac was counting on. The Jellic family sounded like good folks, but he'd gotten comfortable with who he was.

Josh S. McBride of the Philadelphia McBrides.

Mac, to all his friends.

He prayed that wasn't about to change.

Chapter 16

With the sound of the doctor's praising her excellent constitution ringing in her ears, Roxie returned home only a week after they carried her into the hospital.

But twenty-four hours later the walls of her tiny apartment off rue Bonaparte were closing in on her and she was dying to get back to work. Something Charles Fortier refused to consider until he was satisfied she was well enough.

She'd countered by saying, "How much effort does it take to sit down and sketch out ideas? It's my left shoulder that hurts, not my right." He still wouldn't budge.

Roxie had taken her first trip downstairs this morning. A trek to the nearest newspaper kiosk to prove she could manage on her own. And had, despite Nieve, the Portuguese concierge, throwing up her hands, protesting that Roxie would kill herself.

Back in her apartment, she scanned the headlines. The Sevarin scandal had taken two days after she'd landed in hospital to emerge, and still hadn't abated.

But was the public indictment enough?

Folding the newspaper, she picked up Michel Sevarin's diary, the one she'd found in the château.

She'd read it from cover to cover, many times. It still disgusted her, but at last she stopped dithering and made a decision.

There was a journalist she knew...

Certainly, he dealt mainly in fashion and gossip, but if she knew Jules, he would relish an exclusive, and the diary was certainly that.

She huffed out a long breath.

The movement pulled at the newly healed wound on her back, an added incentive to use what she had found.

Yes, she would do it. Not for herself alone. For Grandmère and Madame Fortier, plus all the members of their Resistance cell alive or dead that Michel Sevarin had betrayed.

They deserved some portion of revenge.

Three days later, the red roses in Mac's hand performed the old open-sesame trick and let him into Roxie's apartment building.

Madame liked the idea that *"la petite"* had a lover. And there was no other way to get past the fierce concierge guarding Roxie's privacy.

However, Mac decided the lady didn't have enough teeth to prevent Javier if he'd a mind to go after Roxie.

That's why he was there.

What had she been thinking by releasing Sevarin Senior's diary to a journalist who dealt in scurrilous speculation?

The day after the story came out, every form of media, print, radio and television had leapt on the story like wolves.

There was no way Javier Sevarin could have escaped knowing what she'd done. Especially since it hadn't taken long for Roxie's name to come out.

He supposed that's why her phone was off the hook.

Six flights up without a lift later, Mac demanded entrance, with the back of his knuckles against her impossibly flimsy door.

No reply.

"Come on, Roxie. It's Mac, let me in."

It took her less than a minute to throw open the door and demand, "What do you want?"

He hadn't seen her in ten days, and anything she wore would have looked fantastic, and did. But her rosebud-pink wrap-around ballet top that matched the round-toed pink slippers peeking out under slim-fitting black pants made her look smaller than he remembered.

Her eyes lighted on the roses he was holding as she stepped back to let him enter. "Reduced to bribery now, are you?"

"Reduced to groveling, but not to you, to the concierge."

He stopped in the middle of the floor and looked around. The room felt cramped. "You couldn't swing a cat in here."

She pouted at his insult to her residence and said, "I've no wish to. Its beauty is that for this close to boulevard St. Germain, the rent is reasonable, and I can walk everywhere but to work. For that I take the Metro."

"There are a lot of stairs here."

"I know, but look at the rooftop view. I can see the Eiffel Tower."

He strode to the window and looked over the crowded hodge-podge of metal roofs to the tower, then cast his gaze down into the street. "No place to park your car around here?"

"Doesn't matter, it didn't belong to me."

"Ah," he nodded. "FIS undercover carpool. We have those, too," he said for the sake of making conversation. For the first time since he'd arrived, he'd taken a clear look at Roxie without the window backlighting her silhouette and it hurt.

She looked fragile. No way could he leave her in this mouse hole to defend herself.

But dammit, that wasn't all. It had taken only one glance to convince him how much he'd missed her, a fact that had already pressured him to do his utmost to keep her safe.

So far, he'd been too busy following up leads on Javier to attend to that himself. Instead, he'd had a regular rotation of men watching her apartment since she'd left hospital.

He'd bundled the costs in with the rest of the expenses of their search for Green Shield.

His resignation was hanging fire. Floating somewhere in limbo until Jason Hart, who had been delayed, found the time to speak with him personally, meanwhile...

On top of everything else, he'd just found out that he wasn't actually the person—the son—he'd thought himself from the moment he could see.

It was as if life just had to get another kick in while he was down. But dammit, he still wasn't out. No way!

It might take another few days, but sooner or later he'd get his head around the news, and he'd told his parents *not* to come to Paris until then.

Mac dived into the subject he knew Roxie would hate. "You know you can't stay here, don't you? Javier will find you sooner than later."

He stated with assurance, "My place would be more secure."

He didn't have to wait for her protest. She hardly gave him time to draw breath. "But he knows your address in Le Sentier!"

"No, he knows where Jeirgif Makjzajev lives. Mac McBride resides in the Seventh arrondissement. The Hotel Margeaux on rue Montalembert."

Mac could tell from her expression she'd never heard of it; not many people had. That was the beauty of the place, where most residents, like him, had long-term bookings.

"You don't honestly expect me just to take off and go stay at your place?" She laughed up at him as he crooked an amused eyebrow at her. "Just as I thought, I've got it wrong."

He stepped closer before saying, "No, it was my mistake you found the suggestion amusing. I don't simply *expect* you to come with me, I *demand* that you do, and if need be, I'll put you over my shoulder and carry you."

The scent of her filled his head, made him ache, but now, as with their first meeting, when he'd had to react quickly to save her life, he had no time for distractions.

She tilted her chin at him, challenged him. "So bold and brave now, with your demands, when you've never come near me since that day at the hospital."

"Since Dumont warned me off, you mean? I've known where you were every second of the day." He slipped a finger under her chin so he could look into the depths of her eyes, into her soul.

The pale pink she wore today made her look younger, like a sign that flashed "hands off."

He ignored it. "Did you really think I wouldn't?" he asked, dipping closer to brush his lips against hers.

It wasn't enough.

He gathered her to him, until the whimper she made cleared his head. "God, *chérie,* I've hurt you. That's not what I wanted."

Her eyes were bright with tears and he cursed himself for his clumsy-handed overture. To make amends, he softly brushed the back of his fingers down her wan cheek. "Please, *bébé,* help me out here, come with me."

"Did…" she started uncertainly, "did you mean what you said at the hospital?"

His heartbeat quickened as he remembered the hash he'd made of his declaration. Not the dab hand with the ladies he'd imagined when it came to the real thing. "That I loved you?"

She nodded, and he said, "More than ever. Why do you think I want you to stay at my place?"

"To get me back in your bed."

A wry grin surfaced and he let it show. "Yeah, well that, too, but honestly, I think Javier will be out for revenge and I couldn't bear him to get to you."

He touched a finger to her lips to put a halt to the protest he saw in her expression. "I know you're hurt, and I promise I won't make any demands while you aren't fit. After? Well, it will still be up to you. I can't say fairer than that."

Mac sucked in his gut so Roxie wouldn't get the idea he was lying. He couldn't be around her without wanting her. The hard ridge under his zipper was a dead giveaway, and trust had become a big issue last time they spoke.

Keeping his hands off her would be difficult, but needs must when the devil drove. Their relationship had begun with what for most couples was the penultimate point. Begun with a honeymoon for strangers, and now he wanted to rectify that.

To give her the courtship she deserved.

The trouble was, now he knew how it felt to be inside her. Knew the way her body welcomed his.

Keeping his distance was going to be hell.

Especially since once again there was only one bed.

He looked down at her, saying nothing, waiting for her answer.

"You'd better help me pack," she said, and at last he could breathe again.

"Well, if you won't let me work with you, at least you could let me return to work. I'm tired of being hidden away," Roxie complained.

"It's only been three days," Mac reminded her.

"A lifetime." It had taken her only three days to fall in love with him. Not that she'd dared put it into words.

She'd spent three nights of torture lying beside him in the darkness. Wondering each time he rolled over if he would touch her. Roll her over onto his chest and kiss the living daylights out of her. But he didn't.

h a Stranger

ite casually.
ed his eyes,
like a neck-
ways.
felt he and
ll I've un-
Dumont
ckly, *ma*
ords. "I

lly loved her as much as he said.
ut I don't want to be worrying
hed over the breakfast table and
with three feet of cherry wood be-

fore seemed part of Mac's context, she
was frightened of.

th Charles. What could be better than
other people all day? I'll let you drive me
up at night. Is it a deal?"

s. hen went back to his half-eaten croissant.
n on a winning streak," she continued, "I want
you promise to let me be there when you finally close
in er."

quest made him cough on the buttery flakes of pastry.
take that as a yes, and let you finish your *petit déjeuner*
whi change into my black suit. I hope it won't take you too
far it of your way."

So far he hadn't told her where the IBIS agency had their
Paris headquarters. And it was annoying that he still didn't trust
her not to give the address away.

What did he think she would do with the information? Take
out a banner on the Internet Web site of Spies Are Us?

Though the tightness in her wound hampered her as she
dressed, she was determined not to keep him waiting. If he
wouldn't treat her as a lover, the next best thing was to be treated
as an equal. They were both in the same business, after all.

At least she thought she was, but an hour later Charles
wasn't so sure. "Dumont thinks your usefulness to FIS may
be over."

"What?" she exclaimed from her seat on the wrong side of
Charles's ornate desk.

His surroundings might be elaborate—hardly the scene for

official intrigue—but Charles himself dressed qu
Wearing a light blue cashmere sweater that match
topped with a silk self-patterned silver scarf knotted
tie, over pale gray pants, the man was soigné, as alw

But Roxie was more interested in the mistake she
Dumont were about to make. "After all I've done, a
covered, not to mention getting shot for his cause
thinks he can just toss me aside?"

Charles's habitual smile thinned. "Don't bite so qui
petite puce." He threw in the endearment to soften his v
told him he was jumping the gun, to wait and see."

But his face grew grim as he twisted the pen in his
"It was the diary that made him nervous. Maybe you sho
have released its contents."

An angry urge to jump up and stamp her feet shot th
Roxie. She controlled it. Charles might put up with tan
from a top model; a wannabe designer was a different matt
had to…for Grandmère's sake. Anyone would have done
same—Dumont even."

"Dumont is not such a one." Charles put aside the pen he'd
been playing with and stood. "We are lucky, you and I, *little flea.*
Intrigue may run in our veins, but we have our true calling to
fall back on. Not so Dumont."

He came around the desk to Roxie and took her hand, pulling her to her feet. "No, you can go back to your drawing
board and continue your work on the ready-to-wear collec-
tion. Did I tell you I have great hopes for our March release
of your line?"

Placated, Roxie did as he asked, but as the day passed, it appeared the House of Fortier's clientele weren't as worried by her
sojourn in the media as Dumont was.

The Kincaid family wasn't the only one with an axe to grind
with the Sevarins. Other politicians' wives applauded her courage, but then they didn't gossip as much as they used to.

But as another two days passed, Roxie had more to fill her thoughts than if her use-by date with the FIS had arrived. Such as who would catch up with Javier and Green Shield first?—the FIS or IBIS?

The rivalry on Dumont's side was like a living, breathing dragon—the fool expected her to report on Mac.

But more important, she was constantly wondering just how long Mac was going to make them both remain celibate.

Leaving a gaping concierge hiding below in his rooms, Mac raced up the stairs of an old building in Montmartre, with Thierry and two other armed agents on his heels searching for Javier's apartment.

They'd had a positive sighting of Javier that morning and the agent had followed him here. Of course, in the true spirit of co-operation, they had informed Dumont about it when they were approximately two blocks away from the corridor they were hurrying along now.

When they all reached the door, Mac looked the others straight in the eye as he whispered, "The rules don't count here. No warnings, no playing fair, just take him down anyway we can. Got it?" That said, he turned and kicked in the door.

The locks held but the hinges gave way and two seconds later they were inside, but though they'd had someone watching the exit, Javier wasn't.

"Goddammit! If someone tipped him off, I'll have his head on a platter." He eyed the others, but nobody flinched. "Search the place."

It was Thierry who came across the radio receiver, the type that picked up police frequencies. "What do you think, Mac? Which band does FIS use? Would Dumont have radioed his men after we gave him the heads-up?"

Mac looked up from the small freezer door under the fridge. He'd tossed a few unopened packs of vegetables out onto the floor of the minute kitchen, but for someone his height, it was hard-going to see the rear of the low compartment.

"I can't think of a better explanation," Mac said, more than willing to blame Dumont. The man rubbed him the wrong way.

Thierry agreed. "We were watching the front, but the bedroom window is open, so he could have climbed down the back way."

"So, my friend, our only hope for a good result, is if he kept Green Shield here, and didn't have time to take it with him."

That said, Mac reached into the back of the freezer and found a couple of one-liter ice cream cartons. "Do you think Javier might have a sweet tooth?"

"Judging from the bare cupboards, I wouldn't have said he was eating here."

Mac cautiously straightened his knees till he reached his full six feet five inches. "Yet his freezer is filled with frozen vegetables and ice cream. Let's see what we have here."

He plugged the porcelain sink and ran the hot water over packs to soften the contents before opening them. "If all we have here is ice cream, I'll wash it away, but if it's Green Shield, I don't want any of it to reach the drains."

He lifted the lid of the first carton and, with a spoon he'd grabbed from a cutlery stand, gingerly scraped away the top layer. The curved steel edge soon scraped against glass.

"That makes one. I'll leave the other carton until we get back to the agency. No sense in getting covered in ice cream on the way home. I want it out of here before Dumont arrives."

"Thierry." He nodded for his friend to join him. "You stay here and see what else you come up with. I need someone who won't take any nonsense about jurisdiction from Dumont. Costes, you come with me. I need a driver, a careful one."

And that's how he retrieved Green Shield—very, very carefully. If the end of the world were to be on anyone's shoulders, it wouldn't be his.

* * *

Mac was a little late picking Roxie up from work, but thankfully she'd had the sense not to wait for him on the sidewalk. It was safer that way.

With Javier still not under lock and key, he would be twice as dangerous now that they'd stolen his only means of making a deal with the authorities.

The doorman had gotten used to him picking Roxie up, and Mac knew he would tell her he'd arrived. He was right; soon she was flying down the three steps fronting the House of Fortier and diving into the passenger seat.

"I've had a wonderful day—wait till I tell you," she chattered excitedly, hardly waiting for him to respond. "Charles loves my ready-to-wear line. So much so that he says he will design a new label just for me."

She beamed at him and he couldn't hold back a grin. He had a lot to be pleased about, too. "That's fantastic. I bet you can't wait for March."

"He says that my name will look better for the younger clients he wishes to attract." She chuckled. "Imagine it, Roxie, and underneath, House of Fortier. I'm going to be famous."

"I thought you already were—famous, that is." Mac reminded her that some of the more serious the magazines had now caught up with the story of her grandmother and Sevarin.

"Oh, that? *Comme ci, comme ça.* Fifteen minutes of fame is nothing compared to a lifetime of my own name on a label. One day I may even have my own business. I'll keep it simple, just one name—*Roxie.*"

Her excitement lasted all the way to Hôtel Margeaux. Mac knew it was cowardly, but the longer he put off telling her, the longer her excitement would last.

Once they were in the lift, he pulled her toward him and kissed her. It was moments like these, moments when they touched, that he knew he wasn't going to be able to keep his hands off her much longer.

She melted into him and confirmed she felt the same. Her soft, svelte body conformed to the hardness of his.

And he heard himself say, "I'm really proud of you, *chérie*. Let's go to bed to celebrate. It's been torture lying next to you each night without taking you in my arms."

"I was thinking more along the lines of champagne, but yes, that will do, Mac. Mmm." She stretched up to kiss him. "I can't think of a better way to celebrate," she said, sounding happier than she had in a long time, happier than she'd been since he'd known her.

November had only tumbled into December the day before, so that wasn't even a month. He just hoped she retained her exuberance when he told her about his day.

The elevator reached his floor. "No reason we can't have both. I'll ring down for a bottle almost as soon as we reach my suite. But before then, there's something I have to tell you."

"You sound so serious. It's not something bad, is it?"

They reached the door and he unlocked it, turning to look down at her as he pushed the door wide. "Actually, I was kind of pleased about it, but I didn't want to steal your thunder."

Roxie danced around him while he unbuttoned his topcoat. "Tell me, tell me now." Then she quieted down and asked, "Is it Javier? Have you discovered where he is?"

He slipped his arms out of the sleeves before answering while he tossed the coat over the back of the sofa more casually than he might be tossing away his relationship with Roxie.

"Yeah, someone sighted him buying lunch and followed him back to his bolt-hole, but then we lost him."

"Oh, no-o-o. You lost him. How?" she gasped.

"We think Javier might have been tipped off by a message on the police-band radio we found in his apartment. When I gave Dumont the news that we'd sighted Javier he seemed pretty excited."

Especially since IBIS was a jump ahead of him.

Her mouth dropped open. "You lost him," she repeated.

"Yeah, I know it sounds careless, but although we'd kept radio silence, we think that's how Dumont rounded up his agents, since Javier was all set up to monitor the FIS frequ—"

She cut him off midsentence, crying out as if she was in pain, "But Mac, you promised I'd be there when you caught Javier!"

Before he could catch his breath, she was racing for the bedroom. "Hey, *chérie,* I didn't get to the good part. We recovered Green Shield."

She slammed the door in his face.

Chapter 17

Roxie charged across the room to the bed, intent on throwing herself across the covers, then hiding her head in the pillows. Like an ostrich burying its head in the sand, she didn't want to believe Mac had deliberately excluded her.

But with no lock inside the bedroom door to prevent Mac following her, she had less than two seconds to regroup her emotions. Mac was too quick for her.

As the door swung inward behind her, Roxie dropped onto the edge of the mattress and seized the nearest weapon to chuck at him—her shoe. "Get out, Mac!"

"This is my room, remember?" he said, continuing to advance.

She remembered, all right.

Remembered he'd broken his promise to let her be part of taking Javier down. She threw a second shoe.

Mac was too big a target to miss. And her aim didn't go askew; he simply dodged, let it sail past and land in the sitting room with the force she put behind it.

Roxie leapt off the bed before she realized her mistake. In four-inch heels she was still somewhat smaller than Mac.

Without them she was at a definite disadvantage.

And never more so than when his hands clasped her shoulders. "*Chérie*," he coaxed, "*Bébé*, I'm sorry, I know how much it meant to you, but your being there wouldn't have made a difference. The bird had flown."

She hardened her heart against his soft talk, telling him, "That's only an excuse. The truth is, you still don't trust me enough to take me along with you. You decided I would slow you down. Instead, *you* let *me* down by breaking your promise."

He let out a sigh that stirred her hair, tickling her cheek. "If we are going to be pedantic about it, I never actually promised. My mouth was full of croissant. I couldn't speak."

"That's right," she retorted. "You didn't say anything. The word *no* never crossed your lips on the subject." Frowning at his semantics, Roxie tossed her hair back from her face. "And you've had days to put that right."

"Dammit, Roxie," he barked. His voice sinking to a low growl, he continued, "I love you. I couldn't bear the thought of you getting hurt again."

Tension vibrated through his hands, a signal that his emotions were involved, but that wasn't enough.

She twisted away. "That's not a good reason for keeping me out of the fun," she said bleakly, keeping her head down, but he wouldn't let her get away with hiding her face.

He swung her round and wrapped her in his arms, pulling her high against his chest in a bear hug that meant the only way not to face him was by closing her eyes.

His breath whispered across the bridge of her nose and her eyes, with his lips in quick pursuit, peppering her with kisses.

"I love you." Mac's voice was raw with emotion. "You don't know how it felt to watch you lying there, your life's blood flowing onto the ground. I thought I'd lost you." He kissed her again. "God, it really felt as if my life was over."

Roxie's eyes blinked open. His expression matched the emotion quivering in his voice, and she looked at him with wonder, knowing what it must have taken for a man of his caliber to open his heart and mind to her that way.

His features were finely drawn, the lines dark as if penciled in. "I…I didn't know," she whispered, tears welling in her eyes. Joy or sadness, it made no odds, her emotions overflowed.

"*Bébé*, you were out cold, and I thanked God for it. I didn't want you to watch me killing those men. I didn't like the idea of that memory in the background of what I knew we could have together, God willing."

"I know…" she began.

"That's just it, you don't know. You think you had your revenge on Sevarin by blackening his name? The one I took was worse. Final."

He sank down onto the bed and took her with him so she landed on his lap. His lips were on her hair, at her ear, as he murmured how much he loved her. "You and everyone else believe I burned Sevarin's château down to kill off Green Shield and keep the world safe. That's true, but it's not all."

Mac hugged her close and groaned as her hip pressed into his groin. She put up her hand and felt the slow, heavy thud of his heart against her palm. She felt too moved to speak.

She heard him swallow before he went on. "There is a deep dark core inside me that I hadn't discovered before that day. What the hell, I burned down his château because he prized it and it's history above everything else. You'd only noticed the money he'd spent on it, but if you had heard him talk…"

He shook his head and let out a short and sharp huff through his nose. "And here is the sad bit. I was damned delighted to blow up that kitchen where you had to cook for those animals."

Roxie wrapped both arms round Mac, then, with the top of

her head tucked beneath his chin, she held him tight, gulping back the residual fear from the day she'd thought Yves would rape her.

"I wanted to obliterate the place where Yves had put his slimy hands on you. When I thought Sevarin had taken you, the one person I really cherished, from me, I wanted to destroy the one thing he really treasured."

Mac was on an emotional high. Nothing she said to him could top the outpouring she'd just heard, not even *I love you.*

So she didn't attempt to compete.

Instead, she lifted her mouth to his and kissed him hard, wrote him a love letter with her lips.

For a long time the bedroom drowned in silence as they spoke from both hearts instead of minds. Told of their emotions with a sigh or a touch. And when at last Mac lifted his head and his gold eyes glittered down at her, she knew exactly what he wanted.

He wanted her.

He shook his head as if to set it straight again. "*Chérie,* there's one promise I don't intend to break. I promised you champagne, and champagne you will have. I intend to celebrate your success in style. How does a bottle of Krug sound?"

Mac stood her in front of him to let him rise from the huge bed they'd kept their distance on since the day she'd moved in with him. "It sounds absolutely perfect," she said.

Her head swimming, she watched Mac's long-legged stride carry him to the open door. He had a spring in his step that contrasted with the confessions she'd heard fifteen minutes earlier.

Her heart pounded when she thought of all he'd done in the name of love. Love for her

Reaching the doorway, he turned, a big grin on his face. "Of course, I'll expect you to be naked when I get back."

And Roxie was, but tucked under the covers, still slightly shy of this huge man, and the hidden depths she discovered in him.

* * *

Mac had felt wrung out with emotion, but lying in Roxie's arms refreshed him. He just hoped she wouldn't expect him to let it all hang out on a regular basis.

It wasn't as if he had no more secrets to spill.

He still hadn't told her what he'd discovered. That he was the bastard son of Milo Jellic, some ne'er-do-well cop. Or that his birth mother had once been married to the most wanted king of crime in New Zealand.

Now, there was a pedigree that left Sevarin's in the dust.

There was no room for all of that in the bed with Roxie.

And if he still hadn't come to grips with his parents' failure to tell him he was adopted, though they'd had thirty-one years to tell him the truth, too bad.

He was a fraud. His blue-blooded American genes were non-existent. In fact, he had the perfect profile for a spy; he'd been living a lie all his life.

No wonder Jason Hart had picked him from all the American intelligence agents he'd had to choose from.

He was the real deal.

But he could forget all the uncertainty when Roxie welcomed him into her arms, to her body.

Then, she was the only thing on his mind.

She still hadn't returned the gesture and said she loved him, but he could read the truth in the way she opened her body to him and rocked him in the cradle of her hips.

They'd already done all the romantic stuff, crossed arms and sipped champagne from each other's glasses, and punctuated their consumption of Krug with kisses that sparkled.

Now there was only the rhythmic slap of their hips coming together as a background to the melody played by their passionate sighs and moans.

He thrust deeper, faster, imprinting his taste, smell and feel on her synapses, binding her to him with his love.

His life had been full of revelations lately, and if it hadn't been for Roxie it would feel as if he was all alone, like standing on top of Everest, the highest mountain in Nepal, the country where he'd met a half brother without knowing it.

Only one person had the power to make or break him now, Roxie, and she was locked in his arms, high with passion and elation, communicating her love through simply being *Roxie*.

The sheets were in a tangle around them and the air locked in Roxie's throat as Mac rolled her over so she lay on top of him.

"Sit up and take control, *chérie,*" he panted, his chest heaving against the tender, well-kissed points of her breasts.

A man of contrasts, Mac was willing to give her control in bed, yet wouldn't let her work alongside him in a field he considered too dangerous.

The question was, too dangerous for her, or for any woman?

His hands gripped her hips to steady her, then reached for her breasts as she rode high above him. She'd never known her skin could be so responsive, but maybe it was only Mac's touch that could wring this pool of sensations from her.

They moved together, Mac's hips undulating up into her with each powerful thrust.

He looked up at her from under heavy eyelids, the glitter in his eyes a gold touchstone that set her on fire.

Mac had taken her up this high over and over, without letting her tumble, but his expression told her he couldn't hold out any longer. Knowing sent a shudder through her she couldn't control.

This time they were going to fly.

He pulled the pillow from her side of the bed and in one swift movement tucked it behind her hips, "Lean back, *bébé*. Place your hands on the pillow for support.

Mac was nothing if not inventive at finding new ways to increase their pleasure, so she did as he asked, arching her back and leaning her weight on her hands as he continued to thrust.

"Now, look down. Look down and see what I see." His palms curved round her hip bones, his thumbs stroking the small curve of her belly.

Heavens, she'd never felt so open before, so vulnerable to his gaze, not even that first night in the bath.

The look in Mac's eyes as he watched them move together was enough to send her over the edge. "No, don't look at me, look at us," he groaned. "Watch me slide into you."

It felt like eroticism at its highest. Not lewd, but a loving act between two adults who only wanted to please each other.

Her breathing became labored, but she couldn't look away. Couldn't drag her eyes from the dusky column that lifted her higher with each plunge and compelled her to protest in fear each time it drew back.

"You're killing me here," she moaned as heat and exhaustion made her scared she would collapse before they leapt.

"Time to go, *bébé,* time to blow the roof off this place," he roared, his thumbs sliding down to stroke the pulse above the point where their bodies met.

Once, twice, a third time and the ceiling lifted.

She saw the stars. Shooting stars. Was there ever anything more glorious than lifting off with the man you loved shouting your name as he jetted his life force inside you?

Roxie collapsed onto Mac's chest, enervated, and just before she fell into a mind-numbing stupor, she said, "We should buy a mirror, a big mirror."

The next day went wrong from the moment they woke up, late.

Mac was already running three-quarters of an hour behind schedule when he dropped Roxie off in front of the House of Fortier, wearing a red suit she said was an expression of her happiness.

He'd left her standing on the sidewalk with no time for a goodbye kiss, just a "See you tonight."

Then he arrived at IBIS's Paris headquarters to find Jason Hart there before him. *Three hours before him.*

"Okay," said Jason, "you can start by showing me these vials of Green Shield, then I want your suggestions on how to deal with the green beastie."

Mac led him along the corridor to the locked lab, where he'd stashed it in the freezer. "Personally," Mac told him, "I want to see it destroyed, and there is only one way, extreme heat." He laughed, then continued, "Sir, if I had my way, we'd burn it in a furnace, then seal it up and ship it to the Arctic for burial."

Jason's laugh contained no humor. "It's that frightening?"

"Yes, sir, I've seen it in action, and I don't believe we should take any chances."

"Too bad the people behind it are all dead. I'd like to string them up for unleashing this on the world."

"Not all of them. We still haven't captured Javier Sevarin."

Jason Hart looked at Mac and held his gaze with a wealth of meaning behind his almost nonexistent expression. "I have this feeling he won't live very long after we do find him."

"You could be right, sir," Mac answered, catching his drift. Sometimes waiting for justice to take its course meant waiting forever; however, Mac would make sure it was considered a fair result even if the attempt killed him, as well.

"You're correct about Green Shield, it has to be destroyed. I'll leave you to take care of that," Jason Hart said as they reached the forensic laboratory where the vials were under guard.

They had to wait a moment until the guard let them through, before Mac could say, "But I resigned. I might not be around."

"Well, hell, Mac. You didn't really think I was going to accept that, did you? I had a promotion in mind. Now your cover's ruined in Paris...."

God, don't shift me from Paris. Don't send me away from Roxie.

"How does head of the Paris bureau sound?" Without waiting for a reply, Jason continued, "Cliff Eagles is a good man, but he's hankering to get back to the States. Washington will suit him just fine."

"I don't know what to say, sir." Mac felt stunned. He'd been waiting for the axe to drop, and instead he'd gotten exactly what he needed to stay close to Roxie.

"Say yes, Mac. It's a nice simple word."

"Yes, sir." Mac felt like saluting, but his days in Naval Intelligence were long gone. So much had happened since Jason had recruited him out of there after 9/11.

He opened the freezer and carefully pulled out the plastic ice cream cartons. "This is it."

Jason Hart took a grim look inside the common containers, which were the only thing standing between the world and disaster, if you couldn't count on IBIS.

"Repack it, Mac. Do it yourself. Pack it in something really flammable like polyurethane foam and wood. Then carry out the rest of your plans. Just don't tell anyone what you're burying in the Arctic."

They left the lab side by side, shoulder to shoulder, two men who had taken on the security of the world and everyone in it.

About the time they reached the end of the corridor, Jason said, "'Course, you know what I'd really like to do. I'd like to take those two vials, march into the French Minister of Defense's office and scare the crap out of him."

"Amen to that, sir."

"He's as guilty as the rest of his department for giving this research the okay. You can't create a monster and expect to keep it under control."

Jason gave a cold smile. Mac had seen it before, each time they took out another terrorist. "As it is, the minister will lose his job. I'll see to that. I've a meeting with the French president this afternoon."

And Mac knew he would carry out his plans. Jason Hart was formidable at getting his own way.

"The French were eager to sign up with me and IBIS, so they knew what they were getting into, and like the rest of us they have to abide by the rules, otherwise the bad guys will win."

Mac always marveled at Jason Hart; barely forty, he yielded considerable power, yet it never looked as if it rested heavily on his shoulders.

He still had a lot of youth and vigor in the hand that shook Mac's outside Cliff Eagles's office. "I'll go and give Cliff the good news. You have a good day, now."

Mac thought about Roxie.

He certainly intended having a good night.

It was as if his luck had turned from this morning.

That was before he got a call from his parents.

They were ensconced in the Hôtel George V and would like to talk with him. He remembered his parents sending for him to give him a talking to when he was young, usually for some form of mischief or another.

Tonight, most of the talking would come from him, and his parents' explanations had better be good.

Roxie's new cell phone vibrated against her hip. Vibrated because Charles abhorred the sound of tinny electronic music in his salon, claiming it spoiled the ambience.

"Roxie, I'm sorry I can't pick you up from work tonight." As she listened to Mac's voice, the hairs at the back of her neck prickled and her stomach churned.

He only ever called her at work if it was important, and today his voice had a tense, edgy ring she couldn't explain away as the fault of her cell phone.

"Thierry will come and collect you instead." He laughed then, but it had a hollow ring. "Don't let him talk you into going for a drink with him. The guy is too handsome for his own good, or should I say, my peace of mind...."

"But, Mac, where are you going?"

"It's too long a story. I'll explain when I see you tonight." He paused for a moment. "*Chérie,* I'm sending him because I trust him to keep you safe. Take care, I've got to go."

Roxie closed the cell phone and slipped it back in its pouch as she pondered Mac's obvious agitation. There had been no sign of this morning's protestations of love.

Then it struck her.

Javier!

He was going after Sevarin's son and leaving her out of the loop, *again!*

She hated to compare Mac to Dumont's antifeminist stance, but he'd been another who thought women shouldn't go into the field. That the perfect use for her skills was gathering gossip.

Was it any wonder she'd barged into Mac's apartment when she'd had a chance to prove herself?

Margaret McBride watched her son, Joshua S. McBride Junior, pace the floor of their suite. He was angry.

"How could you let me believe I was someone who doesn't exist?"

Margaret was familiar with her son's expression. Though it had been almost twelve years since they'd had daily contact, she could still read him like a book.

"Of course you exist," grumped her husband. "Don't be melodramatic. You tell him, Meggy."

For a seasoned diplomat, her husband was good at passing her the buck in family matters. "Darling, you've always known you were born in New Zealand. It's on your birth certi—"

Mac didn't let her finish. "Yeah, and all that told me was I couldn't run for president, not that I wasn't *your* son."

Though she was eleven inches shorter than him, she stopped his restless pacing simply by placing her hand on his arm.

"Of course you're our son. We loved you the moment we saw you. It didn't matter that you were bright red with bawling your head off or that your auburn curls clashed with the color of your face. The moment I held you against my heart you were mine, my son."

Actually, she hadn't realized his hair was auburn until Josh had mentioned it after they left the hospital. She'd fallen in love with Mac…with her son, at first sight.

"So, you *bought* me?" Mac covered his eyes as if he couldn't bear to look at her and pains of regret shafted into her heart.

But that wasn't what he wanted to hear. "No such thing," she told him, hurt even more to hear him speak to her that way. Mac might have been stubborn growing up, but he'd never been disrespectful.

She loosed a sigh that began somewhere near her toes. "Yes, we did give your birth mother money, but not because she asked for it. Her only concern was for your safety, to get you away from New Zealand before her husband found you and killed you as he had your biological father."

Tears welled in Margaret's eyes as she remembered how desperate the woman had been to save her son's life, and her grief because the death of her son's father left her no place to turn to for help. Not without placing the people in danger from her husband's wrath. Margaret had never felt as frantic as that woman, until now.

She dragged Mac's hand away from his eyes. "Look at me."

It cut her deeply to listen to the low moan that seemed to come from his heart as he turned his back on her.

Josh put his arm around her shoulders, but even her husband's touch couldn't ease her pain, just as nothing she said seemed to comfort her son.

But at least one of the McBride males was on her side for he cautioned Mac, "Don't you disrespect your mother that way, son. Sure we made mistakes, but it was with the best of intentions."

"Yeah, yeah, you paved my way to hell with them. Why didn't

you see fit to tell me all this while I was growing up?" Mac asked through tight lips, as if he hated them to know his pain.

Josh tightened his hold on her upper arm. He might not have said much apart from leaping to her defense, but she knew he felt this deeply. Today was the day they'd hoped would never come.

Her husband took over now. "Sure, we gave your birth mother money. As much as your life was in danger from her husband, so was hers."

Margaret took over the explanation, smoothing the rough edges of her husband's statement. "We gave her the money to escape New Zealand. How could we live with her death on our conscience? She gave birth to you, the most precious gift we ever received."

"Quite right, my dear." Josh backed her up, and she could tell he was just as affected by the memory as she was. "Her husband is still alive. We've made a point of keeping track of him over the years. He's a *very* bad man."

"Darling." Margaret went over and put her arms around Mac, hugging his stiff-with-resentment body close. "We did talk about telling you, but we know you too well. Your sense of honor and justice is too ingrained to just let it end at that."

She stepped back and looked up at her son. "We were frightened you might go haring off to New Zealand, intent on seeking justice for the murder of your biological father."

The strain eased from Mac's face and a wry twist of a smile shaped it. "Yeah, you know me," he said. "That's exactly what I'd have done...might yet." Margaret felt her heart sink, knowing the son of her heart was a man of his word. She feared for him.

Feared to lose him even more than they had by their silence.

Chapter 18

Lights glowed on the wet sidewalk. Long pale slashes of yellow reflecting the windows of the House of Fortier. Roxie's edgy silhouette broke up the gleaming pattern as she paced.

Thierry was late.

She pulled the black pashmina closer, wrapping it tightly around the shoulders of her red suit for extra warmth. Fifteen minutes. That's how long she'd been waiting for the French agent, growing more agitated during the last five of them.

Passing the stone columns of the front entrance once more, she saw the Russian doorman check his watch. "Mademoiselle Roxie," he called out, "I have to go off duty now. Please come inside to wait."

"Don't worry, Gregor, I'll be okay. My ride should be here any second. Mac's friends aren't the kind to be late because they think it de rigueur."

The words were hardly out of her mouth when a car pulled up and double-parked opposite her with the engine running.

The man inside waved and she stepped off the sidewalk.

It was an older-model car than Mac usually picked up from the IBIS undercover carpool. Down one side a long scrape in the paintwork showed bare metal.

She hesitated as the window nearest to her rolled down.

The car interior was dark. The driver, silhouetted against the lights of passing cars, looked as if he, too, had muffled up against the cold. He waved again. "Mademoiselle Kincaid?"

"Thierry?"

"*Oui.*"

Roxie heaved a sigh as she reached for the door handle. "I thought you were never going to arrive. Not that I mind really. It's just that Mac is always punctual and I make sure not to keep him waiting."

She swung her legs into the car and shut the door. Then, remembering the scrape down the side, reached for her seat belt.

"I had car trouble. Someone misjudged the distance and hit me," he said, looking over his shoulder at the traffic flowing past on their side of the street.

Roxie grinned as the vehicle shot out into a space between cars. "I know. I just saw the evidence. I hope you don't have too much paperwork to fill out because of it."

She held her breath as Thierry hunched over the wheel like some demon driver and risked their lives and limbs as he cut another driver off while changing lanes, saying, "I think if anyone has a multitude of forms to fill, it will be Mac."

"Tell me the truth," she demanded. "Has he gone after Javier and left me behind again?"

The driver turned and faced her as if oblivious to the speed they were traveling. Eyes shining pale blue in the lights from the bridge over the Seine as they crossed to the Left Bank, he informed her, "If that is so, I can assure you, he will be very disappointed."

Roxie's breath caught in her throat as she watched him smile and realized Dumont was right to let her go. As an agent she was too stupid to live.

The soft fluorescents overhead disappeared in a blur as Mac raced along the corridor to the control center of the bureau's Paris branch, shouldering open the door with reckless haste.

"Where the hell is she? Haven't you found her yet?" he demanded, fearing to hear the worst.

He'd had two phone calls earlier, both from Thierry.

The first, while Mac was still in his parents' suite at the Hotel George V, to say he'd been in an accident causing him to be delayed collecting Roxie.

The second, after Thierry had hammered on the door of the fashion house trying to attract the attention of someone inside, and Gregor, the doorman, had informed him that Mademoiselle Roxie had already been collected. By *Thierry*, no less.

It took him a moment to realize the voice answering was Jason Hart's. "There's no news yet, Mac."

No good news.

Had to be, if they felt it necessary to bring the boss into the situation. But Mac was too anxious for the normal *Yes sir, no sir, three bags full...* "Fill me in, sir. What have we got?"

"Thierry just arrived before you did. He got a description of the car. We've put out a bulletin for it and brought FIS in, as Roxie did work for them."

"Still does," Mac chipped in.

"Not according to my information," Jason told him. "But that's neither here nor there. Thierry had already noted the number. It's the same car that sideswiped him before he could get to the couturier's."

Mac's head was spinning, his thoughts racing round and round. Dear God, he couldn't have found her just to lose her again.

Not like this. No wonder she hated the Sevarin family. They were every bit as bad as the vermin living in Paris's sewers, rats. Just when you thought you'd got rid of them, they popped up and took another bite.

"What do we do now?" asked Mac.

They were all staring as if they didn't recognize him, but they'd never seen Mac when the woman he loved had been kidnapped from under IBIS's nose, or when he had ever felt so helpless.

Jason Hart came up and put his hand on Mac's shoulder in much the same way his pop had before he'd left his parents' suite.

Hell, after they'd resolved the situation that had haunted his parents for most of Mac's life, he'd told them, "Prepare to welcome a daughter-in-law into the family, I intend on getting married."

The congratulations were still ringing in his ears when the news arrived that Roxie was missing.

Cliff Eagles joined Mac and Jason. "Mac," his SAC said, "we've done everything we can for now. The police have joined us, and the FIS, in the search for the car. Somehow, though, I don't get the impression that his motivation is revenge for that story in the diary reaching public. If that was it, he would have tried to get to Roxie before now."

With a jerk of his head, Cliff directed Mac's attention toward the bank of computers in the room. "Why don't you sit down over there with Thierry and do what you both do best."

Jason followed Mac in the direction of ten or more screens, flashing pictures of everything from written information to maps and satellite feed. "He's going to call Mac. Take my word on that. We have something he wants in exchange for Roxie."

Mac shook his head. "We had. I took care of that business we spoke of this morning." He checked his watch. "It's probably over the Atlantic onboard one of our courier planes right now."

Jason's smile held a trace of wickedness. "You know that and I know it, but Javier Sevarin doesn't. That's all that counts. Go work out a few scenarios to counter whatever Javier can come up with."

Mac grinned for the first time since he'd left Roxie that morning. "Don't worry, sir. We'll be ready for anything he throws our way."

His equilibrium no longer felt as if it had spun off the curve of the world. Mac was ready to get on with what he excelled at.

Fighting terrorism, whichever face it was wearing that week.

Though it was 6:00 a.m. on a cold winter's morning, Mac sweated blood until the call arrived on his cell phone, just as his confidence had begun to fade.

"McBride speaking," he answered crisply, as if his personal world wasn't falling apart.

"Honesty at last, no more Monsieur Makjzajev…."

"Who is this?" Mac kept up the pretense, stalled as he checked the signal and read the phone's screen. Number untraceable…

"I think you know full well who is calling. I have with me a young lady who has been living with you, one Mademoiselle Roxie Kincaid. If you want her back alive, you will do as I say—"

"Javier! If you harm one hair on her head…" Mac spoke through clenched teeth, no more pretense. The gloves were off and Mac was in the mood for a bare-fisted bloody-knuckled fight.

"That, my friend, is entirely up to you, so be quiet and listen. I want Green Shield. You were not the only buyer—"

"We'll pay whatever you want," Mac cut in once more, very conscious of having destroyed his only bargaining chip.

"No amount of money is enough. Years of work went into that biotech weapon, too many. It was my idea, my genius that conceived it and I want Green Shield back."

Mac heard Javier catch his breath as if he had said too much, then he went on… "Listen up, this is what you must do if you want your *petite amie* back in one piece."

"I'm listening."

"At 10:00 a.m. precisely, I will bring the girl to President Mitterand's precious glass pyramid at the Louvre to make the exchange. Come alone or the girl dies. And don't be late, or the result will be the same."

Javier hung up before Mac could reply, and it was then he realized everyone in the control room had been standing around him, listening to one side of the conversation.

He looked at Thierry. "So, which one of our scenarios can we put together in less than four hours that involves a crowd of tourists and a glass pyramid we don't dare use guns around?"

She'd walked straight into his trap.

But at this stage of the game, Roxie was simply congratulating herself on not endangering her life by losing her temper.

It had been a close-run race. Everything about Javier Sevarin prickled her skin with tension and made her feel she was in a fight with daggers drawn.

However, since she'd been tied up in a dark room all night, thinking she'd never see Mac or the sun again, it was great to be out in the fresh air, even with said dagger nudging her side.

Somehow, he'd managed to find parking close by, then walked her through the long tunnel of Passage Richelieu.

Once they came out into the Carrousel du Louvre, Javier hustled her across the wide Cour Napoléon.

The courtyard lay over the subterranean hall of the same name, a place that drew in daylight from the huge glass pyramids above it. And by staying outside, he'd made sure there would be no challenge at the metal detectors.

Every step she took was agony. He kept one arm around her

like a lover's embrace, so tight it dragged on the scar near her shoulder blade, making it difficult to keep her balance.

"You are fretful to see your lover, *non?*" Javier whispered his version of sweet nothings against her ear. "I, too, am anxious to meet up with him again."

But not for the same reason, I bet.

Roxie was certain if Javier had his way, neither she nor Mac would come out of this alive.

No matter that Javier had spoken of an exchange. After a few hours in his company, she was positive his warped sense of justice called for more than that, much more.

His father's death alone must have been enough incentive to spark Javier Sevarin's need for revenge. Yet, that and his good name only accounted for a small portion of the blame he'd heaped on Mac and her.

Oui, he wanted them dead.

She'd been so mad at Mac when he'd kept her out of the loop; even his explanation—though beautiful—still hadn't quite healed the hurt of feeling *less.*

Less of an agent than he was.

Less of an agent than she'd thought.

But Mac had been right.

Simply wanting it wasn't enough.

The wars that men like Mac fought had few similarities to the one Grandmère had clawed her way through.

Simply being a Kincaid didn't automatically make her capable of becoming an agent. She had the fire in her belly, but not the experience, or the training.

And Dumont hadn't gone out of his way to insure she got any.

Like most Frenchmen, Dumont paid homage to women, but he'd never been able to conceal his antifeminist streak during his dealings with her.

This last episode had probably helped confirm his decision to tell Roxie that her services were no longer required.

His excuse? The last thought made her lip curl.

He said Roxie had become notorious through revealing the Sevarin family history to the media. At the time she had thought, *Spoken like a man who has skeletons in his closet.*

Though, maybe Dumont had been right about her, for she still hadn't found the courage to tell Mac she'd been fired.

And now maybe she would never need to let him know.

Javier had given them far too long to prepare, and that worried Mac. He'd come to the conclusion Sevarin's son didn't actually care about retrieving Green Shield.

Oh, sure, he'd probably be happy to take the vials and make a bolt for it, but his real targets had to be Mac McBride and Roxie Kincaid. Human sacrifices that would help quench the mean streak running through Sevarin's genes.

The receiver in Mac's left ear had kept him up to date on Roxie and Javier's progress from the second they had exited his car and set off through the passageway to the Carrousel.

Two more minutes and they should be in *his* sights as well as those of his men on the rooftops.

Mac had placed snipers at the highest points of the Richelieu and Denon wings, whose honeyed-stone facades looked out at the fragile crystalline construction as if it were a diamond set in the middle of a gold pendant.

And taking no chances, he had placed another two snipers atop the Sully wing that formed the base of the *U.*

Their chances of getting a clear shot were minimal, though, as once the Louvre opened, the tourists came pouring in, wandering around the court to take photos.

Today, for some reason, the pools surrounding the pyramid were empty and the fountains dry.

And as well as the chance one of their shots might strike the pyramid, flying glass could endanger visitors in the basement reception hall beneath the pyramid.

Yeah, Javier had put some thought into picking his meeting place for the exchange.

Roxie scanned the way ahead, certain *she* would easily pick Mac out from the visitors circling the area. The pools were empty, which was unusual, and a couple of workmen were bent over examining the base of one of them. To her it seemed quiet without the sound of running water.

For all her certainty, Javier beat her to it by spying Mac first. "There he is, there's McBride."

He ground Mac's name through his teeth as if he'd prefer to make hamburger of it as he dragged Roxie in Mac's direction. "So obliging of your *gallant* to come save his *petite amie.*"

She swallowed the lump of emotion blocking her throat. That's how it looked to her, as well. But all she felt was guilty.

Mac had said he loved her, but the little thread of resentment that he'd gone after Javier without her, niggling at the back of her mind, had prevented her returning the favor. Stopped her from spilling the words that were always on the tip of her tongue while they made love.

I love you.

The phrase leapt into her thoughts so easily, but Mac wasn't a mind reader.

Javier hauled her to the back of the pyramid and down one of the paths separating the normally fluid triangular pools from glass. He stopped by one of the thigh-high walls that kept the water contained. "This will do. He can come to us now."

She saw Mac was holding a container—Green Shield!

Roxie knew she couldn't let Mac give it to Javier. It was too big a sacrifice even to save the woman who held his heart.

She would have to watch for her chance, grab it and run.

Mac got within eight feet of Javier before the Frenchman called out a threat. "That's close enough, McBride. Another step and I'll show you how easily my knife slips between your woman's ribs." He heard Roxie's swift intake of breath, feeling no doubts that Javier would do as he said.

Keeping his eyes on Roxie, as if that would give her courage, he answered, "There's just one problem. I can't reach across that distance to make the exchange."

Mac continued to stare at Roxie, willing her to react as soon he opened an opportunity. "That's what we're here for, isn't it? I give you Green Shield, and you give me the girl."

One narrow glance from Javier indicated he didn't intend making it that easy for Mac.

"Quite clearly, you can see my half of the bargain." Javier smiled as if at a sick joke. "I'm hiding nothing from you but my knife." He laughed then, and glanced away momentarily.

A couple of Spanish-speaking tourists wandered past and Mac could see the wheels turning in Javier's mind, wondering if they might be undercover. Unfortunately, his indecision didn't last long enough to give Mac an opening.

Hell, he thought, Thierry was a master of disguise, but his strong features would make a damn ugly woman. No, Thierry was actually one of the men pretending to work on the pool lining.

Pulling Roxie with him, Javier stepped close. "I have to be certain that the container holds Green Shield."

Harsh with frustration, Javier's voice almost didn't carry the distance. Max raised his. "What did you say?"

"Open the box!"

"Just give me a second." Mac fumbled with the catch, his fingers not showing their usual dexterity. From under half-shut eyelids he watched Javier crane his neck for a glimpse of the contents.

Opening the lid, he tilted the container toward Javier.

"You'll understand, Sevarin, that the ice cream didn't keep, but I doubt whether you would have eaten it. And we couldn't take a chance on Green Shield ending up in the Paris sewer system."

Javier appeared satisfied.

And so he should. IBIS had gone to great lengths to make the vials look exactly the same as the ones Mac had had destroyed.

He watched Javier's shoulders relax slightly as the tourists walked out of range around the corner.

"Soit," he said, "that will do. Close up the box and slide it over to me."

Mac followed half of the instructions. Leaving the lid up, he spun the box like a curling stone skimming across ice, and just as he'd hoped it failed to make the distance and hit the wall.

"No problem, I'll get it," he called to Sevarin, who looked as restless as an unbroken horse, skittish and unstable.

If he lost control there was no denying that knife might end up between Roxie's ribs. He couldn't let that happen. Damn, he should have had Javier shot straight off.

To hell with the rules of fair play. Javier wouldn't think twice about breaking them.

Roxie stayed still as any of the statues inside the Louvre and didn't begin breathing again until Javier shouted, *"Non, halte!"*

Thrusting out his free hand, he warned Mac off. "Stay back, *I* will retrieve it."

With that same hand, he reached in front of Roxie, grasping her opposite wrist to spin her out wildly between the two men, all the while edging closer to his goal.

Though more by chance than skill, Roxie's feet collided with the container, kicking it farther away.

The next few seconds went past in a slow blur as time stretched in a series of still-life pictures.

"Salaud," Javier shouted as she threw herself onto the paving stones, pulling him off balance with her weight and fueling his anger by tugging hard to release the hand circling her wrist.

The knife moved in a bright arc of light in front of her face.

She blinked, shutting her eyes as if what she couldn't see couldn't harm her. Rolling across the paving, into Javier instead of away from him, Roxie came to a jarring stop as her shoulder thumped into his shin.

He didn't even yelp as he released her wrist to step over her. She was free.

Javier didn't seem to have noticed. Eyes fastened on his goal, he stretched for the box of deadly vials, snapping it shut as he pulled it up into his arms.

Intent on slowing his escape, Roxie grabbed Javier's ankle.

Mac's shadow loomed across them. "Get him!" she shouted, dodging another swipe of the knife that left her clutching a slice of men's suiting, thankful that the fingers on that hand still numbered five.

Mac was conscious of the weight of his 9 mm Glock against his back, but the thought of a stray bullet hitting Roxie stayed his hand. Just one more item on his list of reasons for preferring *not* to work with the woman he loved.

The danger to her put a huge constraint on his highly honed instincts, slowing them to the point where he wasn't doing his job at all well.

Conscious of Roxie on the ground at their feet, he dived at Javier. A feint with the knife sent Mac dancing out of reach, far enough away for the Frenchman to grab a slim vial from under the lid of the container. Then, head down, Javier made a break for freedom, leaping over the barrier to sprint across the surface of the empty pool.

"No, you don't," Mac shouted after him. Whipping around, he hurdled the wall and ran in Javier's wake.

Roxie pushed to her feet, hair wild as she shook it back from her eyes, her red suit covered in dust. Not a great advertisement for her new *Roxie* venture.

Mac's shoes slipped on the slippery pool lining. Ahead of him Javier took a tumble, but not hard enough to slow him down.

Praying Roxie would have the good sense to leave the guy to him now, Mac didn't have enough time to turn and check, or count on her obeying.

Though he desperately wanted to take Javier Sevarin down, he was conscious of the snipers on the rooftops and the chance of his body blocking a clear shot from on high.

Then the worst happened as he drew level with the entrance side of the pyramid. Enough visitors to fill a bus began flowing off the escalators and out into the courtyard.

Reaching for his gun as he ran, Mac heard Roxie yell, *"Au voleur!* Stop, thief!"

Her cry set up a clamor, women squealing and men yelling, "Who, what, where?" The last thing Mac needed was any more help.

Javier didn't slow down or act as if he'd heard Roxie.

Plunging through the crush, he emerged on the other side, leaving an older woman on the ground from a push in the back.

Curses and protests filled the air. Mac had to contend with the aftermath, dodging through what was evolving into an angry mob. He ran faster, the soles of his shoes repeating the thud of the Frenchman's footsteps on the paving as they both drew away from the crowd.

Up ahead lay the Carrousel du Louvre, an inverted pyramid centering a circle of grass, ringed by finely trimmed box hedges.

Javier leapt over the hedge. Out of the blue, Mac had a clear shot. He skidded to a halt, raised his arm and leveled his gun at Javier's retreating back, slowly squeezing the trigger.

"No-o-o-o." The word was ripped from Roxie's throat as she saw Mac aim at Javier. What was he thinking?

The fine green sward that was some gardener's pride and joy, abounding with Keep Off the Grass signs, didn't even earn a glance from the man galloping across it.

But all Roxie could see were the consequences.

If Javier fell on the grass and broke the vial there would be no more grass to worry about.

No more grass in the whole of France, Europe even.

Mac fired. The report rang in Roxie's ears like a death knell for *la belle France.* The country she loved and had made her home.

She saw Javier stagger, twist to face them as he uncorked the vial, and throw it as he fell backward onto the toughened glass covering the inverted pyramid.

Slipping out of her shoes, Roxie brushed through the hedge. Ignoring the wounded man she raced to the spilled vial.

Desperate now, she pulled off her jacket, mopping up liquid she could hardly see as tears streamed down her face.

It was a thankless task, she knew, having seen Green Shield at work, but she had to try.

She couldn't stand by and do nothing.

Mac crouched on the glass and touched his fingers to Javier's neck, as if unaware of the faces gazing up from the hall below.

No pulse.

Mac's sense of relief discharged in a pent-up sigh.

He couldn't say he enjoyed killing, but if it had to be done, it was best done swiftly.

It wasn't until he straightened, stood and looked around for Roxie that he noticed his audience and the attendant dragging on Thierry's arm, calling, *"Non, non, ne pas approcher."*

"Let him through," Mac yelled, and saw the man's jaw drop, shocked, he supposed, by the body at Mac's feet.

For once Mac was all wrong. "But the grass, it is not allowed!" came the pompous protest.

"There will be no grass in the whole of Paris if someone doesn't help me." This last complaint from Roxie.

Then Mac realized what she was doing and loped to her side, pulling her up off the grass and into his arms. Prying the damp jacket from her fingers, he tossed it down onto the grass.

"No, Mac, don't!"

The tears from her gray eyes overflowed onto her cheeks like liquid crystals.

To him she had never looked more beautiful.

Mac brushed away her tears with a swipe of his thumb. She looked so sad, but all he wanted to do was smile. "Ah, *chérie,* your beautiful suit, it's ruined. You looked so chic in it, too."

"How can you be so calm," she ranted. "There is Green Shield all over the lawn. I couldn't mop it all up, and now look."

They both glanced down, then Roxie realized. "The grass? It isn't brown or dead. Did I save it, or…?"

He pulled her into an embrace that would have done justice to a bear as he laughed. "*Chérie…*" He grinned. "*Bébé,* not even for you would I have let him have Green Shield. Besides, I'd had it destroyed long before he made his demands."

"Ah, Mac," she sighed, "that's why I love you, you always seem to think of everything."

"What did you say?"

"That you think of everything. You always plan ahead—"

"No, not that." Mac held his breath.

"I said that's why I love you."

"Well, it's about time. I thought you were never going to admit it," he said, his voice gruff with relief.

He pulled her up higher in his arms and she fell into his embrace, lifting her face for his kiss, oblivious of the crowd of onlookers lining the ring of trimmed box hedges.

Mac poured everything he had, all that he was, into that kiss.

He'd gone through two days of hell.

First the meeting with his parents and the sinking feeling that he had had never really known them.

That he was a stranger in his own skin.

Then, discovering that Javier had Roxie.

If she'd died, he didn't know if he'd be able to go on.

He'd never known that love could take you like this, like an unannounced storm where hot air clashes with cold high in the atmosphere, all heat, energy and flashes of pure brilliance.

By the time he lifted his head, the gendarmes had arrived on the scene as well as Dumont, and the groundsman was arguing against stakes being hammered into his lawn to hold the crime-scene tape.

"Life will go on, *chérie,* ours especially, but first we have a little mess to clear up." He gave her a small kiss on her forehead, then let her slide to the ground as Dumont approached.

He pushed the hair back from her face and said, "Quickly now, tell me."

Roxie quirked her head to one side as she looked up at him, her eyes sparkling as she understood where he was going with it. "Tell you what?"

"Say, I still love you, Mac."

"I still love you, Mac."

"That's good, for I'm never going to stop loving you."

Epilogue

The French had always believed they had the copyright on love.

L'amour.

They certainly knew how to put it in the right setting, and in Paris at night, the Eiffel Tower stood out as the diamond in the City of Lights' crown.

Mac was more than willing to take advantage of that setting.

He kept his arm round Roxie, holding her close to his side as they traveled up in the elevator to the viewing platform.

As a matter of fact, in the week since the confrontation at the Louvre, he'd seemed unable to keep his hands off her, or bear her to be out of his sight.

Not that he'd heard any complaints.

Mac looked over the railing, pointing out the smudge of lights as a tourist boat sailed through the mist covering the river Seine.

Christmas would soon be upon them and Paris was decked out in her gaudiest jewels to welcome its arrival.

Mac turned his back to the rail and leaned back, pulling Roxie into his arms. He'd brought her up the tower to propose, but before that he had some apologizing to take care of, and started with, "There's something I have to tell you, *chérie*."

She blinked up at him as if surprised he'd said *tell* instead of *ask,* and he knew his so-called secret plans hadn't fooled her one iota.

Her eyebrows quirked, making the bridge of her nose crinkle. "Okay, you've got me going, what is it?"

He thought, *cute,* but noted the thread of apprehension in her question and decided that putting them both out of their misery was his best option. "Here I am, going on thirty-one years old, and just over a week ago I discovered I was adopted."

Mac heard the soft intake of her breath, but she didn't say anything, just leaned closer. Her warmth was what he needed right now. That, and her understanding.

"My parents are in Paris at the moment and I love them dearly, but I don't always understand them. My birth certificate says I was born in New Zealand, it doesn't mention another mom or dad."

He forked his fingers through her hair and massaged the base of her skull as if that would help. "But that's not the point, not what I wanted to say…. I want to apologize for the way I treated you. Now I know how it feels from personal experience, to discover someone you love doesn't trust you. It hurts."

"Oh, Mac, I don't think we can compare the two. You had a job to do. And it's been proved that I didn't have enough experience to be a good agent. To be like you."

"You flatter me, *chérie.* I made a ton of mistakes. At least you had the courage of your convictions. Me, I thought I was case-hardened, after my last romantic experience with a beautiful female agent ended with her sticking a knife in my ribs. I guess I ought to tell you about Lucia."

Roxie put a finger to his lips. Tales about romantic adventures in his past were something he didn't have to share. "Mac, hush. Do you really think this is the best time to give me a list of your old lovers?"

She reached up and placed her palm along his taut jawline, smooth as silk for a change, but hardly surprising. She'd heard him shaving only minutes before the cab arrived to carry them to what had started out as an undisclosed destination. It was so like her secret agent lover to plan the evening covertly.

"I can empathize with your feelings," she said. "Trust has to come with love. But knowing the man you are now, the person your parents brought up with high ideals, a sense of honor and a huge love for his country, I can't believe they kept your adoption secret without a very good reason."

Roxie slipped one hand around his neck, and before he could say anything, she stretched on tiptoes to bring his mouth closer for her kiss.

As her heels touched the floor again, she asked, "Do you really think being adopted has changed your values overnight, or could make me think less of you?"

He pulled closer, took her into his arms in a close embrace and bathed her face in kisses. "No, I never thought that of you. I just had to make sure it didn't give you pause about our relationship. If we have children, how can you be sure I won't pass on some genetic quirk?"

"Children? Oh, my goodness, Mac. I knew you had to have brought me up here for more than confessions about your heritage or ancient love affairs. You want to ask me to marry you."

"How did you know?" His voice was gruff with tenderness, but he hadn't denied it and the knowledge filled her with elation.

Overjoyed, she had a sudden urge to tease him. She leaned back in his arms until she could see his face, read his expression, and said, "Didn't I tell you? I'm a secret agent. We're good at working things out, given certain evidence. And that said, as for genetic problems, you're a spy. If you want, you can discover all you need to know and we'll take whatever comes in our stride."

He shook his head and grinned, then pulled her close again. Close enough for her to feel the slow, heavy thud of his heart. Close enough to take in the male scent that spelled out Mac McBride. A scent she would recognize blindfolded.

"God, I love you, Roxie," he told her, and then held her away to give her a quizzical look. "What evidence?" he asked.

Really, for a clever man he'd left himself wide open for a little naughty repartee. "I can feel a bulge in your trousers that's too small to be what you usually keep there for me, so it can't be anything else but a ring box."

He laughed, a large, joyous bellow that rippled through her.

This was Mac, the man who had taken over her life, filled it with love, warmth and a hundred other blessings, until she couldn't picture the rest of her days without him.

"I cannot tell a lie. It's a ring box."

Roxie waited...and waited. "Aren't you going to ask me then?"

"Ask you what?"

That was another thing about Mac. He knew how to win. She capitulated. "Ask me to marry you."

His expression grew serious, his eyes a dim gold that reflected the lights of Paris behind her as he pulled out the ring box and opened it.

Her heart began to race as she looked at the large emerald-cut diamond set in platinum. It was really going to happen.

"Roxie, when I say the words 'till death do us part,' that's exactly what I mean, a lifetime together. I love you. So, will you marry me? Be my wife in whichever corner of the globe life takes us and stay with me always?"

She quivered as she said, "I will, till death do us part," knowing that in Mac's line of work, that was more likely to come sooner, than later.

Mac's voice was rough as he told her, "Before we seal this promise with a kiss, there's something else you ought to know."

Her heart flip-flopped in her chest as she prepared for the worst, prepared to hear he'd been given an even more dangerous assignment than the last.

"Jason Hart has asked me to become SAC of the Paris bureau. That means no more undercover work. As a designing female, how do you feel about being married to a desk jockey?"

"Oh, you big tease." She batted her palms against Mac's broad shoulders. "I'll love it."

"Great, and since our original honeymoon was between strangers, how about setting our sights on New Zealand? There are family there we both need to meet, four brothers and a sister."

Mac had asked her to be his wife in whichever corner of the globe their life would take them, and if that meant going to the end of the earth, she would follow him there. New Zealand was a long way, but not quite that far.

And with Mac by her side, she'd go willingly into this new adventure. For wasn't that the nature of love?

"Whatever it takes, *chéri*. I'll be by your side."

* * * * *

THE HIGH-STAKES ACTION AND ACCESSORIZING CONTINUE IN

Ms. Longshot
by Sylvie Kurtz

December 2005

THE LATEST INSTALLMENT IN

Rich, fabulous... and dangerously underestimated.

Don't miss the rest of THE IT GIRLS books by some of your favorite Bombshell authors:

Available at your favorite retail outlet.

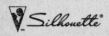

If you enjoyed what you just read,
then we've got an offer you can't resist!

Take 2 bestselling love stories FREE!

Plus get a FREE surprise gift!

Clip this page and mail it to Silhouette Reader Service™

IN U.S.A.
3010 Walden Ave.
P.O. Box 1867
Buffalo, N.Y. 14240-1867

IN CANADA
P.O. Box 609
Fort Erie, Ontario
L2A 5X3

YES! Please send me 2 free Silhouette Intimate Moments® novels and my free surprise gift. After receiving them, if I don't wish to receive anymore, I can return the shipping statement marked cancel. If I don't cancel, I will receive 4 brand-new novels every month, before they're available in stores! In the U.S.A., bill me at the bargain price of $4.24 plus 25¢ shipping and handling per book and applicable sales tax, if any*. In Canada, bill me at the bargain price of $4.99 plus 25¢ shipping and handling per book and applicable taxes**. That's the complete price and a savings of at least 10% off the cover prices—what a great deal! I understand that accepting the 2 free books and gift places me under no obligation ever to buy any books. I can always return a shipment and cancel at any time. Even if I never buy another book from Silhouette, the 2 free books and gift are mine to keep forever.

240 SDN D7ZD
340 SDN D7ZP

Name	(PLEASE PRINT)	
Address	Apt.#	
City	State/Prov.	Zip/Postal Code

Not valid to current Silhouette Intimate Moments® subscribers.

Want to try two free books from another series?
Call 1-800-873-8635 or visit www.morefreebooks.com.

* Terms and prices subject to change without notice. Sales tax applicable in N.Y.
** Canadian residents will be charged applicable provincial taxes and GST.
  All orders subject to approval. Offer limited to one per household.
  ® and ™ are trademarks owned and used by the trademark owner and/or its licensee.

INMOM05   ©2005 Harlequin Enterprises Limited

eHARLEQUIN.com

The Ultimate Destination for Women's Fiction

Visit eHarlequin.com's Bookstore today for today's most popular books at great prices.

- An extensive selection of romance books by top authors!

- Choose our convenient "bill me" option. No credit card required.

- New releases, Themed Collections and hard-to-find backlist.

- A sneak peek at upcoming books.

- Check out book excerpts, book summaries and Reader Recommendations from other members and post your own too.

- Find out what everybody's reading in Bestsellers.

- Save BIG with everyday discounts and exclusive online offers!

- Our Category Legend will help you select reading that's exactly right for you!

- Visit our Bargain Outlet often for huge savings and special offers!

- Sweepstakes offers. Enter for your chance to win special prizes, autographed books and more.

Your purchases are 100% guaranteed—so shop online at www.eHarlequin.com today!

INTBB104R

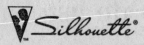
COMING NEXT MONTH

#1395 FEELS LIKE HOME—Maggie Shayne
The Oklahoma All-Girl Brands

When Chicago cop Jimmy Corona returned to his small
hometown, all he wanted was to find a mother to care for his
son while he took down a perp. Shy Kara Brand, who'd once
had a youthful crush on him, was the obvious choice. But
danger soon followed Jimmy to Big Falls, and only Kara
stood between his little boy and certain death....

#1396 MOST WANTED WOMAN—Maggie Price
Line of Duty

Police sergeant Josh McCall came to Sundown, Oklahoma,
for some R & R and fell for an alluring bartender with a dark past
and an irresistible face. Josh was determined to uncover Regan
Ford's secrets despite the distrust he saw in her eyes. Would
persistence and energy win this troubled woman's
heart…or endanger both their lives?

#1397 SECRETS OF THE WOLF—Karen Whiddon
The Pack

Brie Beswich came to Leaning Tree for answers about her
mother's tragic death. But all she found was more questions
and hints of an earth-shaking secret. The small town's handsome
sheriff seemed to know more than he was saying. As danger
loomed, could Brie trust this mysterious man and the passion
that threatened to consume them both?

#1398 OUT OF SIGHT—Michelle Celmer

After a treacherous life in a crime family, divorce counselor
Abbi Sullivan finally found a place to call home in the bucolic
wilds of Colorado. Her dream world came screeching to a halt
when FBI special agent Will Bishop came after her and demanded
she testify against a brutal criminal. Now she had a choice to
make: flee again, or risk her life for the man she loved.

SIMCNM1105